GIRL PLANS, GOD LAUGHS

Sharon Francis

Sharon Francis

Copyright © 2020 Sharon Francis

All rights reserved

The characters and events portrayed in this book are fictitious. Any similarity to real persons, living or dead, is coincidental and not intended by the author.

No part of the book may be reproduced, or stored in a retrieval system, or transmitted in any form or by any means, electronic, mechanical, photocopying, recording, or otherwise, without express permission of the publisher.

ISBN: 978-1-8381173-0-6

Cover design by: Clevera Creative

CHAPTER 1

It took Violet's entire bodyweight to push open one side of an enormous pair of smoked glass doors. Strange how an hour earlier the slightest touch was enough to make it swing freely inward, drawing her into the buzzing hotel lounge, yet now it felt like lead. She sidestepped through the gap as the door nudged her out into the bitter cold. Her wool coat flapped around her in the wind, buttons left undone in her rush to leave, exposing her black dress and stocking-clad legs to the night air. She pulled it tight as she paused to gather her thoughts in the doorway.

A laughing couple, arms intertwined, smiled a greeting as they passed in the other direction. For a moment Violet was in no man's land: part still in the warmth, music willing her feet to join the party; while the other part felt the sandblasting of sleet against her skin, hair snatched from its chignon and heard the roaring of engines in the street.

Everywhere she looked there were signs of the season: fairy lights twinkling in shop windows; advertisements for Christmas films emblazoned on the sides of buses; even her own breath condensing into frosty brume was a brutal reminder of the time of year. She had been so hopeful this year, so sure this one would be different. Now, she wished it was over: every fir tree ripped down; sickly-sweet gift adverts replaced with January sale banners; the sheet music for every carol padlocked away. She shrank with disappointment, shoulders sagging with the weight of it. The tremor of her hand was obvious as she tidied a lock of hair behind her ear. 'Look at you,' she chastised herself. 'How did you get to this state?'

Violet thought back over the last few months, the intricate scheme she had designed like a spider's web, each silken thread adding elegant detail and strength, and she had almost brought it to completion, her masterpiece, until today, when an ugly ladder tore straight through the middle. She had thought her plans were perfect, marvelled at how simple it would be, how everything and everybody would fall into place. Where were those plans now?

She remembered an elderly aunt, from childhood. Aunt Muriel spent hours industriously sewing a cross stitch, stabbing away with her needle, filling every gap with colour. She produced magnificent pieces of art, but when you turned them over, the back was chaos, an ugly tangle of thread. Until tonight, all Violet had seen when she studied her master plan had been the cleverness, the pretty colours, but now she saw the knotted mess behind the scenes.

She looked down at the glitzy shimmer of her shoes, shiny silver and recklessly high. What had she been thinking? She would be paying them off her credit card until March and why? They, like many of her recent choices, had not been good ones; they had been weighted by an unfounded confidence. She had had such faith in herself, faith in the plan, faith in...what? Her hand moved to the cross at her neck, index finger rubbing over the face of it, tracing the fine engraving, before she let it drop away. What was there she could possibly have faith in now? She dragged her gaze up, past the buildings across the street; past the illuminated high rises in the mid-distance; up to the sky beyond, mostly charcoal but for a few low, lighter grey clouds softening it as they raced south east. There were no stars to be seen, no silver linings obscured by the nimbostratus.

She whispered into the ether. 'Listen, God, I don't get it. I thought we had an arrangement. I've kept to my side of the deal. I did all the things I said I would, followed the plan to the letter, so, I don't get it. Did I miss something? Did I get something wrong? What do you want from me? I've tried...'

A black cab pulled up beside the kerb, at the foot of the wide steps below, and she became conscious of her appearance; leaning against a building as if she couldn't support herself; talking to someone who wasn't there. She looked like a sad, dejected drunk. The cab door jerked open and she recognised the high-pitched laughter within – Tara, from HR, - she with an eye for spotting gossip a mile off and a mouth for sharing it. In her current, fragile state, Violet couldn't cope with her sticking her nose in. She quickly scanned her surroundings for an escape route, but there was nowhere to go, except back inside or directly past her colleague. Neither option was perfect, but she still had resources to fall back on. She grabbed her phone from the clutch bag under her arm, pressed it to her ear, assumed a fake smile and hurried down the steps, making a bee line for Tara, improvising a one-sided conversation as she went. Whatever happened, Tara would not go into the party with stories of her leaving, tail between her legs. Violet would not be the talk of the office next week, at least not for that reason. No, she was leaving pride intact.

Utilising her rusty, but passable, acting skills from years past in drama class, she would give a clear impression of someone moving on to a bigger, better party. She would face a few questions on Monday, the odd raised eyebrow, but better that than pity, any day of the week.

'Yes, I've escaped at last and I'm on my way.' Pause for effect. 'I know, but it's got to be done, you know, networking and all that, ha, ha!'

She drew level with Tara and her handsome male escort and briefly raised a hand in acknowledgement, making it obvious her attention was on the phone call.

'No, no, it's fine! I'll grab a cab and I can be there in ten, fifteen tops.' She lowered her voice suggestively as she met Tara's questioning gaze. 'No, I can't wait either.'

Violet made to sidestep Tara, who was staring, radar fully alerted. 'Can I hijack your cab, Tara, honey? I'm in such a hurry!'

As she reached for the door, Violet's heel caught in the grille at the edge of the pavement, forcing her to pivot ninety degrees. With the other hand still clasping the phone to her ear she had no way to steady herself and felt her body tip spectacularly backward, off the pavement and into the road. Her fake smile transformed into a wide-eyed, open-mouthed grimace of complete shock, her limbs flailing.

Violet's shoulder was the first thing to make contact with the tarmac, the force punching breath out of her with a loud oomph. 'Come on, God, give me a break!' she fumed silently. Then her head hit the road and everything became still and distant. She could hear Tara screaming, the clatter of feet rushing from all directions. A vaguely familiar face, with warm dark eyes and a scar above his left brow, hovered above her. His lips were moving and someone was asking if she was all right, but the two didn't fit together. They were out of sync and it was confusing, taking all her concentration to decipher the words.

Violet's brain began to withdraw, like a slow slide down a tunnel. *I bet there's light at the other end,* she thought. *You're not supposed to go to the light, are you? Because that means death, or heaven, or something.* Logic chipped in. *Hang on one minute, heaven means God, and I have a mammoth-sized bone to pick with him.* She allowed herself to continue floating away from her bruised body.

Her senses closed down one by one: the taste of blood from where she had bitten her tongue dissipated; the smell of rain on wet tarmac disappeared; the hustle and bustle above her faded from colour, to black and white, to shadow and then darkness. She remembered reading somewhere that hearing was the last sense to go, but that was not her experience. When sound finally became so faint it no longer reached her, she became aware of something else: a residue of feeling, one final connection with the world, peripheral but constant - the warm, comforting sensation of her hand being held.

Girl Plans, God Laughs

The descent had been gentle and controlled, but that small touch of human contact created a dilemma which steadied and gradually tightened its grip. It anchored her. She longed to hold on to it, that tingle of rightness, starting where her fingers were enveloped by a larger, stronger hand and crept all the way up her arm. But, at the same time, she yearned to go on. She wanted her moment of truth with God; wanted to look him square in the eye and hear his excuses. She needed to have her say, to shout and complain: to make him listen. She wanted justice. She deserved justice. Squeezing the fingers which held hers, she felt a gentle compression as they squeezed back, but the decision was made. Releasing herself from the grasp, she let go of everything which finally connected her with the world. She shut down and time stopped.

The nothingness, the empty blackness, could have lasted moments or a million years. She was lost, free-falling and content in her separation from everything, the freedom of non-existence. Eventually though, a subtle but definite alteration to her state, cut through the fog, caused her to hesitantly explore whether there was anything there, beyond her own being. Her eyelids fluttered open, like a new-born discovering the world for the first time, uncomprehending, unfocussed, until vague colours and shapes became vividly clear and she realised with a start what she was looking at – a pair of piercingly-blue eyes, staring right back, only inches from her face.

CHAPTER 2

The eyes, in such close proximity to her own, caused Violet to recoil in her chair so violently it would have toppled over had it not been fixed to the floor. She grabbed the armrests, body curled in readiness for fight or flight, as soon as she decided which was required.

'Violet Harper? I'm sorry to alarm you, but I've been paging you for ten minutes, so I thought I'd better come and find you, or you'll miss your transfer.' The soft, calm, Deep South American drawl was comforting, but firm. 'It is rather urgent.'

Violet's gaze darted around. She felt exposed, like she had been caught daydreaming in class. Transfer? The last thing she remembered was hitting her head, but now she seemed to be in a vast waiting area. Everywhere she looked there were rows of sumptuous chairs in cream and chrome, separated by pale wood tables, littered with reading material and old coffee cups. At least half the chairs were occupied by people who, unlike the bland but tasteful furnishings, were a hotchpotch of colours and dress. People were wandering around too, individually, but also in groups, huddled around electronic information boards and picture windows, overlooking a view she could not see from her perspective.

'You are Violet Harper, aren't you?'

Violet's attention swivelled back to the middle-aged face, framed by silver-blonde hair, neatly pulled back into a bun. It was attached to a prim body in a crisp royal blue skirt suit and a matching cravat. The air quivered with expensive perfume. The woman was studying a clipboard rather than invading Violet's space now, her air non-threatening and patient.

'Where am I?' Violet stammered. 'How did I get here?'

A half smile softened the woman's expression. 'You're confused, and that's completely understandable. It can be daunting when you arrive quite as suddenly as you did.'

She seemed to make a decision to slow things down. Perched in the seat alongside Violet, knees tilted to one side, clipboard resting on her lap, she spoke softly. 'Violet, you're not supposed to be here. Tell me, what do you remember from before – before you woke up?'

Violet searched her memory, unravelling twisted threads to make sense of it all, shame washing over her as, by degrees, it drip-fed back. 'My work Christmas party.' She winced as the pictures cleared in her mind. 'And I remember making a complete fool of myself in front of the hotel, tripping flat on my face in the road. Then I remember falling and falling. Then I woke up here.'

The woman patted Violet's shoulder. 'Good, good, all present and correct.'

Correct or not, Violet was no clearer than before. She glanced around, looking for something, anything, to fill in the gaps.

The woman became aware of Violet's distraction. 'Now then, Violet.' Violet obediently turned to her guide. 'Time is very much of the essence. Basically, you are where you should not be, therefore it is imperative we get you to where you should be, tout suite.'

Violet, frustrated by unanswered questions, insisted, 'And where exactly is that? Where am I?' Adding as an afterthought, 'And who are you?'

'All equally good questions.' The official tapped a name badge on her chest. 'I'm Grace and my job is to get you home. The reason you feel so out of sorts is simply because you don't belong here. You feel that, don't you?'

Violet shook her head, confused and irritated. 'I don't have a clue where here is, so how could I know if I belong?'

Grace, ever the professional, ignored Violet's petulance, her drawl staying as level and precise as her hairstyle. 'Very good point. Now, you said you remember falling, am I right?'

Violet nodded, suddenly close to tears. She felt like a small child, separated from her mother at the shopping centre. She sucked in the corner of her bottom lip, gripping it between her teeth.

'And if you had to guess, where do you think you were falling to?' Grace spoke slowly.

Violet recalled her descent, the feelings she had experienced, the thought processes she went through as she fell. 'I thought I was dying.' At first, she felt sheepish at the whole idea, but then realisation hit her hard. 'Am I dead? Is that it? Is…is this Heaven?'

Grace threw her hands up to halt the onslaught. 'No, no, you're not dead; not yet anyway, and this is not Heaven – goodness what an idea, no. You see, what seems to have happened is some sort of anomaly. Yes, you knocked yourself out, but then you were supposed to come round, spend a night in A & E and then go home and get on with your life. The issue appears to have occurred somewhere during this unconscious period. Rather than wake up and resurface, you continued to fall, but as that was not on your agenda, we had no choice but to intercept.'

Violet was not to be put off in her quest for answers. 'So, if I'm not in the world and I'm not in heaven, where am I? Where else is there?'

Grace's attitude hovered between patience and patronising. 'You see, you're neither here nor there. You're in between. We specialise in redirecting people like you, who are lost in the middle, between objectives.'

'Lost in the middle? How do you help me? Are you an angel?'

A modest blush forced its way to the surface of Grace's foundation-covered cheekbones. 'Well, it is a phrase that's been bandied around from to time to time, but no, I'm not an angel. I'm merely an operative, a facilitator, if you will. I work here, in the Location and Intervention of Misdirected Beings Office. Simple as that.' She crossed her legs, slapped the clipboard against her chest and folded her arms in front of it, as if no further discussion was necessary.

Violet's lips shaped themselves silently around the words as she twisted and turned them like a kaleidoscope inside her head. At the same time, she looked across the vast network of beings roaming around, her gaze settling on an enormous signage board, displaying the office title in giant letters, the initial of each word emboldened. *The Location and Intervention of Misdirected Beings Office.* She paused, the penny dropping. 'Limbo? I'm in Limbo?'

A horrified look spread across her face and she pushed herself up, out of the chair, frantically searching for the nearest exit. Her body had finally and independently decided on flight as the best course of action, though where she would fly remained uncertain. Grace rested a reassuring hand on her shoulder and steadily held her gaze.

'Violet, don't worry. It's only temporary. You're not stuck here. You're moving on immediately or, rather, you're moving back. I need to return you to your body, pronto.' Confident she had countered Violet's panic and was back in control, she turned her attention to the clipboard, continuing under her breath, 'Before some clever clogs switches off your life support.'

The aghast expression which had faded from Violet's face, reinstated itself instantly and Grace recognised her faux pas.

'Forget I said that. It hardly ever happens and we are monitoring the situation closely to be on the safe side. Come, Violet, walk with me and I'll explain en route.'

Violet examined her meagre options. What choice did she have?

Her legs were weak and unsteady. However, the solidity of the marble flooring beneath her feet bolstered her and her balance gradually recovered. Grace held out the crook of her elbow and winked. 'Come along, my dear. You hold on to me, or you'll have everyone thinking you've been on the Bourbon. I'll see you right.'

Violet slipped her arm through that offered, the sense of urgency to return to her body rising, giving her the strength she needed to hobble along. 'Where are we going?'

'Not far, down the end here, take a left and through the double doors marked "lost baggage".'

Violet examined herself, incongruent in party dress and shoeless feet. Suddenly the garb of those around her slotted into place: a man in an orange boiler suit and matching hard hat; a young woman in a gold bathing suit; an entire family in pyjamas, as if they had simply stepped out of a moment in their lives and straight into Limbo. 'Oh yes, of course. I don't have anything with me. My bag must be in there.'

'No, no. Nobody brings baggage here, that's left back in the world. It's of no use whatsoever, either here or on the next leg of the journey. I think the sign was someone's idea of a joke – some of us have been here rather a long time and we have to provide our own entertainment.'

'So, what is in there, the place we're going? Why do we have to go there?' Violet's interest was piqued by the oddities around her. Despite concern for her own welfare, she was fascinated by this place.

'It's simply a transportation point. We pop you in a compartment, program coordinates and, before you know it, you're waking up in Saint Francis's ICU and all's well that ends well.'

'What if... what if we're too late?' Violet was almost too afraid to say the words aloud. 'What if they have switched off the life support? What happens then?'

'Oh, you are a one for questions, aren't you?' Grace's patience appeared to be waning. 'It is not on your agenda, so it's not going to happen.'

'My coming here wasn't on my agenda either, but it happened, so sometimes the agenda is wrong,' Violet persisted.

'Yes, well, there will be a full investigation into that, in due course.' A defeated edge crept into Grace's voice. 'For the life of me I can't see how it happened. Everyone was in the right place, everything occurred in the right order, at the right time, so I don't know, but we will get to the bottom of it, eventually. I don't suppose you are able to shed any light, are you? Tell me about your journey here.'

Violet shrugged. 'Like I said before, I was falling, at first fast and then slower and slower.'

'That all sounds right.'

'Then I almost stopped. I remember feeling a tug upwards, something pulling me back, but I didn't want to go, so I let go and started to fall again.'

Grace halted and turned, mouth agape, her Texan drawl ever more apparent. 'You let go? Why on earth would you do such a thing?'

Violet concentrated on the crooks and crannies of her mind, until the thought popped to the fore like an air bubble surfacing. 'Because I was angry. Because I wanted to have it out with God.' She met Grace's stare. 'He let me down.'

Grace shook her head in consternation. 'Oh dear. Oh dear me. Have it out with God? Whatever next? Some people,' she huffed. 'Clearly it was you. You sabotaged your own life.' She put her fingertips to her forehead, supporting its weight for a few moments, before allowing her hand to drop away. 'Oh well, we all make mistakes, I suppose. Come along, let's get this mess sorted out and you back to your body.'

She grabbed Violet's arm and pulled, but Violet planted her feet where she stood, strength finally fully returned to her limbs. 'Actually, no!'

'Pardon me?'

Violet guessed Grace had never before had her authority questioned, such was her expression, pencilled eyebrows rising sharply. Violet felt heat building in her stomach, spreading to the rest of her body. Her free hand crept to the cross, still at her throat, as she inwardly examined the turbulent flow of emotions. 'I said no. I'm still angry. I still want to have it out with God. He owes me an explanation.'

Grace pursed her lips in a pout worthy of any catwalk model, one eyebrow returning to its rightful place, while the other remained north, her voice monotone. 'I don't think you want to do this, Violet.'

Violet wasn't sure either, but anger bubbled inside her like a lidded pan and she did not want to spend the rest of any life she may have simmering. 'Yes I do. I'm not going back until I have answers. How can I live my life with this hanging over me? Thinking God has reneged on a deal? I want a hearing.' She was shocked by her own courage, empowered by it.

Grace dropped Violet's arm like a grenade, patience evaporating. 'Have it your own way, but from here on in, you're on your own.' She pointed to an escalator behind them, an infinite flow of grey, dimpled steps emerging from the floor, and heading upwards, so high Violet couldn't see the top. 'That way. All the way up, then the red door facing you, marked "Complaints".'

'And what's in there?'

Grace rolled her eyes. 'Complaints, of course. What else? Good luck!' Her tone did not back up the sentiment.

Violet edged her foot on the first step and was whisked away faster than she could have imagined. She gripped the handrail for balance, her hair flying out behind. The escalator hummed and clicked as Violet's stomach lurched with the haste of the ascent. She looked behind at Grace for reassurance, only to see her ramrod back striding away. Suddenly, she felt lost, alone, in spite of the hoards milling around, now way below her. The staircase seemed everlasting, gifting her with an abundance of time: time to think about what she had done, what she was in the process of doing; time to question; time to doubt; time to wish she had done as she was told for once. She could be on her way back to her body, back to her old life, if only she could leave things alone. She began to think the crest would never come, but at last the peak appeared and she braced herself, prepared to be flung from the top. To her relief however, the steps slowed and she was deposited onto a flat, gridded footplate.

In front of her, as promised, was a single red door marked 'Complaints' in large black letters. Even had she considered changing her mind, she had no option. There was no down escalator, nowhere else to go. She was committed. She faced the door, clenching and unclenching nervous fingers, planning her speech, but no words would form in her mind. Closing her eyes, she breathed one long, deep breath before rapping on the wood.

Violet didn't know what she expected, but a low, throaty voice, with a clipped English accent sharply instructed her to enter. Swinging the door open, she saw a balding man in a white pinstripe shirt, sleeves rolled up to the elbow, and a crooked tie, with a pen behind his ear. He looked up as she entered, a clutch of crinkled papers in one hand, while the other gripped a computer mouse.

'Yes?'

The intensity of his gaze caused Violet to shrink into herself. She was six years old again, facing the headmaster for the first time.

'Are... are you God?' she asked.

'Don't be ridiculous, do I look like God?' He tapped a nameplate, partially concealed among the detritus on the desk. 'I'm the Spiritual Ombudsman.'

CHAPTER 3

Whether due to the sharpness of the ombudsman's voice, the strangeness of the situation or simply the length of the day, Violet's vision took on an ethereal quality. Everything shimmered, as if veiled by a heat haze, the undulations becoming more pronounced, until the entire picture melted and Violet fainted in a heap.

In the millisecond between coming round and opening her eyes, she imagined she was back on the city pavement, head in the gutter, surrounded by ogling strangers, and was very nearly relieved. Then her eyelids opened, reality returned, and she was confronted by the worried face of the ombudsman. He was crouching next to her, hands on his knees for balance. The pen behind his ear pointed to a spot right between her eyes. As she met his gaze he relaxed back on his haunches, wiping his forehead with the back of his hand.

'You had me worried, young lady. Are you ok?'

She mentally scanned herself top to bottom. 'I think so.' She pushed up onto one elbow, the world still swimming. 'At least, as ok as it gets under the circumstances.'

'Fair enough.' He reached for a glass of water from the desktop. 'Here, sip this. I was considering throwing it over your face to bring you round, but I daresay it would be better on the inside.'

'Thanks.' The cold water revived her as it trickled down her throat.

He watched, then in one fluid movement stood up. Relieving her of the empty glass, he placed it on the desk, next to an untidy pile of files. 'Come on, let's see if we can get you up.'

She accepted the proffered hand. Pale, smooth and clammy, it was testament to a life spent behind a desk, but it had a rigid strength and she quickly found herself upright.

He indicated a door she had not previously noticed. 'Why don't you make use of the cloakroom? Then we'll start again. See if we can't get to the bottom of whatever it is you're here for.'

She nodded, smoothed her hands down over her dress and made her way into a luxurious bathroom. As the door swung closed, she leant back against it, enjoying a few moments to get her head together. The apparition in the mirror, above a shiny, white sink unit, was a shock. The walls were stark and the cruel light bounced off, highlighting the smudges beneath her eyes and sallowness of her skin - she looked like a Victorian beggar girl. Her attire, once classically simple, now appeared plain and dishevelled. She splashed her face with lukewarm water, rubbing a damp hand around the back of her neck and squeezing the corded muscles. A pile of white towels were rolled up on the counter top and she pressed one to her skin, revelling in the softness and the freshly-washed smell. She picked up a brush and dragged it through her tangles, relishing the return of order. The image in the mirror was a little more like her now. At least she felt human again.

Violet considered the man on the other side of the door, wondering what qualified him for the title of Spiritual Ombudsman. At first, he had seemed intimidating, scary even, but now she thought he might actually listen. Whether he would be able to help was another matter, but she would give him the opportunity. What choice did she have, stuck in Limbo, miles from her body, her friends and her home? She pulled open the door and re-entered the office.

The ombudsman lounged on a black leather sofa, against the side wall, one grey-socked ankle resting on the opposite knee, flicking through a pile of stapled pages. He glanced up and indicated the other end of the sofa with a fistful of paper.

'Come, have a seat.' He dropped the printed sheets on the floor and retrieved a tablet computer. Then, returning both feet to the floor and shifting in his seat, he gave her his full attention.

Perched on the cushions, her hands clutched her hem, hiding an unsightly ladder in her tights.

'Ok, what's the story?'

She felt at a disadvantage. 'What do you want to know?'

He shrugged. 'Who you are and why you're here, would be a good start.'

'Of course. Sorry. Violet,' she stammered. 'I'm Violet Harper and I'm here because I wish to make a complaint.'

He opened the tablet and typed. 'OK, Violet. What do we have here?' He muttered to himself. 'Ahh. Violet Penelope Harper, thirty years old, TV researcher, originally from the South Hams, lately of South East London.' He glanced sideways at her. 'More lately of St Francis's Hospital I see. Hmm.'

Taken aback by the quantity of data at his fingertips, she watched his morphing facial expressions, the tapping of his teeth with a fingernail, eyebrows rising and falling like a tide. She gripped her skirt even tighter.

'So, what is the nature of your complaint, Violet?' His steady gaze was unnerving.

'Well, I'm not happy...,' she began, her voice petering out as she recognised how petulant she sounded, 'with God.'

His brows reached a new extreme and a poorly disguised smirk crossed his lips. 'Not happy with God? I see. Why is that exactly?'

She felt his mockery as much as heard it and was offended, the sensation fuelling her irritation. 'No, I'm not happy.' Her chin thrust forward. 'We had a deal and he didn't uphold his end of it. I did everything I said I would, and more besides, but he let me down. I want to know why and, to be honest, I'd like an apology.'

'An apology from God?' His tone was patronising.

'Yes, actually, because if you can't trust God, who can you trust?'

The ombudsman turned his attention back to the tablet. He took the pen from behind his ear, waggling it between finger and thumb as he concentrated. The silence lengthened and Violet squirmed in her seat, observing his every move. The solemn replacement of the pen marked an end to the study. He flicked the cover of the computer case over the screen and tucked it under his arm, lacing his fingers in front of him.

'Violet, we have two issues here, neither of which bode well for your case. Firstly, I have never yet investigated a complaint directly against God which could be upheld. Secondly, God does not do "deals".' He made speech marks with his fingers. 'No bargains, no agreements and no pacts. Never has done. Saying that, I am obligated to research all complaints in the fullest capacity if, and I must reiterate, if,' his voice rose on the word, 'you decide to proceed. Think carefully, Violet. It will mean a thorough examination of your thoughts, actions and motivations. Do you wish me to continue?'

Her stomach clenched, the hairs on her arms stood up, toes gripping the carpet, but why? This was what she wanted. Why should she change her mind now? She firmly placed her reservations aside. 'Yes, I'm sure. I know there was a deal, whatever you say. I remember it clearly, last New Year's Eve. It's not something I'm likely to forget. Besides, I have nothing to hide. Please, carry on.'

His stare continued a little too long and Violet wished she could hide within the sofa cushions but, at last, he shrugged. 'Ok then. So be it.'

Jumping from his seat, he waved for her to follow. 'Come, come. No time to hang around.'

She struggled to her feet and stumbled after him, through a door at the rear of the office and along a narrow, grey-carpeted corridor. At the end were double doors and the ombudsman held one open while she passed through, into a cavernous, dim cinema. Tiers of folded padded chairs sat empty, the only light provided by a glowing, but otherwise blank, screen. He urged her to a seat in the middle of the room and indicated for her to sit, before he flopped into the one adjacent.

Rifling in a pocket in the back of the seat in front he pulled out a remote control, covered with an array of multi-coloured buttons. 'Don't you love gadgets?' He smirked.

Violet looked from the screen, to his excited face and back, at a loss as to what was happening.

He settled back. 'Ready?'

She had been expecting questions, note taking, a thorough harvesting of information. 'Ready for what?'

He frowned as if it was obvious, shrugging. 'I did warn you I'd need to assess your thoughts, actions and motivations as part of my investigation. We're going to watch the movie of your life, starting with New Year's Eve, last year.'

An image appeared on the screen, a wide-screen, technicolour, high definition image of herself. She remembered the scene as clear as day, although the perspective from inside her head had been a little different. Her stomach churned as she absorbed the minutiae. Now she saw a rather drunk, bedraggled vision of herself, balanced on a wall, clinging to a lamp post, mascara marking roadmaps down her cheeks, her hair, partly stuck to her face, partly blowing wildly in the wind and rain. As she swung forward and back, she was shouting abuse alternately at the torrid river, broiling metres below, and then at the gloomy, cloud splattered sky.

The ombudsman sucked in his cheeks. 'Is this it? The prestigious moment the deal with God was struck?'

Violet swung like a pendulum from pure humiliation to indignation and back again. 'No actually, it's not. That was later.'

'Oh good,' he replied. 'If someone was making a deal with God, I would expect them to be suitably dressed for the occasion: possibly a power suit; a complete pair of shoes, at least.'

'Don't be …,' She didn't know what to say.

'Don't be what, Violet?' he shook his head. 'Am I supposed to take this,' he indicated the screen, 'seriously? I don't appreciate having my time wasted.'

'I am not wasting your time, I assure you, but you have to see the context. I was going through an extremely difficult period; had a bellyful-.'

'A bellyful of something, that's for sure,' he interrupted.

She pinched her lips together, indignation coming out on top. 'As an ombudsman you are supposed to be unbiased and non-judgmental. You should be listening to the facts, not jumping to conclusions.'

His head bucked at her chastisement, then he nodded. 'You're right, I should. I apologise, but you must admit, this does not promote your case as it stands.'

'As I said, you need to see the context.'

'Then where do you suggest I start?'

She had his attention and did not intend to let it slip away. 'A couple of hours earlier that evening – say eight o'clock. I was meeting my friends at a restaurant downtown.'

As she spoke he was keying away at the controls. 'Eight o'clock, you say?'

The screen changed to a rushing Violet, tripping over her bag in the hurry to climb into a taxi.

She felt a blush rise to her cheeks. 'OK, I was late. Maybe ten past eight.'

He fast-forwarded to a point where she was pushing open a restaurant door, tucking a lock of hair behind her ear and plastering a smile on her face, in anticipation of meeting whoever was inside.

'That's it!' she interceded triumphantly. 'That's where it all started.'

CHAPTER 4

New Year's Eve – A Year Ago

Violet hoisted the strap of her black leather bag over her shoulder, straightening her jacket and brushing down her burgundy dress, consciously breathing steadily, calming her thumping heart. She was aware of the taxi she had stepped out of moving away from the kerb, its wheels crunching through wet gravel, as it merged with the heavy night traffic. She was nervous. Ridiculous really, under the circumstance; it was simply dinner with her best friends. Except, it wasn't. Yes, it was dinner; yes, they were her best friends and had been for years, but the one thing it wasn't, was simple.

The event had been her idea. In fact, she had railroaded them into it, when they would have rather not made the effort. It was a means of bringing them back together as a unit, rather than the splintered mess they were at risk of becoming; a reminder they weren't alone. She felt a keen sense of responsibility to make it a success, mentally preparing for days. There were topics of conversation to be avoided, risky subjects to skirt around, diversionary tactics to be employed, tactical memory lapses and hilarious stories to be brought into play when all else failed. She had to make this work.

Girl Plans, God Laughs

Her heels tapped a rhythm on the damp-stained slabs to the restaurant door. They would be there already, the girls. She was always last, so they would expect nothing more, but usually it was because she was applying another coat of mascara; changing her shoes for the fifth time. Today it was because it would have been far easier to lock the door, pull on her pyjamas and curl up in front of a movie, so everything seemed to take twice as long as usual.

She wondered what sort of atmosphere she would be walking into. The restaurant would be warm, full of delicious aromas, low-level music in the background, as it always was – that she could rely on. The atmosphere which worried her was that directly around her table, like a hamlet with its own weather system. A short, goateed waiter took her coat and she dabbed at her face with a handkerchief, removing the droplets which had settled there. She looked around and could almost have sobbed with delight and relief. There they were, huddled in an alcove, popping up and down like meercats as they spotted her, bidding to get her attention. There were smiles and giggles and tapping of watches, as there had been at every get-together they had ever had before, an air of welcome, blessed normality. She waved a greeting, mentally berating herself. What had she expected? Banners around their necks displaying 'woe is me'? They were her friends, always had been; always would be, no matter what else they had to contend with.

Hurrying to their table, she disappeared in a scrum of hugs and kisses. They shuffled along the padded benches and she stumbled into the space, bag slung on the floor, the chain strap snaking around her shoes. She studied each face one by one, observing the smiles, but secretly searching a bit deeper, below the surface. Lulu sat directly opposite, blonde curls bouncing as her shoulders lurched with laughter following a throw away comment by someone about Violet being early for once, or at least not as late as usual. Ayesha, next to Lulu, had made the comment and backed it up with the evidence she was only on her first drink, lifting a long-stemmed glass of red wine to her matching gloss covered lips as she spoke. Kate was next in the row. Always the quietest, she sat at the head of the table, taking it all in, fingers fiddling with a lock of mousey hair, eyes flitting from one face to another as they took it in turns to berate Violet's timekeeping. Kate allowed the mockery to continue for so long and then stepped in, peacekeeping, conscious no one's feelings be hurt.

'Never mind all that,' she murmured, grabbing Violet's hand across the table. 'She's here now and that's all that matters. It's so good to see you, Vi.'

Another hand snaked in on top of theirs, clasping them both tightly. Isobel was squeezed between Violet and Kate and bobbed in her seat like an excited puppy, knocking them both with jiggling elbows. 'It is. It is.'

Violet grinned as things settled down. 'It's good to be here. Thank you, everyone. I know we're all busy, and I'm sure you've got other things you could be doing, so it's lovely you've come out to keep me company tonight.' She reached for a bottle of chardonnay, already open in the centre of the table and poured a short measure into the waiting glass. Not so confident with the mood yet, she wanted to keep her wits about her.

She lifted the glass high into the air. 'Cheers, girls.'

***

The image on the screen froze on the group of women, faces alight with smiles, glasses lifted in salute, and Violet stared, waiting and willing it to continue, stomach tense with anticipation. She felt like Ebenezer Scrooge with the Ghost of Christmas Past, experiencing once again precious moments in her history, remembering the jokes and laughing again, noticing for the first time expressions on the faces of her friends, significant looks passing between them, body language which had gone unnoticed before. As time passed and nothing happened, she glanced at the ombudsman, who was brandishing the remote control, but staring at her unmoving.

'What?' Her chipped fuchsia fingernails drummed a rapid rhythm against her knees.

He shrugged. 'As rewarding as this exhibition of sisterhood is, we need to move on. There is the small matter of your being on life support and we don't have time to review the entire last twelve months of your life, warts and all. So, where does the relevant action happen? Tell me where it starts.'

She eyed him, disgruntled. 'It is happening, right in front of you. You have to look deeper.'

His chest rose and fell exaggeratedly as he sighed. 'Really? Obviously much deeper. What happened to ruin your evening and bring about the drunken finale? A bad prawn? No profiteroles left?'

Her lips pursed as she struggled to maintain a level tone. 'Metaphors about icebergs and what's beneath the waterline spring to mind. You can't just take things at face value. You need to see the complete picture before you can judge. There is so much more to this scene than merely dinner with the girls. I arranged the get together because every one of them was going through difficult times and I wanted to remind them we were there for each other. If I'm honest, partly it was to make myself feel better, too. Like I was helping them all in some small way, when there really was nothing I could do to help their individual situations.'

'That's all very well, but we don't have the luxury of time to study the complete history of your entire peer group. Look, I'll take it as read you had your reasons for the drunken tomfoolery.'

She made to interrupt, but he waved away her protestations. 'There are two specific points which need to be clarified, whether there was a deal with God, and then whether he broke it, so let's get straight to it. Where and when did this alleged deal take place?'

She plucked the controller from his hand. 'Here, give it to me. Clearly I'll have to show you.'

CHAPTER 5

New Year's Day – A Year Ago

Violet's evening was ruined, but she refused to cry, not that anyone was giving a blind bit of attention to her on this night of all nights. The fireworks marking the beginning of the New Year had ended ages ago and everyone was either too drunk or in too much of a hurry to be interested in what she was doing.

It wasn't her fault it had gone wrong. Well, possibly a bit, but she found plenty of ammunition against providence in her musings, too. Every drip of rain down her back added insult to injury. A vehicle passed too close and a muddy wave crested the kerb, soaking her ankles, and she stopped in her tracks, fists clenched, a pressure cooker squeal escaping her lips.

In fury, she kicked at a loose stone and it flew into the river below. She found the process satisfying and aimed at another, but as it took flight, immediately behind it flew her right shoe. The sight of her precious heeled pump bouncing through a gap onto the ledge, teetering above the water, sent her to her knees in panic. Momentary relief as it settled on the edge turned to frustration as her arm was brought up short by the ornate carving of the stonework. Shuffling along, she tried another hole, but could get no closer.

Staggering to her feet, she considered the options, then, kicking off the remaining shoe, grasped hold of a lamp post and pulled herself up on to the apex, gripping the rough edges with her toes to maintain balance as she swayed. Once up there, it was obvious the only way it could be retrieved was by climbing down the far side, braving the dizzy height and, drunk or not, she simply didn't have the nerve.

Hugging the post, she vented into the dark sky and, if she hadn't feared the possibility of slipping in her stockinged feet, would have stamped in temper, too. Surely there was nothing more the world could throw at her tonight.

'Excuse me? Are you all right?'

A low voice with a soft Irish lilt brought an end to her loud protestations and something like shame washed from her head to her toes. She had given no thought to witnesses.

'Can I help you? I'm sure nothing can be so bad as to...'

Clinging on with one arm, she shuffled around, unable to put a face to the voice from her current angle. 'I'm not trying to jump, you idiot. Do I look suicidal?'

'Well...'

'For crying out loud! Help me down, will you?'

A tall, dark man in waterproofs, with a woolly hat and scarf covering most of his face, stepped forward and lifted her down. She stood back to look him in the eye. 'For your information, I was trying to get my shoe.'

He picked up the one lying on the pavement.

'Not that one. That one.' She indicated the far ledge and he leaned over to have a proper look.

'How did it get there?'

'Well, I was...' There was no way to explain which put her in a good light. 'Does it matter?'

'I suppose not.' He threw himself on his knees and repeated her earlier actions of trying to fit his arm through gaps in the stone,

but with hands far larger than hers, he had no chance of success. 'Sorry, but I don't think we're getting it back tonight.'

'Yeah, I'd pretty much worked that out.' She pulled the one remaining shoe onto her foot and hobbled away, grasping the wall to stay upright.

The man lurched forward, taking her arm to prevent her falling. 'Here. Look. Try these.' He swung a rucksack from his shoulder and pulled out several pairs of flip-flops. 'What are you? Small? Medium?'

She eyed him suspiciously. 'Why the heck do you have women's shoes in your bag?'

Selecting a pair, he dropped them on the floor and slipped them on her sodden feet, handing the remaining high heel back to her for safe keeping. 'Ah, it's sort of my job. Not my day job, just a volunteer thing. I'm a street pastor.'

'A what?'

'A street pastor. Volunteers from the churches come out at night to help people in trouble, make sure they get home safe.'

'What are you, a vicar or something? Are you going to preach me a sermon? 'Cause let me tell you, I am not in the mood.'

He smiled at her contrary attitude. 'I'm in no position to preach to anybody, believe me. Come on.' He hooked his arm through hers and led her away. 'The hall is over the bridge here. You can go in and dry off until we find you a taxi.'

'What kind of pastor doesn't preach? What is the point of you?' Her footsteps halted and he urged her on.

'I've been given the ministry of flip-flops.'

She stopped again as a laugh erupted from her lungs and she bent double with amusement. 'Ha!'

'Funny. That's what I said when they told me, but once a month I walk the streets and rescue ladies like yourself, with broken shoes, no shoes, who can't stay upright in their shoes. I like to think there are less broken ankles thanks to me and my flip-flops.'

Leaning in for a better view of his face, she grasped his collar. 'Think you're some kind of hero?'

'No, no.' He gently straightened her up, pointing her in the right direction.

They reached steps up to the softly glowing entrance of a shabby church building, as a figure appeared in the doorway, swathed in outdoor clothing and brandishing a bunch of keys.

'Aah, Peter, I thought you'd signed out for the night. I was about to lock up.'

'Yes, I thought I was done, then I ran into this young lady on the bridge. A bit of a shoe problem unfortunately.'

The matronly woman looked Violet up and down and smiled. 'Oh dear. That's a nuisance, isn't it?' She pulled up a sleeve to glance at her watch. 'Were you hoping for transport, dear? Do you have far to go?'

Violet struggled to focus, the wind whipping the woman's words away before she could absorb them. She looked from the woman to the street pastor and back again. 'Who, me?'

'Yes, dear. Where do you live?' The woman enunciated each word as if talking to someone hard of hearing.

Violet relayed her address, then concentrated on maintaining balance while the others held a discussion above her head. A few minutes later she found herself bundled into a car, confused, but pleased to be out of the weather.

They pulled up outside her apartment building and Peter helped her from the back seat. The woman hovered in the crook of the driver side door.

'Are you sure you can manage, Peter? I can stay if you need me to.' Her body language and the noisy, gaping yawn between sentences suggested otherwise.

'Margaret, it's fine. I'll pop her in the lift, and my apartment is only down the road. I'll be home in no time.'

'If you're sure.' She drove away before he changed his mind.

The alcohol had sapped the strength from Violet's legs and Peter all but carried her to the front door, waiting patiently as she incorrectly input the entrance code twice, before gaining access. The foyer was an oasis and, as the calm and warmth enveloped her, consciousness ebbed away.

He manhandled her into the lift like a sack of potatoes, propping her body in the corner, his rear end preventing the lift doors from closing. He backed away on tiptoes, but, as he did so, her knees buckled and he dived forward to keep her up right. 'No, you don't.'

The lift doors closed with him inside. 'Well, it looks like I'm taking you all the way home.' Her body slumped into his, her head resting on his shoulder. 'Perhaps it's just as well.'

The trip from the lift into her flat was no easy task and, eventually, having retrieved keys from her bag to unlock the door, he swept her up into his arms and carried her to the sofa.

She opened one eye. 'I don't know you.'

He crouched next to her, at eye level. 'I'm Peter, the Street Pastor. I'm going to leave you now. Do you need anything before I go? Water?' He studied her for a moment. 'A bucket?'

With an almighty effort she manoeuvred herself to a skewed sitting position. 'Street Pastor! Pah! What did God ever do for you?'

An expression she couldn't read crossed his face. His voice was soft and far away. 'I wouldn't know where to start.'

Considering his comment, she closed her eyes to aid concentration.

By the time she resurfaced, the room was empty and quiet, except for a loud banging she had assumed was coming from the flat next door, but was actually inside her own head. She tried to move, but everything ached from the arches of her feet up, and her mouth felt like carpet.

'Eww! I need a drink.' *She pulled herself up, regardless of the pain and, in the dim light from a lamp left on in the hall, made out a glass of water on the little table to her right. She swallowed it in one long draught and dropped the glass back down. The street pastor must have left it for her. Peter. Yes, Peter. What was his game? Picking up women in the middle of the night and... and... and... being kind. As much as she would have liked to, she couldn't think of anything truly negative about him, or his actions, apart from the fact he was clearly deluded. Why would anyone volunteer as a street pastor in this day and age? There was a story there somewhere, she was certain of it. He had history. But he was sure of himself, and he seemed quite nice. Perhaps he was on to something.*

'How much did you drink, girl?' She laughed and winced, but as the chuckles died away, the idea remained. What if he was on to something? What if there was a God and he could give her everything she needed? Practical matters interrupted her train of thought and, aching limbs or not, she stampeded to the bathroom to vomit.

Once her stomach was empty and her heart had slowed to its natural rhythm, she stood at the wash basin and tugged on the light pull. Her face was a peculiar shade of grey and she looked older than her thirty years. It was hardly surprising with what life had thrown at her. She rubbed a hand across her forehead, ironing out the beginnings of worry lines above her nose with a finger.

'I wish my problems would disappear.' Her voice was a whisper. 'Can you sort that, God?' She heaved a sigh, returned the room to darkness and carried a refilled glass and a couple of pain killers back to the lounge. Bed would have been a better idea at this late hour, but it was empty. Of course, the sofa was empty too, but an empty sofa was far less depressing than an empty bed and that was all she could face right now.

As fluids trickled through every cell in her body, the abstract thoughts circled, gradually linking together, forming a whole and a knot of excitement swelled in her chest. Maybe she was still drunk, maybe she was simply ridiculous, but it was worth a go.

Clearing her throat, she began, quietly but clearly. 'Ok, God. Are you listening?' She paused for a reply, then shook her head at the idea. 'I'm going to assume you are.'

As her confidence grew, her voice gained momentum. 'Your man, Peter, he sort of suggested you're a generous guy... girl... whatever. Anyway, the way he talked about you made me think maybe we could help each other out; that you could help my friends out. I'm not after material stuff, I don't want to win the lottery or anything. And, I'm not expecting freebies either. What I'm suggesting is a quid pro quo sort of arrangement; an I'll scratch your back, you scratch mine sort of deal. Starting tomorrow, I'm going to do stuff for you, I don't know what yet, but I'll give stuff up; not do things I shouldn't do; do kind stuff, which in the past I may not have done. And in return, I want your help. Actually, it would be great if you could drop me some clues so I know what you want from me, quite big clues until I get into the swing of it. And, I'm going to make a list, so we're both clear, on who needs what from you.'

Wobbling to the sideboard, she retrieved a notepad and pen from a drawer and collapsed back in the seat. She nibbled the end of the already well-chewed biro. Who needed help? Kate. Definitely Kate. A frisson of shame shot through her as she remembered their interaction at last night's dinner, but this was no time for recriminations. She wrote Kate's name on the list and next to it added "baby". She would leave up to God what variety, size, style of child was provided. After all, Kate wouldn't be fussy. An adamant full stop at the end of the line gave her impetus: suddenly there was no holding her back. One by one, she listed her friends' names and next to them their deepest, most urgent needs.

She didn't pause until the bottom of the page, where her own name had flowed in an inky flourish, but the magic ingredient to her happiness didn't seem so clear cut. Why wasn't she happy?

What was missing? She had money, job, home, a family - not that she saw much of them, but they were there - friends, clearly, that's what this was really about. So what was lacking? She knew, but didn't want to admit it, and writing it down, in black and white, pained her.

'Do I need to write it down? If you're real then you already know, right?'

The absence of a response seemed like an answer in itself, but she waited, in case there was some delay in communication. Nothing. She tapped her teeth with the pen, still loathe to expose herself on paper. The silence stretched, tension mounting.

'Ok! Ok! I'll do it.' She scratched the words "a man" next to her name, then scribbled it out and replaced it with a single telling word, "Love". 'There!' She threw the pad aside and, after one last chew, the pen followed. 'Happy now?'

The whole event had zapped her strength and she felt cold to the bone. She dragged a throw around her, curling up so it stretched right up to her ears. Her head still hurt, though the pain killers had kicked in some time ago, and she knew the only cure now was sleep. She jiggled the cushions to get comfortable and placed a spare one over her eyes. Anything to blot it all out.

CHAPTER 6

'There, you see? There's the deal.' Violet beamed, arms spread wide in vindication.

The ombudsman seemed less impressed. 'No. Not really.'

Her face fell.

'I'm sorry, but all I saw was a drunken young woman rambling. I certainly didn't hear anything from God.' He made to rise from his seat. 'If that's all there is we might as well call it a day.'

'No, wait.' In panic, Violet grabbed his arm. 'I know you couldn't actually hear his side of the agreement, but that doesn't really matter. What matters is that essentially a contract was formed.'

He made to interrupt, but she forged on, determined to get her point across. 'Wait, wait. A contract is essentially a set of promises, whereby one party agrees to do something for the other in exchange for benefit. Yes? Now, you've seen my demands and needs. I wrote them down for the sake of clarity, and my offer was I'd carry out random acts of kindness and personal sacrifice as the opportunity arose. It was then up to God to accept my terms, and although nothing was written down, although there was no actual verbal agreement, his actions spoke louder than words. You've only got to look at the evidence.'

'Violet, you've shown me no such evidence.'

She agreed. 'No, not yet, and I was still doubtful myself at that point. It was when things started to happen, it became obvious God was holding up his end. That's when I knew for certain.'

'Violet, I don't think…'

She pulled on his sleeve, urging him back into his seat. 'Watch some more. I can prove it to you.'

He sat down, the whole row of chairs wobbling with the momentum.

'Just a few minutes more. What harm can it do?' She tried to read his expression in the dim lighting.

Finally, he shrugged. 'Go on then, but make it quick.'

January First

New Year's Day was a washout. The dreadful weather of the night before had continued and Violet was using it as an excuse to nurse a hangover in front of a black and white musical on the television. She cobbled together some leftovers for lunch at about three in the afternoon and, as she bit into a sandwich, the list caught her eye. What had she been thinking?

The doorbell rang, and she hid the notebook in the drawer, away from prying eyes, though she had no idea who could be calling. She wasn't expecting anyone and she wasn't the sort of person people called on without prior arrangement. Her hair hadn't been brushed and she ran splayed fingers through it to achieve some semblance of order, before opening the door.

Outside stood a vaguely familiar figure, a neighbour from the other end of the corridor if she remembered correctly, but the young woman's face was strained and she was as dishevelled as Violet, if not more so.

'Hi?' Violet *was intrigued. They had barely exchanged two words previously.*

'Hi.' The woman leaned against the door jamb, seemingly lacking the strength to stay up right unaided. 'Look, I know you don't really know me, but is there any chance you could you do me a massive favour?'

Violet paused. They were definitely not on "massive favour" terms. This was so out of the norm. Weird. Unprompted, the list shimmied into her thoughts.

'I wouldn't ask if I wasn't desperate. There's no one else.'

The woman had obviously taken her tardy response as refusal and Violet detected a tremor in her neighbour's bottom lip. 'What's the problem?' *Under normal circumstances she would have made excuses, without a second thought, but she couldn't shake the idea this may be her first opportunity to contribute toward the deal.*

'It's Arthur. He's been so unwell. I haven't had a wink of sleep.'

Violet tried to picture a face to fill the void the name had created, a boyfriend, a husband? She couldn't remember seeing the woman with a man. 'Arthur?'

'My little boy.'

Of course. There was usually a pushchair attached to the neighbour. That's why she looked out of place.

'I thought it was his teeth. He's that age, you know, but the duty doctor says it's an ear infection. The poor mite's in agony and I've been so impatient with him.' A tear plopped on to her cheek.

'Oh, I'm sure not.' *Violet patted a shoulder in encouragement.* 'What can I do to help?' *She couldn't turn her away, particularly if this was an opportunity to earn points.*

The woman's demeanour immediately changed, detecting hope. 'The doctor's given me a prescription, but the only chemist open is a mile away and they close in an hour, and I really shouldn't take Arthur out in this weather.'

A quick trot to the pharmacy? Violet could manage that. No problem. 'Of course. Let me have it. I can be there and back in no time.'

'It's kind of you, but I need to pick up a few other bits, nappies and formula. Plus, I feel like if I don't get out from these four walls for a few minutes I'm going to go completely berserk. What I was hoping was that you would watch Arthur, for a little while.'

Violet was torn. On one hand, she knew nothing about babies, was in fact petrified of them, but on the other, the woman was clearly frazzled. The fear must have shown in Violet's eyes, as the woman's shoulders dropped and her voice took on a new tremor. 'I wouldn't be long, I promise. And he's fast asleep in his buggy right now. I could wheel him in here and be back before he even knows I've gone.'

So, this was how it would be. God was testing her mettle from the outset. Could she do it? Was it worth it? If it meant a baby for Kate, or a job for Ayesha, yes, it was. And, if it was all a figment of her imagination, the proof would out and she could fling the list in the bin. Violet took a deep breath to steady her nerves, she was a full-grown woman for heaven's sake. How difficult could minding a baby be? 'No problem. Bring him round.'

The woman, who introduced herself as Naomi, ran back to her own door and reappeared moments later in a waterproof coat, and with a small blond boy with flushed cheeks, in a pushchair, a cuddly rabbit gripped tightly under his arm.

'This is Arthur.' *She parked him in Violet's lounge and handed her a bag.* 'He shouldn't wake up, he's exhausted, but if he does everything you could possibly need is in there.' *She backed out of the door.* 'Thank you so much for this.'

Violet watched her leave then re-entered the flat, heart thudding in her chest. Giving the slumbering child a wide berth en route back to the sofa, she planned to sit in silence until Naomi returned: no sudden movements and no loud noises. It would be all right. As long as he didn't wake up, it would be fine.

The peace lasted less than ten minutes. Violet had watched every movement the little boy made, every twitch and shuffle, willing him to stay asleep. She turned the volume on the television down and the thermostat up to ensure he was comfortable, but there was nothing she could do about the wail from the sirens of a passing fire engine leaking into the room. That, combined with the flashing blue lights, whipping up a disco scene, jolted Arthur so his eyes fluttered open and he stared sightlessly into the mid distance. Violet stopped still, afraid to even breathe, silently pleading with him to close them again, but gradually a frown developed on his brow, his bottom lip protruded, and he turned his head to stare straight at her.

What should she do? She tried a smile, his frown only deepened. Perhaps he needed reassurance. 'Hello, Arthur.' Her words were soft, but they prompted an immediate reaction. His face screwed up into a ball and he screamed as loud as his lungs would allow.

She jumped to her feet. Now what? She couldn't just ignore him, but neither did she know how to do anything else. Think. What would Kate do? She was the most motherly person Violet knew so if she could channel her all would be well. Kate would pick him up, comfort him. Kate definitely wouldn't freak out.

Violet reached out to unclip the buckle secured across the child's middle and untangle his arms from the straps. All the while, his screams became louder and more urgent. Once he was free, she held him at arm's length, his legs dangling in mid-air. How did you hold a baby? She manoeuvred him close to her chest, one arm wrapped around him, the other struggling to keep his wriggling form vertical.

For the next few minutes, she pulled every tool she could conjure from her mental toolbox. She talked calmly to him, jiggled him gently, rocking back and forth. She went to the window, hoping the scene outside would distract him, as well as to check for any sign of his mother coming back. The hullaballoo continued.

What with her own stress and his agitation, her temperature rose and she regretted turning the heating up, so hurried to the hallway to turn it down. The crying temporarily faltered, but as soon as she stopped moving it began again. She studied the little boy. 'You like that, huh? You like the speed?'

She whisked from one end of the room to the other and once again he became quiet. Ok. If exercise was what it took, she could do that. Anything to stop the shrieks. She wished she'd put on her step tracker that morning, but hadn't anticipated moving much further than the sofa, now it seemed she may manage a new daily record.

On her fifteenth circuit from the lounge, to the kitchen and back again the doorbell rang and she glanced down at the boy. 'That'll be your mummy. Hallelujah.'

The boy let out a scream.

Relieved, she threw open the door, but rather than Naomi, it was Peter, the Street Pastor. His attire was a world away from the evening before, hat and multiple scarves exchanged for a sports jacket and jeans, but she recognised him in an instant.

'Oh, hello.' Her heart dropped and she bounced on the spot in an attempt to quieten Arthur. 'What are you doing here?'

He waved a shoe in the air. 'Good news. I managed to rescue your shoe. It's a bit soggy, but it'll be all right if you stuff it with newspaper and put it in the airing cupboard.' As she was unable to take it from him, he stepped inside and placed it on the floor. 'I didn't know you had a rug rat.'

She restarted marching up and down the corridor. 'Oh, no, he's not mine. I'm minding him for a neighbour.' Raising her voice to make it heard over the crying. 'He's not taken to me, I'm afraid.'

'Bless him. He does seem out of sorts. Here, let me.' He held out his arms to take the boy.

'Oh, I don't know. I don't think he likes strangers. He hasn't stopped...'

Peter took the child into his arms and the noise ceased. 'There, there.' He turned to Violet. 'What's his name?'

'Arthur.' She watched, astonished, as the boy calmed, the child eyeing Peter through stuttered breathing and reducing whimpers. 'You've done this before,' she accused.

'My brother's got three back in Ireland,' he offered by way of explanation, then ruffled the front of Arthur's t-shirt. 'Shall we go and sit down? Shall we? Shall we? Yes, we will, won't we?' He made his way to the lounge, lowered himself onto the sofa and reached for Arthur's abandoned rabbit. 'Who's this little fellow?'

Violet watched him talk gentle nonsense, waving the cuddly toy in all kinds of strange angles and was in awe. That was some skill he had. She stepped away, desperate for air. 'Coffee?'

'I shouldn't stop. I'm on my way out.'

Her stomach clenched at the idea of being alone with the baby again so soon. 'Are you sure? I owe you after last night, and for the shoe today. Thank you.'

He checked his watch and shuffled forward in his seat. 'Ahh, no, I should be away already.'

Arthur was deposited back into her arms and she and the child exchanged equally fearful expressions.

'Will you be all right now? He seems to have settled down.'

She didn't know whether to admit her reservations or be offended by the suggestion she couldn't manage, but he continued before she could work out which way to fall.

'Of course you will. Anyway, I'll see you around. Good bye, little man.' With that, he was gone.

Violet tentatively sat back in the chair, mimicking Peter's actions with the rabbit, while Arthur observed with a bemused expression.

Minutes later, she handed the boy back to his grateful mother, who, thanks to the serenity of the scene, was oblivious to the havoc her son's visit had caused. Violet accepted her thanks and promised it was no trouble and waved him away as if they were now good friends, but as soon as the door was closed she headed straight to the kitchen for wine.

With a glass in hand she retrieved the list from the drawer and made a quick note on the reverse. "Sacrifice one – Babysitting Arthur".

'Right then, God. What have you got for me?'

CHAPTER 7

Violet paused the screen.

'So, this is the evidence so far. Exhibit one – the list. Exhibit two – my first act of kindness, which I think you'll agree was no small thing. For exhibit three, we need to see God's response. I didn't have long to wait. In fact, it was only the next day I got my reward. Because my first contribution was babysitting, I expected the result to be baby related, but it wasn't. I didn't fully understand how it worked at that point. The benefit I received actually related to item three on my list, it related to Lulu.'

The ombudsman stared blankly. 'Lulu?'

'Yes, Lulu.'

He shook his head. 'Truly though, all this is irrelevant. I already told you, God doesn't do deals. Why would he make an exception for you?'

She hugged her face with her palms, thinking. 'You need to understand the connection me and my friends have. How important we are to each other. I know we're on a deadline, but can I show you? I do think it's the only way you can properly judge.'

He tapped his watch. 'Ok, ok. According to the stats, we have a little time, provided nothing changes, but if there are unexpected developments in the hospital, we'll have to stop short. We can't risk an overstay, or you may never get back.'

'Great. Let's do this.' She jumped the video back to the New Year's Eve dinner, zooming in on an image of her friend.

Lulu's face was alight, eyes crinkling as she laughed. She made an eye-catching portrait, with tumbling blonde hair and soft blue eyes. Her vivid red dress was overtly sexy, the shoulders and back no more than a breath of lace, the neckline daringly low cut.

'This is Lulu.'

The ombudsman flicked open the case of his tablet. 'Lulu who?'

'Smythe. You'll probably have her down as Louise Ratner-Smythe.'

He frowned as he surveyed the data.

'Lu's parents are politicians, spend a lot of time abroad. Lulu and her sister Rachael went to boarding school and spent most holidays with staff. The oldies had high expectations, and somewhere along the line Lulu's interest in medicine meant they had her earmarked as a doctor, but she's not the academic type. She's not dim, but she was never doctor material. She wanted to go into nursing. They pushed her, but her exam results had the final word. They wanted her to do re-takes, but she refused. I met her, in halls, first year at Uni. Her parents were so put out, they withdrew financial support, put their eggs into Rachael's basket instead – an 'A' student through and through.'

The ombudsman looked bored. 'It's a poor little rich girl tale, is it?'

She nodded, willing to allow him that. 'Cliché, but the reason it's cliché is because it actually happens. Anyway, Lulu worked hard, but those nurses party hard too – I couldn't keep up. When the money ran out she got herself a job in a bar, the result being her studies suffered, and she failed the first year. The Uni allowed her to re-take the year, but the bar work took over and she'd dropped out by Christmas. We were sharing a flat by that time and there didn't seem any reason for her to move out, as long as she could pay her share of the rent. If she wasn't working at the bar, she hung out there. Her life became one long party.'

His eyes darted across the page, reading notes as he listened. 'You're not telling me anything I didn't know.'

'Precisely. That's the story everyone knows. Lulu, with a different guy on her arm every week, always a glass in her hand. Her closest friends know different.' Violet pointed at the tablet. 'Does that thing tell you she's the kindest, most thoughtful person you could meet? She would do anything for a friend, but underneath all the bluster, she's extremely vulnerable. She created this "I don't care what people think" persona, but it's not real. She disappointed herself more than anyone else, and now can't pull herself out of the rut, but she is a really, really good person,' her tone was emphatic, daring him to argue.

He nodded, taking in her comments. 'Accepted, but your point?'

'I'm getting there.' She scrolled through footage. 'At that point I was worried. Look.' She stopped on a scene of Lulu, distracted, checking her phone. 'And here too.'

She flicked through scene after scene, pausing only briefly before speeding on. Again and again, Lulu was shown, checking her watch, glancing at the door, fiddling with her handbag.

'Her sister was diagnosed with leukaemia a couple of years earlier. She was in and out of hospital for all sorts of horrendous treatments, none of which had any lasting impact. Rachael was the only family Lulu felt properly connected with. In fact, she adored her and felt guilty for passing the buck years ago, so all the pressure from the parents had transferred to Rachael's shoulders. Maybe she even thought it contributed to Rachael becoming ill. She was starting to lose hope. Watch this, it says everything.'

New Year's Eve – A Year Ago

Ayesha's head and shoulders were sprawled across the table, while Violet patted her hand. Cold air seeped around them as the restaurant door swung open and closed behind a middle-aged round man, sporting a comb over and Bluetooth. Lulu shuffled to the end of the seat.

'That'll be for us. Get under the other arm, Vi, see if we can get her up?' She hoisted Ayesha's arm around her shoulder and heaved, clearly no stranger to manipulating a drunken body. 'Come on my lovely, up and out.'

As Violet tried to assist, their handsome, young waiter arrived alongside. His Italian accent matched his dark hair and olive skin. 'Did you order a taxi, ladies? Are you leaving us already?'

Violet was conscious of interested glances from the other diners. 'Yes, thank you, Antonio. My friend needs to go home, but we're staying.'

His smile was understanding. 'Let me help you.'

He reached around Ayesha's waist and swept her up effortlessly. Violet grabbed Ayesha's handbag and checked around to ensure nothing had been left behind. He had whisked his burden out, past the other diners with the minimum of fuss. By the time Violet and Lulu caught up with him, he was shuffling Ayesha into the rear seat of the taxi, chattering to the driver.

He backed out. 'If you can give the driver directions, I will fetch the lady's coat. It was the turquoise wool funnel coat, yes?'

Violet looked at Lulu, clueless, having been last to arrive.

Lulu jumped in. 'Yes. Can you also bring the black leather bomber jacket, please? Thanks.'

As Antonio returned inside, Violet hunched her shoulders against sharp pellets of rain and turned to her friend. 'You are coming back, aren't you? It's early yet.'

'Not tonight.' She reached for Violet's hand. 'I have had a good time, so thank you for making me get off my backside and come out. But I promised to see the New Year in with Rachael. You understand, don't you? She's stuck in the observation ward again and she so wanted to be at home. Mum and Dad are in Paris, so it's the least I can do to spend an hour with her, but you guys, you can still enjoy the rest of the night, can't you?'

Violet tightened her grip on the hand holding her own. 'Of course we can, but we haven't had a proper catch up yet.'

Lulu's smile was bittersweet. 'I know. We hardly seem to do more than bump into each other these days, do we? But, I don't know, my heart's not in it tonight. It breaks my heart to see Rachael in that place.' She lowered her voice so it was barely audible as it was carried away by the wind. 'I can't help thinking this could be my last chance. Vi, this could be her last New Year.'

Violet pulled Lulu into her arms, partly to offer comfort and partly to hide her own distress. 'Oh, Lu, I wish I could make it all better for you. If wanting anything enough could make it come true, Rachael would be back to her old self tomorrow. We're all willing her on.'

Antonio bustled out, carrying two coats under his arm and a wide, black umbrella above him, at the same time preventing the door from flying out with his leg. 'Here you are ladies, let me help you.'

Violet released Lulu, flung Ayesha's coat into the taxi and set about checking the seatbelt, as Antonio helped Lulu into her jacket. She stepped back, joining him in the meagre shelter of the umbrella, hugging herself for warmth as she watched Lulu climb into the front passenger seat. 'Happy New Year!' As the door clanged shut, she raised her voice. And give my love to Rae!'

She watched the taxi disappear into traffic, feeling powerless and abandoned.

Antonio's melodic voice recalled her to herself. 'Sometimes goodbye is difficult, isn't it?'

She nodded, blinking to disperse the droplets balanced on her lashes, until they merged with the rain on her face.

'Your other friends are still here for you,' he cajoled.

Violet smiled. She had no reason to feel sorry for herself. Her problems paled into insignificance when she thought of what others around her were coping with. She turned to peer mock suspiciously into his eyes. 'I suspect you're more than simply a waiter, Antonio. I think you double up as an agony aunt and a guardian angel as well.'

He laughed. 'No, no, only a waiter.'

They turned towards the door. 'Do you have someone waiting for you too?' She asked.

'Oh yes,' he admitted. 'Everyone must have someone, somewhere, even if we haven't met them yet. As it happens, my someone is the chef here. A grumpy, bossy man who gets far too stressed about his work. If it wasn't for me, he would work himself into an early grave over something no more important than the seasoning of the soup.'

She laughed aloud. Whether intentionally or not, he had succeeded in lifting her mood. She headed back to the table with renewed determination, to make the most of what was left of the evening, and the

warmth of friendship waiting there.

***

'You see, those women mean the world to me. They're the cement that keeps me together. When I see them suffer, going through...' She shrugged as she searched for the right word to sum it up. 'Stuff, I feel it too, even when other people may not see they're going through anything at all. That was the first time I saw Lulu leave a party stone cold sober, and it's the first time I heard her admit Rachael's situation may not have a happy ending. She put on the bravest face, but inside it was ripping her apart, simply by saying those words out loud.'

He seemed thoughtful as he selected his words. 'It is hard to watch a sad story play out in front of you. I can understand how helpless it made you feel, but Lulu's situation isn't new, it's going on in many lives, in many places, every day.'

'I know.' Violet smiled wryly. 'But that's in other people's lives. When it's your life, or somebody close to you, it's real, isn't it? Hearing Lulu admit she was scared, scared me too. Most of the time I think we're invincible, that I'm invincible, but I'm not.'

'Anyway.' She took a deep, cleansing breath and flexed her shoulders, preparing to continue. 'Back to the task in hand. Do you see? How close we are? How connected we are?'

The ombudsman's frown was pronounced. 'I do, but...'

'But nothing. I would have given anything to make things right for Lulu, and that meant making things right for Rachael too. We have a special bond. What God did next shows he recognised that. Watch what happened, after the Arthur incident.'

She brooked no argument, immediately moving the video on.

CHAPTER 8

January Second

Violet ran across the park, as a short cut to meet with Isobel. The rain had stopped, but the wind hurled heavy drips from the trees in wild gusts, and she had to keep one eye on the path to avoid the puddles. Isobel was already in the café, halfway through her first cup of coffee.

'I've already ordered for you. I'm guessing you're pushed for time, as usual.'

'Thanks.' Violet flopped into the free seat. 'Yes, I've got a conference call at two. Sorry, I couldn't put it off. Someone's pulled out of Friday's show. At this time of year, with so many people still away, it's a nightmare trying to fill the gap.'

'You know you love it.' Isobel pushed a coffee towards her. 'Go on, get some caffeine in you. Have you heard from Lu today?'

Violet felt the hot liquid filter into her system and flexed her shoulders to release the tension. 'No. Should I have?'

A waitress arrived with two salads and conversation paused as they prepared to eat.

'No, it's only, we were talking on New Years' Eve and she mentioned a meeting about Rae was happening yesterday. I wondered what the outcome was.'

'And you haven't rung her to find out?' Violet was flabbergasted.

'Um, no. No, I haven't.' Isobel blushed and the forkful of salad halfway to her mouth returned to the plate. *'I couldn't. What if it was bad news? I wouldn't know how to handle it.'*

Violet pulled out her phone and found Lulu in her contacts. *'You just handle it. Lu could be dealing with this on her own, for goodness sake.'*

She tapped her shoe against the table leg as she waited for the call to connect. *'Lu? It's Vi. I'm with Issy, she told me about the meeting. What happened?'*

There was a brief exchange of words, after which Violet replaced the phone on the table.

Isobel's face was frozen in anticipation. *'Well?'*

'She's only five minutes away, so she's going to get off the bus a stop early to meet us here.'

'But, how did she sound? Was it bad?' She rubbed her forehead. *'Oh Lord, what am I supposed to say to her?'*

'Issy! She's our friend. Don't panic. Whatever's happened, we'll deal with it. Besides, she sounded pretty upbeat.' Violet sipped at her coffee. *'My money's on good news.'*

They picked at their food, one eye on the door. When Lulu entered, the smile on her face immediately dispersed the tension.

'Hi girls.' Lulu swept in to exchange hugs and kisses, then picked up Isobel's fork and stabbed a piece of chicken. *'Are you not eating this?'* Without waiting for a reply, she swept it into her mouth.

'Well?' Violet's patience ran out first. *'What happened?'*

Lulu tried to swallow, then reached for Violet's coffee to wash the chicken down.

'Do you want me to order you one?'

'No.' She swallowed again. *'I can't stop. I need to get to work, but I had to bring you both up to date.'* A deep breath indicated a move to serious business. *'There's good news and bad news.*

Basically, the powers that be had their meeting to discuss Rae's treatment plan and there aren't a lot of options left. The good news is they agreed to try her with a new drug regime. It's a bit experimental, but initial results have been impressive so far. The side effects can be rough, but it's a chance.' She shrugged.

'So, what's the bad news?'

'Bad news is, it's a last resort, so all our eggs are in this one basket. If this doesn't work...' As her words fell away, the determined smile on her face cracked.

Violet jumped in. *'If this doesn't work, there may be another new drug ready to try by then, but anyway, it will work. I've got a feeling.'*

Isobel couldn't bring herself to speak and merely patted Lulu's hand.

'You should have let me know.' Violet grabbed her cup back.

'I would have, but it all dragged on. They were supposed to have the meeting in the morning, but it was delayed until the afternoon. Then, there was a disagreement, some were in favour, but some weren't. They were deadlocked,' she lowered her voice. *'I only know because one of my nurse friends leaked me inside information. Apparently one of the consultants left to take a call and by the time he came back he'd changed his mind and gave the go ahead. It was a mini miracle.'*

Lulu's words hung in the air. Violet caught them and twisted them around, examining their meaning. A miracle? She tried to sound casual. 'So, what time did he give the go ahead?'

'I don't know, late afternoon, four thirty, maybe.' She frowned at Violet's concentration, misreading it. *'I couldn't call you then because Rachael hadn't been told. They gave her analgesia because she's had such awful headaches this last week, with the fever, and it completely knocked her out. She didn't wake up until the early hours.'*

Violet clamped her teeth together in shock as she did the calculation. The meeting was at four thirty. Violet had handed Arthur back to Naomi at four thirty. There had to be a connection.

Lulu stared at her. 'What?'

Violet shook her head, clearing the look. There was no way she was sharing her suspicions at this early stage, but her stomach gurgled with excitement. 'Nothing. No, nothing. It's just, I have such a good feeling about this.' She pulled Lulu in for another hug. 'I can't explain it, it just feels right.'

Lulu and Isobel exchanged glances. Violet was the least likely of their group to succumb to superstition or instinct.

Violet saw the shared look and shrugged. 'Don't ask me. I don't know why, but my gut says this is great news.'

Lulu raised her eyebrows. 'Well, who are we to doubt your digestive tract?'

***

Violet held up a staying hand. 'I know what you're going to say. It's not enough. It doesn't prove anything. And you're right, it doesn't. It was an isolated incident, but it opened my mind up to the possibility something other than coincidence was involved. In fact, it opened my mind up to all sorts of thoughts. Like, it dawned on me, if it was real, what a major undertaking I had signed up for. My list had five items on it, but they were big asks. I would clearly need to make more than five sacrifices. Obviously, an hour and a half babysitting in no way equates to a cure for cancer.' Violet rolled her eyes at her own naivety.

The ombudsman listened in silence.

'I spent a couple of days flicking from one opinion to another and back again. Was it real? Was it not real? But in the end, all I could do was test the system.'

'Probably a sensible idea.' Agreed the ombudsman.

'If it happened again, if I did something good and something from my list took a step forward, then I could be more certain. So, I spent the next few days waiting for opportunities.'

Violet skipped the video forward. 'Yes, this was the second event, a week or so after the last. Here we go.'

CHAPTER 9

Mid-January

Violet climbed out of a taxi in front of her building, weighed down with groceries. The driver followed with more and, after she had accessed the lobby, he dropped them next to her on the carpet and jogged away without a word. She was glad she hadn't tipped him more generously. One bag tipped on its side and an apple rolled across the floor. A large grey trainer stretched out to halt its passage and she glanced up to ascertain the owner of the footwear. It was Peter.

'Oh, hello. Good catch.' She was suspicious of his third appearance in such a short time. 'What are you doing here?'

He bent down to retrieve the fruit and handed it back. 'I should have mentioned my company's taken over the maintenance contract for these flats, among a host of others, from the beginning of the year. I'm afraid you might see me around from time to time.'

'Don't apologise.' She attempted to draw the bags together, ready to transport. 'Perhaps things might actually get done around here. A bulb's been out at the end of my landing for three months, at least.'

'Bulb on level three, noted.' He squeezed his face into a grimace. 'Unfortunately we have bigger issues right now though.'

She interrupted her juggling to look up at him. 'Really? What issues?'

'The lift's out of order.' He shrugged. 'Sorry. I'm waiting for an engineer.'

Her shoulders sagged. The perfect end to the perfect day.

'I would offer to help you, but I've no out of order sign and I need to watch the lift to make sure no one uses it.' He lowered his voice, 'I turned my back for five minutes earlier and Ramon from the top floor got in it. It took me twenty minutes to get him out. He wasn't best pleased.'

She managed a chuckle. 'I bet he wasn't.' Lifting half the bags, she nudged those remaining with her foot. 'It's no good, I'm going to have to make two trips. Can I leave these here?'

'Course. I'll put them round the corner out of the way.'

Her legs were heavy after a hectic day at work, but she was determined to stay positive. By the time she had tackled three flights of stairs twice, she would have earned a long soak in the bath and a glass of wine. She might even light a candle. Depositing the first load in the kitchen, she transferred a bottle of Sancerre to the fridge before heading back down. As she approached the flight to the ground floor, heated voices floated up. She recognised Peter's apologetic tone, but the other was unknown.

'I told my daughter it wouldn't work. A woman my age on the fifth floor, but she wouldn't have it. All mod cons, she said. Always someone on hand, she said. But, it's no good her being just up the road if I can't get to my flat, is it? She's not going to put me on her shoulders and carry me up, is she?'

'I'm sorry Mrs Brent. There'll be someone here to fix it soon, I'm sure. He said he'd be here twenty minutes ago.'

Violet tiptoed into the lobby. She had seen the old woman a couple of times, coming and going with her wheeled walker, but they had never spoken.

'That's no good to me though, is it? I can't stand here and wait until it's mended, can I?'

Violet felt for both the woman and Peter. As inconvenient as it had been for her, having to walk up and down to her flat twice, it was far worse for the woman, and it wasn't Peter's fault the lift had broken down. Her natural instinct was to skirt around the pair, collect her bags and go, the hot scented bath whispering sweet nothings to her aching feet, but a niggle had started up in the back of her mind. She should try to help. She should go out of her way to be a good neighbour. Peter glanced up and met her eye and the niggle became more pronounced. He was getting it in the neck for no good reason and Violet did owe him. There was a beautiful pair of black heeled pumps sitting in her wardrobe, thanks to his actions.

She produced a smile which didn't make it past her lips. 'Perhaps I can help?' A small chance remained the woman would refuse assistance and Violet could still make it to her couch at a reasonable hour.

'What do you suggest, dear?' For all her cross words, the woman's eyes displayed vulnerability rather than anger.

Violet's heart softened. 'Well, we could walk up together. You can lean on me. We can take it slow, one step at a time. I'll come back down for your walker after.'

The woman looked at Peter, considering the offer. Peter was encouraging. 'There you are, Mrs Brent. Violet will give you a hand. You'll be tucked up in your flat in no time.'

There was something very scared rabbit in the woman's expression and Violet felt the need to take charge, as she would at work, with a nervous guest on the show. She took the woman's arm and placed it on her own. 'Come on, Mrs Brent. We've not met properly before, have we? It'll give us a chance to get to know each other.'

The woman edged towards the stairs, her trust growing. 'I'm on the fifth floor, dear. Are you sure?'

'Absolutely. So, tell me, where were you living before here?'

As Mrs Brent lifted one knobbly foot onto the first step, her concentration moving on to relating stories of her past, Violet looked over her shoulder. Peter gave a quick wink and mouthed 'thank you', before turning to deliver the bad news to another arrival at the front door. Violet felt a warm wave of pride spread through her. It wasn't a feeling she was used to.

The journey was an eventful one. By the time they reached the third floor, Mrs Brent was struggling and Violet nipped into her own flat for a chair. Hearing the commotion, Naomi joined them on the landing and revived the old lady with a cup of tea. As the woman sipped and sighed with pleasure, Violet glanced at her watch. The evening was ticking away.

It was a relief to both of them when they reached the fifth floor and Mrs Brent's door. Violet helped her into a floral armchair, where she exchanged shoes for well-worn slippers. 'Thank you, dear. I couldn't have done it without you.'

'You're welcome, Mrs Brent.'

'Rhoda, dear. Call me Rhoda.' Her smile was weary as she took Violet's hand. 'Do you know, I've been living here six months and until today I didn't know anyone else in the building? It's a nuisance that thing breaking down, but silver linings, eh? I've met two new friends.' She kissed her hand, before releasing it.

Violet was touched by the woman's gratitude. 'You're welcome, Rhoda. It was nice to meet you too. Now we won't be strangers when we pass in the halls. I'll leave your walker outside your door in a while. All right?'

'All right, dear.'

As Violet began her descent the residue of warmth from the interaction dissipated and logic took control. If babysitting for an hour and a half had warranted Rachael's acceptance onto a new treatment, what would tonight's escapade earn? She almost couldn't wait to find out.

Peter was busy with the engineer in the lobby, so she helped herself to Rhoda's walker. The thought of the payback for tonight's good deed made her third journey seem like nothing.

She was still imagining good news winging its way to her when she reached her own level in pursuit of her shopping, but there she found Peter waiting, her bags in his hands.

'Here you are. The engineer's on guard duty now. Sorry about all that. You must be exhausted. Was Mrs B all right in the end?'

She unlocked her door, so he could carry the bags through. 'I'll have you know Rhoda and I are now good friends. Yes, she was fine, but you're not wrong, I am exhausted. Is it fixed now?'

'Well on its way. Anyway, I'd better go keep an eye on the engineer. Thanks for stepping in.' He held up a hand as he walked away.

Once in the comfort of her own apartment, Violet whipped herself into a frenzy of organisation, pouring scented oils into the bath. While it ran, she packed away the shopping and put a ready meal in the oven. Ok, so the candle may be a step too far at this late hour, but there was no reason why she should forego the other pleasures she had planned for the evening. She poured the wine, carried it through to the bathroom and eased into the steaming water. Maybe today hadn't been all bad.

Her telephone beeped and she balanced her glass on the lip of the tub and reached to read the message.

It was Issy on WhatsApp. "Don't forget Culture Sunday this weekend. Whose turn is it to choose?"

One weekend of every month, the girls took themselves off to explore something new, to broaden their horizons. It usually ended with cocktails.

Violet reached for a towel to dry her hands so she could reply, but before she had the opportunity Ayesha had chipped in. "It's Vi's turn. Who's coming this month? Can everybody make it?"

Kate was next. "Yes, in fact I'm going to be relying on you guys to help occupy my time from now on. Fantastic news. Ben got his promotion. It means more hours, but also more wonga, which means IVF sooner than we hoped. Yahoo!"

There was a flurry of congratulations.

Violet was thoughtful as the discussion on where to go for their outing resumed. Was this her payback? Kate's policeman husband getting promoted? Of course, it meant another chance at IVF, but that had seemed a mixed blessing thus far, at least to everyone in the group except Kate. The hope offered by their rounds of treatment had been far outweighed by the devastating disappointment and loss actually delivered. Violet's heart sank at the thought of supporting their friend through such another pummelling. Except, if this was her payback, then surely that meant this time it would be successful. Kate would finally get the baby she longed for.

Violet dropped her phone onto the fluffy towel on the bathroom floor and rested back in the cooling water. She didn't know whether to laugh or cry.

***

'Well, I must say the evidence you're putting forward is rather spurious,' the ombudsman said. 'I'm afraid correlation doesn't imply causation. It seems to me you're even doubtful yourself. You certainly don't look over the moon about the news received that particular day which, if it was a step towards one of your five main goals, I would have expected you to.'

Violet's smile was a mere compression of the lips. 'Life's not always that simple, is it?'

'Isn't it? Most matters are black and white, as far as I can see. From what I've observed of life, it's only when we don't want to accept the facts the waters become muddied.'

'Observing something and actually living it are two very different things. I'm sure you realise that.' She watched the frown on his forehead deepen. 'Look, I wanted Kate's dreams to come true, I really did, but I didn't want her to go through more of the stress and turmoil IVF had wreaked previously. You should have seen her in those days. The treatment was unpleasant and the hormones made her super emotional. She and Ben spent a lot of the time at loggerheads, although it was something they were supposed to be doing together. I think seeing her like that tore him apart. In fact, I think if it was up to him he would have given up rather than see her put through it, but for Kate it was never an option. When the treatment failed, it hit her like a tonne of bricks. The last time was the worst. About six months before the New Year dinner. Kate actually did manage to get pregnant, but she miscarried at ten weeks. She was in pieces, for months. It was only the thought of the next attempt that lifted her out of it.'

'I understand how difficult it could be for her, and her friends, but isn't that what friendship is, being there in good times and bad?'

'Absolutely, and if suffering through another round was the only way she would achieve her perfect outcome, then we would all go through it with her again, without a doubt, but it wasn't something I relished. When I wrote "baby" on my list, I had imagined a simpler answer. Not a stupid pay rise.' She kicked out at the leg of the chair in front. 'Me, more than any of the others needed to prove myself. I'm afraid I hadn't been as good a friend as I should have at times, and I was still feeling guilty about my most recent clanger. Me and my big mouth.'

The ombudsman pursed his lips. 'I'm not sure I want or need to know.'

'I'm not sure I want to tell you, but I think I probably should.'

He sighed. 'Are we reviewing the entirety of Kate's life now, as well as your own?'

'No, no.' She flicked through scenes in the video. 'We're only going back to that night again. Believe me, on New Year's Eve it was all happening.'

CHAPTER 10

New Year's Eve – A Year Ago

Numbers in the restaurant had dwindled and the atmosphere began to peter off; chatter reduced to a dull hum, until their diminished group felt obliged to settle their bill and head off. Irish coffees had done nothing to dampen their spirits and they giggled and hugged their way to the foyer, pulling on coats and scarves in preparation for the harsh night. Antonio assisted them with wayward sleeves and professionally avoided wayward hands, particularly Issy's, who seemed inexplicably unable to avoid his bottom. They tumbled out and huddled in the doorway.

Violet was eager for the evening to continue, hooking an arm into the crook of the other girls' elbows. 'Come on. Race you to Arnie's for a night cap.'

Issy was not ready to leave the restaurant behind. 'Antonio should come with us. His shift must be almost over.'

In a moment of daring, it seemed she was about to re-enter to offer up an invitation, but Violet grasped her tightly. 'No, he wouldn't. I happen to know he has other plans. Come on, Kate. Let's go.'

Kate was the least inebriated and had a close eye on the other two. 'Are you sure you want any more? We've already lost Ayesha to the demon drink. You'll regret it in the morning.'

Violet pooh-poohed the idea. 'Oh, one more won't make any difference and anyway a walk in the wind and rain will sober us up. Come on, let's have champagne.' She shouted into the night air, 'It's New Year's eve!'

They wavered along the pavement, Violet in the middle, dragging the others in her wake. Kate laughed at her exuberance, struggling to balance in high heels. 'All right. I haven't been to Arnie's in ages. Come on Issy, keep up.'

Issy's forward propulsion may have been aided had she been looking in the right direction, but her head was firmly focused behind. 'But what about Antonio?' she whined, taking on the tone of a petulant child. 'I'm sure he would like Arnie's.'

Violet halted and drew the others into a confidential circle. 'Between you and me.' She paused, looking around for witnesses. 'Antonio may be interested in Arnie, but he most definitely is not interested in you, Issy.'

'What do you mean?' Issy's whisper was less than subtle, drawing the curious attention of a couple passing in the opposite direction.

Violet waited until they were out of earshot before continuing. 'I'm afraid he's gay,' she announced.

'Gay?' Issy's voice rose with consternation, 'No, he is not! Didn't you see the way he was looking at me all night?'

Violet attempted to hold her gaze. 'Issy, you look stunning tonight. You're gorgeous,' her voice rose with enthusiasm. 'But you're simply not Antonio's type. Trust me.' She turned to Kate for back up. 'Come on, Kate, tell her. She's gorgeous, isn't she? The right man is out there somewhere, but it's not Antonio. Sorry, Is.'

Issy's face drooped, her eyes doleful.

Kate jumped in to soothe hurt feelings. *'Issy, you've got to be patient. Who knows? Maybe this time next week you'll have met the man of your dreams.'*

Violet enjoyed this particular train of thought. *'That's right. This year, I mean the year which starts in half an hour, could be your year. Maybe your perfect man is in Arnie's right now, tall, dark and handsome, waiting for you to walk through the doors. It could happen. Miracles happen. In fact, maybe there's one there for me too. Ha!'* She folded in half with laughter.

'What's so funny?' Issy found Violet's mirth perturbing.

She straightened up. *'Oh, nothing. I just had a vision of all these guys in a row with roses in their lapels and bow ties and glasses of champagne, like Gene Kelly, waiting to dance us into the rain.'* She swung her arms as if she were about to launch into a waltz.

Kate shook her head. *'I think you've actually had enough of the booze already, but let's go.'*

They straightened up, linking arms again, with Kate now in the middle, serving as a pillar of support. Violet laughed as she marched. *'We're like in the Wizard of Oz. We're off to see the wizard. He's drinking shots at Arnie's.'*

Kate chortled. *'As I was saying, more than enough.'*

'Oh, go with it, Kate, have fun for a minute,' Violet encouraged. *'You're Dorothy. Who are you Issy? The cowardly lion? The scarecrow? Or, or the tin man?'*

'Ooh, I don't know. I don't think I want to be any of them. They're all men for starters, and I'm not bothered about being brave or brainy and I've already got a heart, even if it has got some dents.' Her face gurned as she concentrated on the question. *'I know. I want to be the nice witch.'*

Violet halted once more in her tracks, almost pulling Kate over. *'Aww, that's lovely. You want to make everyone's dreams come true.'*

'No, I want to be pretty, and skinny, and have lovely clothes and for people to admire me.'

Kate hugged Issy to her with one arm, at the same time holding Violet upright. 'Issy, you're already pretty and you have a great body and we do admire you. Don't we, Violet?'

'Yeah, and you have lovely clothes too. Look.' She pointed at their reflection, clear as day in the shop-front window.

The three of them stared at the image, a bedraggled vision of friendship, their bodies expanding and shrinking as they swayed in front of the street light illuminating the scene. They were very different bodily: Kate tall, upright and willowy; Issy petite and rounder to the point of voluptuousness and Violet somewhere in between, but they made for an attractive picture, despite their hair blowing wildly with the gusty wind and their slightly dishevelled attire.

Violet pointed as steady a finger as she could manage at the trio staring back. 'We are fabulous, and don't let anybody tell you different.'

A mass of young men bustled past, their faces briefly appearing and disappearing alongside the girls, as they strained to work out what they were staring at. One of them muttered something about women and shopping and the whole group guffawed as they continued on their way. The girls looked at each other and laughed.

'Come on, let's get to Arnie's, or we'll miss midnight,' Kate encouraged, and they moved forward again, with a new sense of purpose.

Issy returned to the topic. 'Seriously though, Vi, what would you ask the wizard for?'

'Oh, I don't know. A fortnight on a desert island somewhere maybe, or a lottery win? It's not like you'd actually get what you asked for anyway.'

Kate raised her eyebrows at the sudden dip in enthusiasm. 'What happened to "go with it, Kate"? "Let yourself have fun, Kate"? Huh?'

They all turned into a corner, past a queue of taxis lining the pavement, nudging along every time the front car took passengers on board and moved away from the kerb. The quiet rumbling of engines ticking over and the acrid aroma of exhaust fumes warmed the air.

'You've seen the film. He lets everybody down, like every other man in history. What's new?' Violet blurted.

Isobel winced, raising her voice as music spilling out from the wine bar, still half a street away, began to invade their relatively peaceful approach. 'Ouch! There speaks a woman scorned.'

Violet thrashed her head from side to side. 'No, no, no! Don't tell me it's just me. Look at some of the shockers who've have done the dirty on you. Look at Martin for goodness sake. The evidence is all on my side.'

Kate pulled her in firmly, out of the way of slow-moving revellers, passing in the opposite direction, all at varying speeds and levels of intoxication. 'No one's arguing there aren't bad guys out there, and I know you're still sore after Ryan, but there are good ones too. Look at my Ben? He's a treasure.'

'Oh, Ben. Yes, I suppose I'll give you that, but he is a treasure, a rare and valuable thing that's hard to find. In fact, he might be the only one left. Good men are like dodos. Perhaps me and you should give up, Issy.'

Isobel's duck pout was back as she pondered Violet's negativity. 'You're right,' she breathed. 'It's hopeless. We'll be old maids, with nothing but a house full of smelly cats for company.'

Violet's shoulders slumped in tandem with her ebullience and she leaned around Kate to hug Isobel into her side, almost tripping them all up in her momentum. 'Let's get slaughtered,' she whispered conspiratorially.

Kate, as ever, was the voice of reason. 'Come on, girls. You know that won't help anything. You'll only feel worse in the morning.'

'I'll worry about the morning in the morning,' Violet pronounced. 'Tonight I want to blot it all out.'

'You know I'm right.' Kate's tone was cajoling.

'Leave us alone.' Violet moaned, leaning against the tall wooden frame of the pub front, almost yelling above the now intrusive noise level, drum and bass vibrating the glass next to her. 'It's all right for you, with precious Ben to go home to. We're alone and hopeless and getting drunk is all there is.'

Exasperation began to win out, 'Good grief, Vi. What happened to "It's New Year's Eve!" and Gene Kelly and all that palaver?'

'It got rained on.' She straightened her shoulders and gestured ahead emphatically, her pointing finger repeatedly stabbing at the night air. 'The door to Arnie's is right there and I'm going in and I'm getting wasted. That's the end of it.'

'Oh, Vi. I think you'd be better off getting the next cab and going home. You'll thank me in the morning.'

She turned on Kate with venom. 'Kate, I am not a child. Go and practice your mothering skills on someone who's interested, why don't you?'

Kate dropped Violet's arm like a hot potato and turned stony faced to Isobel. 'Look, Issy, I've had enough for the night. I don't want to cramp your style. You two have a good time and I'll speak to you in a couple of days.'

She hitched her bag over her shoulder, straightened her jacket and marched to the front of the waiting line of cabs, got into the back seat and was driven away, without a backward glance.

Violet was dumbfounded. 'What's her problem?' she wailed, torn between bafflement and chagrin.

Isobel met her gaze, wide eyed. 'Oh, Vi, that was the wrong thing to say. You know she's fragile right now. She only came out because Ben's taken an extra shift to help pay for another round of IVF and he didn't want her to be home on her own tonight.'

Violet's hand flew to her face, covering the mouth which had let her down so badly. She closed her eyes, muttering expletives into her palm. All her preparation, all her rehearsing before leaving the flat and it had all gone to pot. How stupid was she?

Isobel's arm snaked around Violet's frame as she pulled her into an embrace. 'Don't worry, Vi, it will all be forgotten in the morning. You didn't mean anything by it.'

'What a stupid cow I am. Poor Kate. She'll never forgive me.' She was distraught at her thoughtlessness.

Isobel gripped her tighter momentarily, before releasing her shoulders and grabbing her hand instead and pulling her towards the entrance. 'Don't be silly. This is Kate we're talking about. She never held a grudge against anyone for more than five minutes. Come on. Let's have that champers.'

Violet could barely meet the gaze of the ombudsman, so ashamed was she of her hurtful outburst. 'And then there were two. From one disaster to another. You see why I ended up in a stupor on the bridge?'

'I see you said something you wish you hadn't.' His brow was furrowed. 'Many a harsh word is uttered in haste. Your friend was right, I'm sure. No doubt you were soon forgiven?'

'Oh, yes. Kate is the most forgiving angel on the planet, but it's not so easy to forgive yourself, is it? That's why she was top of my list. She deserves so much more, and I felt so guilty.'

Silence stretched as Violet pulled herself together. It was no good sitting there feeling sorry for herself when the clock was ticking and she had so much more to show the ombudsman.

'So, post Ben's pay rise, I realised I had to up my game. It wasn't enough that they could start saving for more IVF, I needed to make sure it was successful, so from then on, I began actively looking for good deeds I could do. Waiting for something to fall into my lap was too slow.'

She skipped the video forward. 'For two weeks I was like a new person. I tried everything I could think of, giving up my seat on the tube, putting my change in the charity collection boxes, reaching things from the top shelf in the supermarket for old ladies.'

'Commendable, I'm sure.' His dry tone suggested he was less than impressed.

'I knew they wouldn't be enough on their own, but I thought maybe all those little things would mount up, you know, clubbed together they might warrant a reward, but there was nothing. It was here the next big sacrifice took place. The beginning of February.'

CHAPTER 11

Early February

Violet was late for work and it was purely the fault of the bus. It had nothing to do with changing her outfit twice, or checking her inbox when she should have been brushing her teeth. Buoyed by the idea of item five on her list and wanting to oil the wheels wherever possible, she had signed up to a dating agency. Her friends wouldn't have approved had they known, but she had been selective in choosing the agency, opting for one with five-star reviews and aimed at professionals, but so far the response had been disappointing to say the least. Every time she did something remotely kind or compassionate she would log in to check for messages, but so far there had been nothing to inspire. She could only assume insufficient sacrificial credits had accumulated as yet.

She hustled into the high-rise office building backwards, cup of macchiato held out in front of her, handbag clutched under her elbow. Her colleague, Khalid, hovered by the lift doors, shuffling from foot to foot, resplendent in a pink paisley shirt, as he checked his cuticles.

'I know, I know. It would have been quicker if I'd walked. Honestly...'

He interrupted, his news far more urgent than the usual rant about public transport. 'It's all kicked off. I couldn't let you go in there without warning you.'

The lift doors opened and, after waiting for the space to clear, she stepped in, but Khalid grabbed her shoulder and pulled her to one side, her coffee slopping onto her wrist.

'What the heck?' She put her wrist to her mouth to ease the scald.

'Violet, this is serious. Stop a minute.'

She rolled her eyes. Khalid was prone to exaggeration, the drama queen in him often taking control.

'Raymond has left the building.'

She shook her head. This was not news. Her manager had been absent for a fortnight "for personal reasons" but they were all well conversed in their duties and his non-appearance barely caused a ripple, apart from the usual office debate about what "personal reasons" constituted. Violet's own bet was on marital problems, mainly thanks to Raymond's reputation with the ladies. 'I know, but...'

'No, Violet, I mean he's gone gone.'

Her mouth fell open. 'For good?'

He nodded as the information filtered through. 'For good gone. And what's more, his mystery replacement is in with Cheryl and Dwayne right now. He's going to see us all before the end of the day. Maggie is frantic. She thinks she's for the chop after the balls up with the cast from the West End show last month. I know it was a nightmare, but she needs to let it go.'

Violet's finger shot up in front of his lips. 'Don't.' She wouldn't put it past him to burst into song to emphasise his point.

'Hey, you should be thanking me, lady. Anyway, rumour has it, big changes are on the way and I thought you should know.'

Violet's mind worked overtime. Big changes could mean anything, positive or negative but, if she was honest, she was pretty comfortable with the status quo. If recent events had taught her anything though, it was to embrace new ways of thinking, new ways of behaving, and she wondered how she should handle whatever the day would bring. It would take a while to percolate.

'Khalid, how many times have I told you? Never listen to rumours. It'll only drive you mad. Come on, let's get up there.'

He followed her into the lift. 'Well, you've taken this better than expected. Poor Maggie is in bits. She's already surfing for jobs. Do you think there'll be cuts?'

Her stomach clenched at the prospect, but she reeled in the panic. 'You're getting ahead of yourself, Khalid. There's no reason to assume the worst. Calm down.' She followed her own advice and took a couple of slow deep breaths. 'We should carry on as normal, show we're quite capable of getting on with the job. The show will still have to go on as usual tonight, so we can't let everything grind to a halt.'

Khalid stared at her and sucked in his cheeks, clearly baffled by her reaction.

Violet patted his arm in an unusual show of empathy. 'Don't panic.'

She stepped onto their level and strode toward her office, Khalid trailing, his head darting left to right as he scanned the horizon for fresh outbreaks of stress or upset. The room was subdued considering the number of bodies it contained, but there was an underlying air of tension, as if everyone was watching and waiting.

He leaned in towards the reception desk as they passed. 'Anything?'

The receptionist shook her head, but as she did so the phone rang and her hand shot out to answer it. Violet and Khalid hovered, watching the girl's face as she took instructions, before replacing the handset.

'He wants to see the three content execs first. Maggie, then Howard, then you, Violet.' She stood up to search the office. 'Any idea where Maggie is?'

'Last time I saw her she was heading to the ladies.' Khalid's face was a picture of horror. In fact, Violet hadn't seen him this pale since the incident with the film of a cow giving birth during Nature Watch week last spring. They had unanimously agreed the footage was unsuitable for tea time viewing. 'She's not going to like this. Poor Maggie.'

'Maggie will be fine.' Violet pushed past him, refusing to give in to the threatening hysteria. 'I'll find her.'

Marching past staring colleagues into the hall, Violet paused in the oasis of calm outside the toilets. This was a new situation for her. In the past she would have kept her head down, let events play out, not got involved. She had no idea how to handle Maggie, they mainly communicated via their assistants, but something told her it was the right thing to do to step in. She tapped on the door and walked in.

Maggie was sniffing over the sinks, dabbing at pink, swollen eyes with a tissue, smearing mascara further across her face rather than removing it.

'Hi, Maggie. The new guy is asking to see you first.'

'What? No! No, I can't possibly see him like this.' She leaned closer to the mirror, examining the damage close-up, although Violet couldn't help thinking it was perfectly visible from six feet away. 'I might as well pack my bags now.'

Violet's natural instinct was to tell her to get a grip, but she clamped her lips with her teeth to contain those words while she conjured alternatives. 'Maggie, you're fine. It will be fine. It's only a meeting.'

Maggie's pencilled on eyebrows rose in defiance. 'Fine? You know he's already been in with Cheryl, and Dwayne? They won't have been singing my praises, will they? Not after last month's mix up. Dwayne told me straight he wanted me fired.' She dissolved into renewed sobs.

Violet knew he had said exactly that, both to Maggie's face and behind her back. Cheryl and Dwayne were the hosts of "Prime", *the early evening show they all worked on, and were as highly strung and demanding as their exorbitant pay cheques suggested. Dealing with divas was a downside of the job Violet otherwise loved with a passion. The injustice of their attitudes towards the support staff hit her with a new clarity.*

She stamped a foot, indicating she was deadly serious. 'Maggie, nobody listens to Dwayne. You know what he's like and I'm sure the new guy, whoever he is, has dealt with characters like him before, or he wouldn't have got the role. Besides, one mistake doesn't wipe out years of hard work, loyalty and inspired thinking. You're great at your job.'

Maggie's eyes squeezed to slits as she listened to Violet's praise, a deep frown forming on her brow. 'Really? You think I'm good at my job?'

'Absolutely.'

'Honestly?'

'Of course.' *Violet was gaining momentum.* 'Now, grab your things, touch up your make up and get up there.'

She had peaked too soon.

'I can't go in there looking like this. Look at me.' *She glanced sideways at Violet.* 'It's my mother's fault. She was an ugly crier too. Is there no way we can put him off?'

Violet had to admit, Maggie's appearance would raise questions, but what options were there?

'Would you go instead? Make my excuses? Give me time to sort myself out?'

'Oh, I don't know ....' *Violet shook her head. How would it look? Overriding the new boss's first and simple instruction.*

'Yes. Yes, it would work. Tell him I'm in a meeting with, um, with a guest for tonight's show and I won't be free until later. I'll go to the lunchroom and put my face in the fridge for half an hour and Bob's your uncle,' *Maggie pleaded.*

That would mean Violet was going in blind. She had intended to use the next few minutes to Google the new guy, get the heads up about his past and his reputation so she could go in with a plan.

'Please?'

Maggie's tone was pitiful and Violet felt a now familiar niggle start up at the back of her mind, a flutter at the base of her stomach. Was this the opportunity she had been waiting for? Could this be the chance to earn serious points? Only one way to find out. 'Ok. I'll do it.' But it didn't seem quite enough. She should do more. 'In fact, I'll make sure to point out how essential you are to the office, while I'm there.'

'You will?' The dubious frown was back on Maggie's face.

'Yes. I will.'

With that, Violet marched out of the ladies and back through the main office, pausing only to inform the receptionist of what was happening before heading upstairs, colleagues straining in their seats wide eyed, watching her go.

Her confidence lasted until she reached the next floor and knocked on the door, when it struck her she was so unprepared she hadn't even found out the man's name.

'Come in.' His voice was strong and deep, but otherwise gave no clues of what to expect.

When she entered, he was standing at the window with his back to her, studying a clipboard. He turned and held out his hand and her breath caught in her throat.

'Hi, Maggie. Niall de Havilland. Pleased to meet you.'

Muscle memory caused her arm to rise to clasp his, but all attempts at controlled movement had abandoned her. He was...there was no other word for it but, magnificent and, from the weakness in her legs, it would appear her knees had been first to recognise the fact. She heard her voice blurt a greeting and her body was pleased to follow his instruction to take a seat. He continued reading for a few moments before dropping the board down and giving her his full attention.

'Sorry about that, Maggie, a lot of information to take on board today. You'll have to excuse me if I refer to my notes. Now...'

At once she realised she had been too busy concentrating on the rise and fall of his muscular chest beneath his crisp, white shirt to set him straight on her identity. 'No, sorry. I'm not Maggie.'

Confused, he retrieved the board from the desk.

'I'm Violet Harper. Maggie and I have swapped around because she has a pre-arranged meeting about tonight's show. I hope that's all right.'

'Yes.' His pout suggested otherwise, as he flicked from one sheet to another and back again, but otherwise his face gave nothing away. 'Yes, of course. The show must go on.' The room became quiet as he read.

'So, Violet.' He picked up a pen and bounced it on the desk a few times before grasping it between both hands. 'Let's not beat around the bush. I'm sure you've heard by now, I'm taking over Raymond's position. I hope that's not going to cause tension between us?'

'No, why would it?'

His shoulders relaxed. 'Oh good, so you're not one of his...' He coughed. 'Oh, good. Anyway, to cut to the chase, everything's happened at a great rate of knots. Raymond is no more. I mean, Raymond is still Raymond, he hasn't died or anything, but I am the new Raymond. Actually, I'm not Raymond at all, I certainly don't want a reputation like that. Let me start again...'

He was a handsome man and she had found it difficult to concentrate on anything but the movement of his mouth as he spoke, but she was beginning to find his inability to say what he needed to say slightly frustrating.

'I'm sorry. I was all set to speak to Maggie and knew exactly what I was going to say to her, but seeing you first has thrown me off kilter.'

His stumbling allowed Violet to recover somewhat. He no longer seemed quite the intimidating figure he had at first, although he was still impressively chiselled. She had been wondering how to carry out the promised promotion of Maggie and now she saw her chance.

'About that…'

'Yes?' He peered from beneath dark, neat brows.

'What you were going to say to Maggie. I know it's not my place, but knowing the only people you've spoken to on the team so far is Dwayne and Cheryl, I'm concerned you may not have received a full and accurate picture of…' She should have given this speech far more thought. 'Of Maggie.'

'Is that right?'

'Yes.' She wished she had had time to consider her campaign, but instead had to make something out of the ramblings rattling around her brain. 'I mean, we all make mistakes.'

His head dipped to one side as he studied her. 'We do?'

That had been the wrong thing to say. Pull it back. 'Yes, absolutely. Only little ones, of course. Nothing major.' A lack of response on his part forced her to continue, but she wasn't sure where she was going with it. 'And she's always ready for broadcast, even if it is a bit of a rush at the end. The incident with the parrot was totally a one off.'

'The parrot incident.'

'Yes, definitely. Could happen to anyone.' She felt she was finally getting her point across. 'And we all get emotional, on the odd occasion. I mean, who hasn't had a little cry in the ladies on a bad day?'

The intensity of his focus reawakened her nerves and the perfection of his jaw line seemed to interfere with her thought processes.

'Actually, I don't suppose you've done that.' It was time to shut up. 'Basically, Maggie works really hard and does a fantastic job and I thought somebody should let you know that.'

He nodded slowly. The intensity of his gaze made it seem as if he was trying to read her mind. 'And Howard?'

'No, no. Howard has never cried in the ladies, at least, not as far as I'm aware.' What was she saying? He would think she was a complete idiot. *'You didn't mean that, did you? What I should say is, Howard also works hard and, well, you know…'*

'OK. Thanks for bringing me up to speed. I'll take it on board.'

A cough indicated a change of subject. *'Anyway, I'm sure you appreciate the environment we work in is an exacting one. Things have to constantly change to stay fresh. Budgets get stretched, belts get tightened,'* he paused. *'Job roles get updated to be fit for purpose.'*

Job roles changing? That sounded like code for cuts, and she had spent the last ten minutes praising Maggie and Howard to the hilt. What would this mean for her?

'How do you think the team will cope with change?'

She shrugged. *'It depends on the change, but pretty well I'd say. We have to cope with last minute hiccups on a regular basis – it's the nature of live TV, and I think we deal with most challenges head on.'*

'So you think the team is up to it? You yourself, you're happy to face the challenge?'

She was still unclear whether these changes would be for her benefit or otherwise, but all things considered, now was not the time to be negative. She forced a smile. *'Bring it on.'*

'Great. Good to have you on board.' He stood up and held his hand out, indicating the end of the meeting.

His handshake was firm, if slightly sweaty, and she enjoyed the feel of skin on skin. At least she now knew she still had a job.

***

'What was the point of that?'

The ombudsman stared at her as if the whole thing had played out in double Dutch, but she could see his point. The scene was not at all as she remembered it. 'I really don't know. In my head, I left the office feeling like I'd done something amazing. I thought I'd done Maggie a huge favour. What did I do?'

'Basically you highlighted all of her short comings.'

'But, that can't be right…Can it? I mean, if that is actually what I did, why did I get a reward? It doesn't make sense.'

He raised one eyebrow. 'I have to be honest Violet, not a lot of this is making sense right now.'

She ignored him and leaned forward, gripping the back of the seat in front, trying to work out a logical explanation.

'Let's move on, time is of the essence. Clearly this section is of no use to the investigation.'

'No, no, no. This was important. The events that day had a massive impact on my life. It's got to mean something.'

His fingers drummed the arms of his chair, patience wearing thin.

'Unless, perhaps it wasn't what I did which scored me points, but my intention. Perhaps because what I intended to do was a good thing, the fact I failed isn't important.'

'That's stretching the parameters somewhat.'

'What parameters?' She met his gaze. 'We don't know what the parameters are, but I can tell you I received a reward that day. I moved a step closer to item five on my list. Niall is the fulfilment of number five.'

His eyes narrowed as he studied her expression. 'Niall is the answer to your search for love?'

'Oh, yes. I knew from the moment we met. There was an immediate connection, no doubt about it. A…' She searched the air for the right word, her whole body tingling at the thought. 'Frisson.'

'Frisson?' He sniggered.

She ignored him. 'This was the first step towards the end result, the first step of many as it turns out, and the second step came in the afternoon.'

The ombudsman groaned.

'Trust me. This is short, but you'll see what I mean.'

Early February

Violet tidied her desk, moving piles of papers from one tray to another in readiness for the morning. The show had run smoothly and she could go home to relax without any recriminations about her performance. Even Cheryl had muttered a well done when she bumped into her in the corridor, which for her was praise indeed. The arrival of Niall de Havilland on the scene that morning had upset her equilibrium for a number of reasons, but she was confident a chat with the girls about him, over a glass of Prosecco, would soon set her to rights. She grabbed her handbag from the back of the chair and was about to leave when the man himself knocked on the door and stuck his head around it.

'Ah, Violet, you're still here. Good. Can you spare a minute?'

Considering he was the boss, she took that as a rhetorical question and stepped back to allow him room to enter and close the door. He nodded at her seat and she sat down, while he perched on the small sofa at the edge of her office, usually used for informal chats with guests. It was soft and luxurious and the length of his legs meant his knees were almost as high as his chin.

'You might remember I mentioned changes when we touched base this morning?'

Her stomach clenched. She was fired after all.

'Basically, although I'm taking on Raymond's role, I'm still carrying on in my old position too, with Daytime. The morning show? You know it?'

Did she know it? It was only one of the biggest daily shows the corporation ran. 'Of course.'

'Of course you do.' Even smug looked good on him. *'What's happening is a semi merger of Prime with Daytime. They'll both still have their daily slots. They'll both still have their individual hosts and so forth, but there will be crossovers, shared themes, etc. We need to keep abreast of the times. We need to maintain ratings, which means we need to keep it sharp, which means we have to push the envelope.'*

Her nerves were fraying and all she managed was a brief nod.

He was on a roll. 'We need more guest hosts to take things up a gear. We want more celebrity interaction. They use us to promote their latest films or albums, but it's no longer going to be enough for them to turn up and sit on the sofa. If they want our support then they need to be prepared to be more interactive, join in with the other segments, give us something exclusive, provide more bang for their buck. We may have to be firm with them. Is that something you could shoulder?'

'I think so. Some A-listers try it on, you know, demanding Nepalese Mineral water on tap at thirty seven point four degrees and stuff, but I say no when I need to. I've never been star struck. The show is what it is and as much as we want to be welcoming there are limits to what we can offer, and I make that clear from the outset. I've never had any complaints.'

'Good, good.' He rubbed his hands together. *'The truth is, I can't be everywhere at once and I can't do my old job and this one. I don't have the bandwidth. So, someone needs to step up and I was hoping that someone could be you.'*

She was taken aback. 'Are you offering me Raymond's job?'

'No, no.' He coughed. *'I'm doing Raymond's job, I'm just delegating most of it to you.'*

She tried to figure out the difference.

'It will mean a nominal pay rise, and it will mean us working together quite closely. Maggie and Howard will report to you, as will whoever takes your current role, and you will report directly to me. How does that sound?'

It sounded like a massive reward for all the good works she had done over the last two weeks. It sounded like a promotion she had only ever dreamed of. It sounded like an opportunity to get to know the delicious Niall de Havilland a lot, lot better. It sounded too good to be true.

He stood up and handed her an envelope before moving towards the door. 'HR has put the offer in writing, so there's no confusion about what's involved. It's a lot to think about, so I'll leave it with you, but, as you will appreciate, we need to move on this, and I would be grateful if you could let me know ASAP. Ok?'

Her lips manufactured a smile, while her brain attempted to sort the conversation into some kind of order. How did their garbled meeting of that morning result in the offer of a promotion? After he had left the room, she looked at the envelope, resting in her open hand like a foreign object and, rather than read it, shoved it into her handbag for later, when she was more confident she was in her right mind.

***

Violet shrugged at the wide-eyed expression of the ombudsman. 'Tell me that's not divine intervention.'

'That's not divine intervention.'

She almost detected the roll of his eyes without seeing it. 'What? Surely you can see my point? I would never have seen that coming in a million years.'

'Actually, I think it was inevitable.'

'What? How can you…'

He shook his head as he spoke. 'Obviously I don't know all the intricacies of your particular office politics, but from what I've seen, there were only three of you in the running for the somewhat dubious honour of the job in question anyway, you, Maggie and Howard. I think it's fair to say you wrote off Maggie's chances with the "we all make mistakes" fiasco, and you didn't exactly highlight Howard's accomplishments either. Which leaves you.' He shrugged. 'I rest my case.'

She considered his point, chewing on her bottom lip. This put a whole new perspective on the event, one she wasn't overly keen on. 'So, you don't think it was a reward at all? You think I orchestrated it myself?'

'Yes, Violet, I do.'

She stroked her chin. 'I'm not sure I agree with you, but that's ok. I've got plenty of other evidence to back up my case, and even if meeting Niall and my promotion wasn't payback, other things happened as a result of that day which did move the list forward. I had seen those events as by-products, but maybe they were small instalments in themselves. Maybe I've been oversimplifying things. Maybe God is a lot more complicated than I first thought.'

'I've heard a lot of words to describe God in my day, but I don't think complicated is one of them. Let me refer to my manual.' He pulled a hefty book out from under his seat and flicked through the closely typed pages.

'That's a Bible.'

He turned to the black leatherette front cover embossed with gold writing. 'So it is. Now then. It's here somewhere. Ahh, yes. "God made us plain and simple. It is we who made ourselves complicated." Ecclesiastes, seven, verse nine.' He closed the book with a snap and tucked it away again.

'It doesn't say God is simple though, does it?' She shrugged. 'Anyway, let me show you what else happened as a result of that day. You can judge for yourself.'

CHAPTER 12

Early February

Violet had been keeping her head down all day. An email had been cascaded first thing that morning informing the staff of her new role and, although she had no qualms at accepting the offer – considering the circumstances, clearly it was her destiny - there was an underlying discomfort about the fact Maggie and Howard were both older and more experienced. She hoped there would be no bad feeling. Late in the afternoon however, the need for caffeine forced her into the staff room. Almost immediately Maggie sneaked in behind her and closed the door.

'I was hoping I'd run into you.' *She sounded breathless and Violet suspected she had sprinted from her own office with the sole purpose being to intercept her.*

'Hi, Maggie.' *She kept her tone light, but was steeled for confrontation.*

'I heard about the promotion.' *Maggie's tone was non-committal, leaving Violet unable to gauge her mood.*

'Aah.'

Maggie suddenly grasped Violet's hand in both of her own and shook it with vigour. 'I'm so pleased for you. Congratulations.'

'Oh. Oh, thank you. I wasn't sure how you'd feel about…'

'I'm over the moon for you. And also, I wanted to say, thank you, you know, for the other day. In the loo.' She mouthed the last few words and glanced over her shoulder as if wanting to be sure nobody overheard. 'And for what you said to Niall. I don't know what it was, but it certainly did the trick. He was nice as pie when I saw him, and I was able to go in looking presentable too. I do appreciate it.'

This was going far better than Violet had expected. 'Well, you're welcome.'

'Until then I had no idea how highly you thought of me. I'd always thought you saw me as a bit of a weak link, but now, well… Thank you.' A distinct dampness was brewing around her eyes and her voice took on a tremor. 'You know, I've had such a lot to handle at home and I thought you were oblivious. It's so nice to know my colleagues have my back.'

Unused to being praised in this way, Violet's confidence soared. She had no idea what Maggie's issues were at home, usually preferring not to get involved, but the impulse to be magnanimous temporarily overwhelmed everything else. 'That's ok, and if I can ever do anything to help, please ask.'

'Really?'

Maggie's enthusiasm slammed the brakes on Violet's empty offer. 'Mmm, of course. Anything.' She bit the inside of her lip, cursing herself for not knowing when to keep quiet.

'Well, there is something…' Maggie waved her hand, denying the possibility. 'No, no, never mind. I'm sure you're too busy.'

It had gone too far for Violet to back out now and whatever it was might not be too onerous. She hoped. Please be something easy. 'Go on. What is it?'

'There's a little event I'm running at the weekend, Sunday afternoon. A tea party to raise money for a supported living facility close to my home. They're in desperate need of funding and they really are a vital service to their residents.'

'A tea party?' She scanned her mental diary for excuses, but none materialised. In fact, her whole weekend had been blessedly free. Thinking about it though, this was the perfect opportunity to make a sacrifice and she had coped with worse. Besides, if payment for a few kind words in a meeting amounted to an introduction to the love of her life, what would giving up a Sunday afternoon warrant? 'I'll do it.'

'You will?' Maggie clasped her hands together before throwing them around Violet in a brief, but violent hug. 'Oh, that's brilliant. I've put posters up in the staff room and around, but nobody has come forward. I thought I was on my own. Oh, that's excellent.' She turned to the door. 'I'll email you the address and the time as soon as I get back to my desk. A couple of dozen cakes or scones should be enough and they don't have to be fancy. I'm doing lemon drizzle and tipsy red velvet.'

Maggie disappeared out of the room and Violet stared after her. She had anticipated pouring tea; smiling at strangers; making small talk even, but not actual baking. In fact, it was doubtful anyone would want to buy anything she had baked anyway. It was not a skill she possessed. Oh, Lord. What had she done? But then, surely that would qualify for even more brownie points. Her mind trailed off on a tangent. Mmm, brownies. Surely they couldn't be too difficult.

***

Violet barely paused for breath. 'That was the offer.' She kept her eye on the screen, the images fast forwarding at high speed. 'And this was the day of the tea. It was actually more fun than I first expected, but it was also more challenging too. I have to say, when God was handing out talents, he completely forgot my pinch of domesticity. Baking is a complete and utter mystery to me. Luckily I've got friends who got double dibs.'

Mid-February

Violet hovered in the forecourt of her building, resplendent in a Hawaiian bikini-girl apron. Peter was addressing the crowd gathered there, his voice raised above the hollering smoke alarm.

'Ok, ladies and gents. I'll do a quick check around the whole building and then you can go back in.' He sucked in his cheeks as he turned and spotted Violet among the throng. 'No prizes for guessing who was cooking up a storm.'

Laughing, Peter disappeared back inside while everyone else turned to stare at Violet. She cringed and held up a hand, apologising through gritted teeth. 'Sorry guys. Sorry.'

Naomi appeared alongside, an oblivious Arthur strapped to her chest in a papoose, and slipped her free arm around Violet's shoulders in a show of support. 'Oh, Violet, are you ok?'

'Better than my cakes.' She rolled her eyes. 'A bit embarrassed is all, but goodness knows what I'm going to do now. They were supposed to be for a charity thing this afternoon. I don't know what happened. I only stepped away for a minute to check my emails. How can a few cakes create so much smoke?'

Naomi tightened her grip for a moment. 'Don't worry. It could be worse.'

'Could it?'

A fire engine swung around the corner into their road, sirens blaring.

Violet closed her eyes and sighed deeply. 'I don't actually think it could.'

Like all things embarrassing, it seemed an age before the forecourt cleared. First the fire crew drove away amid a round of clapping, although nothing had been required of them beyond turning up, but according to Naomi, that was enough to make her day. Violet and Naomi lingered longest, shaking hands and apologising again, like an odd wedding party, as one by one, chatting groups disbanded and filtered back to their own flats. Thankfully, they had been more amused than angered at being inconvenienced and had taken it in turns to pass witty comment. Outwardly Violet took it with good grace, although inside she was dying of shame.

As they approached the landing to their floor, Violet and Naomi met a breathless Rhoda, painfully negotiating the stairs, still on her way down. They both rushed to her aid.

'Oh, Rhoda. Are you all right?'

She clung to the banister. 'Yes, yes, dears. I'm just waiting for my second wind to kick in. Did I miss the firemen?'

Peter bounded up the stairs behind them, but halted when he saw their predicament.

'Mrs B, I didn't see you when I was doing my rounds. Where did you spring from?'

She avoided his eye, nose in the air. 'I was otherwise engaged when the alarm went off. I got here as soon as I could, but I must say, my old legs have had about as much as they can take for one day.'

'Please allow me.' Peter swung her effortlessly into his arms. 'Now, where are we going? Back up to your flat?'

She gazed into his eyes, all bluster dispersed. 'You can take my anywhere, young man.'

Violet and Naomi laughed. 'Will you come into my flat for a cup of tea? Assuming the smoke has cleared. I am responsible for this palaver, after all.' She walked ahead to unlock the door.

'You, dear? My goodness, what has been going on?'

Peter followed on. 'She's only been baking, Mrs B. Would you believe it?'

'Well, considering the outfit, I think I might.' Her shrunken body seemed swamped as he deposited her in the armchair. 'Not very successfully though, I take it?'

'No. I can't understand it. I found the simplest recipe for brownies I could on the internet, bought all the right ingredients and tins. The only thing was, my oven won't go anywhere near the temperature it said on the instructions, so I put it on full whack and left it a few extra minutes to make up for it.'

'Aah. I think I might know the problem.' Rhoda nodded sagely. 'If the recipe was American, the instructions were in Fahrenheit instead of Celsius. Poor cakes must have been cremated.' Her whole body wobbled as she giggled.

Violet shook her head. 'That's it. I'm never cooking again. I'm just not cut out for it.'

'Nonsense, dear. When you fall off a horse, get straight back on, and lucky for you, you've got an old hand to point you in the right direction. School cook for thirty years, I was.'

'Oh, Rhoda. I couldn't. You've been through quite enough…'

'Nonsense. Prop me on a stool, give me a cuppa and I'm in my element. Come along.'

Naomi excused herself with Arthur, who was still blissfully unaware of all the excitement, and Peter followed her to the door.

'Go on, young lady. Do as you're told.' He winked.

Violet stuck out her tongue.

***

'Don't give up your day job.' The ombudsman muttered through a mouth full of something.

Violet looked at him from beneath one raised eyebrow. He was helping himself from an enormous carton of popcorn, the warm, sweet smell of which tainted the air.

He lifted it in her direction. 'Sorry, did you want some? All the talk of cake made me hungry.'

'No. Thank you.' She couldn't help wondering where the carton had appeared from and had the galling idea he had slipped out to fetch it when he should have been watching her life. 'Besides, I did warn you I couldn't cook. That's why my trying to was such a gesture. Anyway, in the end Rhoda helped me make one tray full and I telephoned for reinforcements for the rest – Issy works in a deli-come-bakery in town.'

His cheeks bulged like a chipmunk, as he crammed in another handful.

Violet pouted and stared at his working jaw, then her stomach growled. 'Actually, yes, I do want some. Pass it here, and watch this.'

CHAPTER 13

Mid-February

'Where do you want these?' Violet was met at the open door by Maggie, who was rushing in the other direction.

Maggie's face lit up and Violet was only protected from the violence of her hug by the bulk of Tupperware bolstered between them. 'Oh, good, good, good, you're here.' She waved her into the hall, past a number of large hand-drawn arrows, through to a large open plan living area, hardly pausing for breath. Patio doors stood open, leading out to an enclosed marquee, where tables and chairs were set out for guests.

'I think we're in for a big turnout. People have started to arrive already. Mainly relatives of the residents, but they've told friends who've told other friends. I hope we have enough to offer.'

Maggie pointed at a trestle table along the back wall. 'Take your pick. One end or the other. I'm going to get my last load from the car. This is Jan, by the way.' She pointed to a flustered woman, next to a stand set up with the accoutrements for making teas and coffees, and who somehow managed to look excessively warm despite the cold February air rushing in from the garden. 'She's on beverages. Jan, this is my very good friend, Violet.'

The two women nodded greetings as Maggie scurried away and Violet was soon gathered up in the whirlwind of preparations for the imminent arrival of the masses.

An hour later they were still waiting. The few early comers had drunk their coffee, eaten their sweet treats and drifted away and Maggie was decidedly less optimistic. She constantly adjusted the cake stands and straightened tablecloths as if a neat display would somehow draw in the crowds.

'I'm sure they'll be here soon,' Maggie fretted. 'I hope I put the right time on the posters. We're hardly going to cover costs at this rate and Primrose House so needs the funds.'

'Here's someone.' Violet tried to be reassuring, but was concerned her offer of help would count for nothing if there was no one to serve cake to.

A young woman tiptoed through the door, wide eyed at the piles of food, hands appearing and disappearing inside the sleeves of her duffle coat as she clenched and unclenched her fists. There was something familiar about her, although Violet couldn't recall having seen her before. She was a pretty girl, with pigtails secured by pink ribbons, which made her look younger than she probably was and her features carried the signs of Down's syndrome. Suddenly she spotted Maggie and flew across the room to hug her.

'Hello, Mummy.' She beamed and twirled in a complete circle. 'This is amazing.'

Maggie's worries seemed to have disappeared as her face returned the glow. 'Hello, you. I wondered when you'd arrive.'

'It's my day for lunch with Daddy and Irene. He brought me back.' The girl bounced on the spot with excitement.

Maggie smiled at the girl's enthusiasm. 'Say hello to my friend Violet, then go and see Jan for a drink and come back to choose your cake, my treat.' She turned to Violet. 'This is my daughter, Caroline. She lives here at Primrose House.'

'Hello, Caroline.' Violet held out a hand, but was instantly enveloped in a bear hug.

'Hello, Violet.' She turned back to her mother. 'I'm going to get Bella. She's waiting in her room for me. She didn't want to come on her own.'

'All right then, my lovely. See you in a minute.'

She bounded out of the room and Maggie turned her attention back to the empty room. 'Look, I'm going to go and have a word with the other helpers and thank them for coming. I don't think you'll struggle to manage without me.'

There was a droop to her shoulders as she walked through to the marquee. Violet watched with a gripe in the pit of her stomach. This wasn't at all what she'd anticipated. She'd expected to leave the event with a nice, warm fuzzy feeling, as she had when she'd helped Naomi with Arthur, and Rhoda when the lift was broken. She was also concerned the remit for reward was shrinking fast, but what could she do? What they needed were people. Just a few would make a difference, but a good-sized crowd would turn the whole event around.

Violet reached for her mobile and quickly drafted a message. "Please, please, please, come and eat cake at Primrose House this afternoon. They need your support." She added a link with the details and sent it into the ether to everyone in her contact list. It was a rare thing for her to call on friends for assistance. As a rule, she was proud of her self-sufficiency and, having not tested the system before, was dubious there would be any response at all, but at least she had tried, for Maggie's sake and her own.

Maggie had just suggested packing up early, when the first friendly face arrived at the open door.

Lulu wafted in, fumbling in a large shoulder bag. 'Sorry ladies. I can't stop, but can I buy some cakes and run?'

Maggie's face brightened a tad. 'Of course. You're more than welcome.'

'Which are yours, Vi? I don't want to take any risks. Rachael's doing so well, I'd hate to knock her back with food poisoning now.' She chortled at her own joke.

Violet shuffled from behind the table to draw her into a hug, ignoring the jibe. 'Is she really doing well?' She searched Lulu's eyes for an honest answer.

'Yes, she is. So far, so good, touch wood. A way to go, but, you know...' She hunted around for something resembling wood to touch, but settled for the laminate table-top.

'That's good to hear. Ok, so what can I get you?'

Lulu made her choices and Maggie crafted a box out of folded paper plates to keep them safe for the onward journey, but before she could leave, Kate and Ben swept up, Ben wrapping his arms around Lulu from behind, so her feet almost lifted off the ground. They exchanged a quick greeting before Lulu scurried off.

'Thanks for coming, guys.' Violet was touched by their appearance.

'No problem. This looks lovely.' Kate examined the laden table. 'Ben, babe, why don't you get us some teas and I'll pick some cakes.'

As always, he immediately obeyed instructions and Kate leaned in close to Violet. 'We were at Ben's mum's for lunch. I was glad of the excuse to get away early. That woman...' Ben returned with two steaming mugs. 'Ooh, yes. One of those muffins, please.' Kate's change of topic and tone was seamless.

Violet laughed, took their money and pointed them to the seating area beyond the patio doors. Meanwhile, Maggie had greeted Khalid and his boyfriend, who was requesting a full list of ingredients and calorific content of each individual cake, and heading up a small trickle of customers. The air rang with coins tumbling into the cashboxes and the atmosphere warmed as more bodies milled around. Caroline and her friend, Bella, were called in as reinforcements, providing waitress service to the tables, as orders backed up.

'Brownies? I don't think we had any brownies, did we, Violet?' Maggie's query broke into Violet's consciousness and she glanced up to see Peter grinning across the table.

'I could have sworn someone said there was going to be brownies.' There was a wickedly mocking tone to his voice.

'What are you doing here?' She was certain Peter's number was not in her contacts list.

'I'm acting as chauffer to a young lady who wanted to come, but didn't have the transport.' He ticked his head towards Naomi, and a sleeping Arthur, just visible in a scrum made up of Jan, Kate and Ben.

'That's nice.' She wondered at the nature of the relationship between her single mother neighbour and apartment maintenance man.

'Aah, it's the sweet tooth. I can't say no to carbs. Anyway, where are the infamous brownies?'

'Actually they're still in the tub under the table. The other cakes looked so impressive, I was too ashamed to put them out.'

'Away with you. Let's have a look.'

Unable to think of a valid reason not to, Violet pulled the box out from its hiding place and removed the lid.

Maggie joined them for the grand unveiling. *'Why infamous?'*

Violet shook her head. She didn't want *that* story making it into the office. She had a reputation to maintain, after all. *'Never mind. Look. They're a bit sad next to Issy's creations.'*

Peter reached in and helped himself to a hefty wedge, then glanced up at her. *'Looks like a brownie to me.'* He took a bite, eyes closed in rapture. *'Tastes like a brownie to me. Mmm, heaven. How much do I owe you?'*

She waved him away. *'It's all right. It's on me after the trouble I caused this morning.'*

Naomi extricated herself from the fan club and arrived alongside with a tray of teas. *'Hi, Violet. This is very nice.'*

'Try the brownies. They're delicious.' Peter relieved her of the tray and headed outside.

An extremely smart, middle-aged woman squeezed in at the front of the queue. *'Who made the muffins? Are they yours?'*

Violet glanced up and was shocked to instantly recognise the face, a minor celebrity and regular on Daytime, the sister show to Prime. Made-up impeccably, her clothes were designer, but demure. Pure class. 'No, I'm afraid not. My friend is a baker. The brownies are mine.'

Casting her eyes from one plate to another and back again, the woman nodded sagely. 'The muffins are fabulous. Tell her, well done, from me. Thanks for this, Maggie. You've put on a grand show.' She sidled to the door and exited the building.

Violet turned, open-mouthed to Maggie. 'Was that...?'

'Mmm, what?' She seemed unaffected by the woman's appearance. 'Yes, Saffron Headland. Bella's her daughter. We often bump into each other here at Primrose. She's such a lovely lady.'

Violet and Naomi exchanged wide-eyed glances.

'I did mention it to Niall. I thought he might pop in considering his connection with both Saffron and I, but...'

At once, Violet regretted the understated jeans and t-shirt and complete lack of make-up, if Niall were likely to turn up. 'Did he say he would come?'

'Mmm, I don't think so. Apparently he was going to check his diary, but probably had too many ducks to get in a row...' Maggie's expression suggested she had no idea what he was talking about. 'And something about herding cats? Anyway, I took it as a no.'

Violet nodded a level of understanding, and considered popping to the ladies to apply lipstick, just in case.

An hour later the event was winding down, and it was just as well as supplies were running short and Jan looked in dire need of a sit down. Violet was up to her elbows in soapy suds, washing up.

Caroline was on drying duty, while the others dismantled tables. 'Are you my mummy's friend?'

'*I work with her at the studio.*'

'*But are you her friend?*' Caroline seemed frustrated by Violet's answer.

Violet thought about it. If she had been asked what Maggie was to her a couple of days ago, she would have said colleague. In spite of working together a number of years, they had never been close, in fact Maggie had barely featured in Violet's life before, she was simply somebody who shared office space, but perhaps that had changed now. '*Yes, I am her friend.*'

The girl threw her arm around Violet's shoulders and pressed a kiss on her cheek. '*You can be my friend too, if you like.*'

The embrace was over as suddenly as it began and Caroline resumed work with the tea-towel. Violet was surprised to feel a wave of emotion wash over her. It seemed an honour to be invited into Caroline's circle. '*Yes, I would like that, Caroline. Thank you.*'

Maggie bustled in, huffing and puffing. '*Right, almost there. Gosh, what a day! I'll finish up if you two want to get off.*'

Caroline immediately threw down the cloth and disappeared.

Violet's conscience intervened. '*I may as well get to the end of this lot. It won't take long.*'

'*You're a star.*' Maggie snatched up the cloth and took over where her daughter had left off. '*And I mean that. Today would not have been the same without you.*'

Violet tried to wave the praise away, but Maggie was not to be silenced. '*And don't think I don't know you sent out for reinforcements this afternoon. It didn't pass me by that that last rush consisted almost entirely of people you knew. We've collected a hefty amount for the charity thanks to you.*'

'*I enjoyed it.*' She hoped the reward for her good deed would not be diminished because of the pleasure she had had in carrying it out. '*And so did my friends.*'

'*Pleased to hear it. And to think I …*' She shook her head, cutting short whatever she had been going to say. '*Never mind.*'

'No, go on.' Violet was intrigued.

Maggie stacked the plate she had been wiping and leaned back against the worktop. 'Well, I've worried about you in the past. It seems silly now, but, I don't know, I always thought you seemed a bit lonely.'

'Me?'

'With your family being so far away, and keeping yourself to yourself.' She breathed a laugh. 'When obviously you have a huge amount of friends to keep you company. You're such a lucky girl, after all.'

The mention of her family rocked Violet. Generally, she spared them sparse thought and even that she felt was more than adequate, but today, having watched the interaction between Maggie and Caroline, she couldn't help but be a little jealous of the mother daughter connection they shared, something missing between her and her own mother. When was the last time they had even texted each other? She pushed the thought away. As Maggie had said, she had friends. 'Yes, I am lucky.'

Jan appeared, pulling on a jacket and preparing to leave and Maggie was called away. Violet picked up the tea-towel and wiped the last of the cutlery and tried hard to concentrate on all the good things she had in her life.

CHAPTER 14

Mid-February

The warm feeling following her good deed had leaked away by the time she was half-way home. The top deck of the bus was quiet, except for a pair of elderly women perched at the front, passing comment about every unlucky pedestrian who caught their eye from the pavement. A young couple snogged noisily at the back. Violet zoned them, and the stale, sweaty odour left by an earlier passenger, out. She was busy mulling over Maggie's comments.

The fact her workmate had labelled her lonely made her uncomfortable. She worked hard to project a professional, confident persona to her colleagues and it felt like failure that one had her down as some sort of weakling. Where had the impression come from? What had given Maggie such an idea? For starters, she wasn't lonely, so it was a totally incorrect impression, but there must have been something, in her manner, her attitude, which made her look as if she was lacking human affection. Maggie had mentioned her family, of course, although Violet couldn't remember ever having a conversation with her about them, so how she knew they weren't close was a mystery. She must have let her guard down at some point, revealing information she normally kept close to her chest. Maybe it was when...

Violet's phone vibrated and she reached for her handbag to answer it. It was Ayesha.

'Ayesh, hi. How are you?' It was unusual for her to call out of the blue. Her usual communication of choice was a brief, functional email.

'Hi, so sorry I didn't make it this afternoon.'

'That's OK. It was only a quick shout out to whoever was free. No biggie. We had a good turnout in the end anyway.'

'Good, good.' Ayesha barely waited for Violet to finish her sentence. 'I would have been there if I could, but I was waiting in for a very important phone call from the US.'

A slight vibrato to her voice pulled Violet up short. 'Really? Should I ask?'

'Oh, Vi.' There was no doubt about it, Ayesha was emotional. 'They've dropped the court case.'

Thank goodness, they were happy tears. 'What? They have? Oh, Ayesha, what fantastic news. You must be over the moon.'

Violet heard a stuttered deep breath as Ayesha pulled herself together. 'I don't know about that. It's definitely a weight off. It means I can avoid bankruptcy, which is great, obviously, but after all this time, it'll be like starting from scratch.'

'Oh, but Ayesh, the last nine months have been hell on earth for you. Now, at least you know you're in the clear to start again. You've done it before and you can do it again. You know you can.'

'I know I can, but do I want to? The last ten years have been for nothing thanks to... I'm not sure I can ever trust people again.'

'Course you can. You've learnt one hell of a lesson and you'll never make the same mistake again. Honestly, you're overwhelmed tonight. Give yourself a couple of days to absorb what's happened and then get right back on the horse.'

'You think?' There was an absence of hope in her tone, but Violet was determined to reignite her friend's zest for life.

'Absolutely. In fact, I think we ought to have an impromptu celebration in the week if we can get everyone together and it can double as a relaunch of the business at the same time.'

'I don't know…'

'Go on. You know you can't resist a party. I'll do the organising,' Violet wheedled.

'Oh, all right then. I suppose it is cause for celebration.'

'Excellent. Leave it to me.'

In the quiet which followed the end of the call, Violet hugged herself. Once again the system had worked. She had given up her afternoon for the tea party and Ayesha had come out of the long dark tunnel which had entombed her for months. On top of which, a party mid-week would certainly put paid to Maggie's suggestion that Violet was lonely. Result.

***

The ombudsman's eyes were not on the screen, they were scrolling through data on his tablet, lips pursed in concentration.

'What are you doing?' Violet was annoyed. How could he judge her case without giving it his full attention?

'I'm reading up on your history.' He scratched his chin, but didn't look up. 'Finding out where your family are.'

Violet's mouth fell open. 'I show you the most straightforward example of sacrifice and reward, backing up my case, and you're checking my family out? That's completely irrelevant.'

'On the contrary, it is most relevant. Family is a major part of a person's life, shaping how they think, how they behave, their belief system…'

'Not on this occasion!' She slammed her hand down on the armrest and the ombudsman shot upright.

'There's no need to shout.' He dropped the computer on his lap.

'Yes there is. Once again you're missing the point. This was about me helping a colleague and my best friend getting a break, and let me tell you it was well overdue.'

'All right, there's no need to get narky. I was simply trying to ascertain a full picture.'

'I'll give you a full picture.' She brandished the remote control with fierce determination. 'A fuller picture than that piece of electronic claptrap will give you, for sure. In fact, if you want to put it to good use, look up Ayesha. Go on, Ayesha Sanderstead.'

She was surprised to see he obediently followed her instructions and immediately began to tap away, eyes scanning side to side, devouring the details.

'Ayesha Sanderstead, only child; same age as you; British father; West Indian mother; grew up in the same town?'

'That's her. I've known her the longest. Ayesha's mum died when she was ten. I met her shortly after, when she transferred to my school. She was such a little scrap, but so strong and determined. We were instant friends.' Her heart flooded with nostalgia, 'I wish I could show you what she was like in those days. She was like a little terrier, fierce and focused; nothing daunted her.'

Violet rewound and paused at a point on New Year's Eve where only Ayesha appeared on the screen, spine straight, shoulders back, head held high, a glass of red wine aloft in her right hand, toasting something or someone. 'She would tell you I took her under my wing, but she's too kind. She scooped me up and then Isobel and we became a gang; an invincible group of buddies'.

The video moved forward slowly, each frame revealing a slightly different version of Ayesha, her eyes languidly closing in a blink; sluggish lips forming into unknown words; her glass lifting to the air and back to her mouth. 'She didn't have it easy. Her dad didn't cope well. I don't know if it was because of her mum, or maybe it was even before then, but he drank – a lot. But Ayesha never said a word against him. I wouldn't have been so forgiving if my dad had turned up for parents' evening completely off his face, but she never said a thing. Instead, she worked hard. I mean, really hard. Perhaps she thought if she did well at school nobody would question what was going on at home, or perhaps she thought if she made him proud he would stop drinking. There were two facts you could rely on where Ayesha was concerned. First, she was always focused and second, she wouldn't drink. Even as a teenager, going to parties and stuff, she barely touched a drop. She would have a glass in front of her, for show, but that's where it stayed. I suppose she'd seen what it did to her dad.'

The ombudsman studied the footage, eyes narrowed. 'Clearly something happened to change that.'

'Yes, it did.' Violet's chest rose and fell as she breathed long and deep, and she pressed a button, the sequence on screen speeding up, the characters cartoon like in their haste, as if she could not bear to watch.

'She was ambitious; an A student through and through. Flew through Uni. Interned and worked at a couple of prestigious companies, all the hours going, learning the ropes. Then she started her own business. I don't think she ever failed at anything, until last year.'

Violet's head tilted and she smiled as she slowed the footage, observing Ayesha on the screen, worse for wear, her drunken hand trying to wipe a stray lock of hair from her eyes and in doing so slopping wine over Kate, in the seat next to her. 'She was hired to promote a band. They were planning a massive tour – UK only to begin with, but if she pulled it off there were rumours of an international contract too. It was a real coup, or it would have been if it had come off, but it fell apart. The band split, just before the tour was due to start and she'd invested heavily. To top it off, there was some mix up about insurance, or something like that, which resulted in litigation. It almost wiped her out. She lost all her clients, her flat, pretty much everything she'd worked for for ten years. She ended up moving back in with her dad. All she could do was take the flack and wait for it all to play out.'

New Year's Eve – A Year Ago

Ayesha had been resting a weary head on her hand, like it was too heavy for her shoulders, but her elbow slowly slid away until her chin rested amongst the debris on the table and she slumped forward. The rest of the party was staring, aghast at the sudden collapse.

While Violet patted her hand sympathetically, Kate frowned with concern as she lined up empty wine bottles.

'I had no idea she had drunk this much. You, me and Issy are on white, so only Ayesha and Lulu are on the red. It's so unlike Ayesha, to get this carried away.'

'It's because it's so unlike her she's ended up in this state. She normally nurses one drink all night, but she's been topping up her glass every five minutes.'

Lulu, returning to the table from the lobby, dropped into her seat. 'She actually drank mine as well. I turned round and my glass had disappeared. Never mind. We all qualify for a blow out every now and again, and Ayesha's was well overdue. Anyway, the taxi is on the way. They're a good firm, I use them all the time. They always get me home and safely in the front door before abandoning me.'

Kate was still worried. 'Do you think she's alright? I mean, I know she's just drunk right now, but the rest of the time, is she coping?'

Issy leaned in, 'I met her for lunch, week before last and she seemed ok - bored with so much time on her hands, but upbeat. In fact, she seemed optimistic about the future, kept talking about contacts and plans for this and that. You know how she is, always plotting something.'

'She is amazing.' *Kate nodded proudly and renewed her efforts of stroking Ayesha's arm,* 'It's been a tough time for her.'

***

'There you saw the disastrous drunken end which was Ayesha's part in my sad old New Year's Eve tale.'

The Ombudsman raised a slow eyebrow in question, 'OK, I admit to being confused. You were upset because Lulu was sober at the end of the night, but, at the same time, you were upset because Ayesha was drunk?'

Violet shrugged at her own contrary notions, 'Humans, huh? Who'd deal with them?'

She took a few moments to pull her thoughts together. 'We thought she was doing ok. We thought she was alright.' She paused, 'Clearly, she wasn't.'

'I'm sure you all did your best.'

Violet was not prepared to listen to his reassurances. 'No. We didn't. We sat there watching Ayesha dribbling into the tablecloth, wondering how we could possibly not have known things had got so bad.' She looked him square in the eye. 'What sort of friend doesn't know when someone's life takes a dive like that? Basically, we failed, I failed, and there's no other way of dressing it up to make it more palatable.'

The ombudsman opened his mouth to speak, but she interrupted. 'So, don't even try!'

He resealed his lips.

Violet shrugged. 'Part of me thinks "you're only human, give yourself a break", while the other part keeps giving me the look my mum used to give me when I was giving her lip in front of my friends – you know, the one mums do, when you're in the wrong but she doesn't want to tell you off in public, but you know you're going to get it when you get home. I should have done more. That's why it threw me so much that night. That's why it upset me. That's why it was so important she got a break.'

Violet turned her attention back to the screen, concentrating on the activity which zipped past, to buy time until she could regain her composure. The ombudsman kept his gaze discreetly on the footage, waiting for her to make the next move.

At last, her face, all except her eyes, smiled at him. 'Are you ready to see the next part of the story?'

The smile he returned was a mere hint, achieving little more than softening his features. 'Ready when you are,' he agreed.

CHAPTER 15

Mid-March

The meeting was drawing to a close. Violet became aware of papers being shuffled as people prepared to leave, but other than that, all she was aware of was the man standing at the head of the table. Niall was intermittently facing the group square on, and twisting to point with one arm at a flipchart, at which point his shirt would pull tight across his chest and if Violet concentrated hard she could detect a six pack. She gently chewed on the corner of her bottom lip as she tried to focus on what he was saying.

'So, guys, the key takeaway is, we need to raise the bar. Bring me ideas; bring me thinking outside the box; bring me plans which have legs. We'll touch base again same time, same place next Monday.'

She wasn't sure if it was her imagination, but she could have sworn he had made significant eye contact with her more than once this morning. She was never scruffy when she came to work, but the last few weeks, Mondays had become more important. On Mondays she paid more attention to her make-up, had been more selective with her outfits, had tried to ensure a good night's sleep the night before so she would appear bright-eyed and fresh, because Mondays were when she knew she would be seeing Niall at the motivational meetings he insisted upon holding. As everyone else gathered up their belongings and filtered away, she lingered, took deliberate care filing her notes and pocketing pens. Something told her today would be the day he approached her, the day he made the first move, because it was about time.

Niall was talking to someone from finance and the conversation went on and on, until Violet could delay no longer. She sighed and made for the door, at which point he leaned around his opposite to stop her. 'Sorry, Violet. Do you have a minute?'

Yes, she had a minute. She had as long as he needed. All day if he liked.

She hovered in the background as he guided her colleague across the room and ushered him out, before closing the door. 'Numbers people. I know they're essential, but ...' He rolled his eyes, before returning to his spot at the table and, rifling through papers, pulled out a glossy, embossed A5 envelope. 'I was wondering if you had plans for Sunday night.'

It took all her strength not to fist pump the air in triumph, but she didn't want to look too eager. Treat them mean, keep them keen. 'Me? Sunday? I don't think I've anything in my diary. Why?'

'You know it's the TV awards, right?' He said it like she would be thinking of nothing else. 'I wondered if you'd like to go.'

Wow! What a first date. A celebrity packed glamour fest. She would have attended with him, without him, offered to waitress to get her hands on a ticket. 'Oh, Niall, I don't know what to say.'

He perched on the edge of the table. 'Both Daytime and Prime teams will be in attendance, but I can't be in two places at once and I have it on good authority Daytime is a winner, so obviously I need to be visual there, which means there are a pair of tickets left on the Prime table.'

Ah. So he wasn't asking her to partner him. Disappointing, but even so...

'You're the most senior member of staff not already with tickets and I'm not sure Cheryl or Dwayne are actually using theirs.

Cheryl's not interested as there's no chance of an award and Dwayne, well Dwayne is best away from the champers right now. Anyway, interested? You can use them yourself or pass them on to select others if you wish, but we need to be sure of bums on seats. TV awards are aspirational. It can't appear as if people don't want to attend.'

So she was a chair filler. Her heart sank, and yet it was the TV awards. It would be madness to turn an opportunity like that down. 'Great. Yes, thanks. I'd love to.'

'Good.' He handed her the envelope.

She felt there should be more. It seemed wrong to take them and go. Perhaps he needed a little encouragement. 'Was there anything else?' Like declaring undying love? Throwing yourself at my feet? She waited desperately holding onto hope.

He didn't take the bait, 'No. I think that's it.' He frowned and tipped his head to one side a little confused, trying to work out if he'd forgotten something. 'Unless you had something you needed to discuss?'

No, she wasn't that brave. 'No, no. Ok, I'll get on then.' She waved the tickets at him. 'Thanks again.'

Tucking the tickets into her handbag, she left the room and stepped into the lift, sighing deeply. Clearly he needed more time to build up the courage to ask her out, although he didn't strike her as the shy type. Or, perhaps he was planning on speaking to her at the awards. Perhaps he didn't feel comfortable approaching her in the workplace. That would make sense.

By the time she reached her floor, she was working out what to wear.

***

The ombudsman was making notes in a pad, lips pursed, and Violet guessed he was questioning the relevance of the scene she had shown him.

'I know what you're thinking.' She pre-empted.

'Yes.' He nodded sagely. 'He's definitely not into you.'

'What? That's not what I was going to say... What do you mean he's not into me? He so is, or was.' She glowered at him. 'I was going to say you have to see what happens next to understand the relevance.'

In disgust, Violet turned her attention to the remote control, but threw one last glance at the ombudsman before pressing play, muttering under her breath. 'Not into me indeed! Honestly.'

Mid-March

When the doorbell rang, Violet stopped in her tracks. Her bed was draped with the slinkiest, sexiest dresses she possessed and a pile of shoes were strewn on the floor alongside and she had intended to while away what was left of the evening trying them on, to gauge the most suitable for Sunday's event. She hadn't expected anyone and, glancing at her bedside clock, realised it was late for guests at any rate. If it was Naomi with Arthur again she would have to turn her away. Preparations for her night out were far too important to be put off for another day, in case she needed to resort to online shopping for the killer outfit.

It was Kate and she was in floods of tears.

'What on earth's the matter? Come in, come in.'

Violet led her to the lounge and pulled her into the sofa for a hug. After a few moments the sobbing subsided. 'So, come on? What's all this about?' She knew Kate and Ben were still way off their savings target for another round of IVF and that was the only thing that generally reduced Kate to this sort of state.

'Oh, I'm sorry. I didn't know where else to go.'

'But what's happened?' Violet handed her a tissue.

Kate's breath stuttered as she attempted to explain. 'It's Ben.'

Ben wouldn't hurt a fly, surely? 'Ben? What's he done?'

'It's not what he's done, it's what he said. He said I don't care about him. He said all I'm interested in is having a baby and I don't give a stuff about anything else. That's not true, is it?'

Aah. Violet would have to be shrewd about how she answered that one. 'I'm sure Ben knows how much you care about him.'

'He says he works all the hours God sends to make me happy and I'm still not satisfied, but I do know. I do appreciate the effort he's making.'

'Of course you do. Listen, can I get you a drink? A glass of wine?'

Kate sniffed into the tissue. 'No, better not. We're not supposed to be drinking alcohol at the moment.'

'Tea, then?'

'Yes, please.'

Violet moved to the kitchen and Kate followed, leaning against the doorjamb as she wiped her eyes. 'So, what brought all this on then? It doesn't sound like Ben. You two never argue.'

'Well, he came in from work and went to get a beer from the fridge, but I'd thrown them out because I read that excessive alcohol intake reduces your sperm count.' *She shrugged.* 'It's for his own good, and I'm not going to be drinking either.'

'Oh Kate' *Violet stopped what she was doing to face her friend.*

'What?'

She held Kate's hands in her own. 'I don't think Ben drinks excessively and it's not like you're having treatment at the moment, are you? You know, he's doing a very stressful job and he needs to be able to relax when he gets home. I'm sure one beer wouldn't do any harm.'

Kate looked down at her shoes. 'I know.'

Violet held her tight for a moment. She knew Kate was teetering on the edge. The last five years of disappointment had taken their toll, until the hope of someday having a child of her own had infiltrated every avenue of her life. There was room for little else in her thoughts and now it seemed even Ben was feeling excluded. If Kate and Ben's relationship were to fall apart, Kate simply would not cope.

'I've been terrible to him, haven't I?'

'No. No, you haven't been terrible.' Violet poured the tea and grabbed a packet of chocolate digestives from the cupboard. 'Come on, let's go and sit down.'

They returned to the sofa.

'I think you've got a bit caught up in the trying for a baby business, which is completely understandable after what you've been through, but maybe you need to back off, just a bit. Remember, Ben's been through it too. When it's time for the next round of treatment, definitely go for it wholeheartedly, but maybe now, while you're waiting, you should try and have some fun. Not take life too seriously. Go out and live a little, as a couple. I mean, you won't be able to when you've got a baby, will you?'

Kate stared at her tea. 'I know you're right, but the problem is he's working all the hours, and when he's not, we don't have the money spare anyway. You can't exactly have a wild night on a tenner, can you?'

The award night tickets caught Violet's eye from the sideboard where she had propped them and their very existence hit her like a slap. A neon sign telling her to offer them to Kate couldn't have been more obvious. She let her breath out very, very slowly as a wave of resignation washed over her. She had to give them to her. It hurt. All day she had been building the event up in her imagination, the stars she would rub shoulders with, the gourmet food, the champagne, what Niall would finally get around to asking, her own response to his asking, but no, it was not to be. Kate and Ben needed them more.

'I may have just the thing. Are you free Sunday night? Is Ben working?' Please, please let him be working.

'Yes, we're free. He's taken an extra shift on Saturday, but Sunday is all ours.'

Kate's face displayed such desperation for good news, it softened the blow of giving the precious tickets away. Violet reached for the envelope and passed it to her friend to open without uttering a word.

Kate took it with a frown of confusion, but as she opened the elegant card out, the frown was replaced with an open-mouthed expression of delight. 'No! You're not serious?'

Violet dismissed her query with a wave of the hand. 'Absolutely. They're yours.'

'But, but what would I wear?'

'Hold on.' Violet ran to her bedroom, shuffled through the pile of dresses until she found the shiny silver sheath dress which she knew would always look better on her sylphlike friend than on her own curves, and carried it back into the lounge with a pair of matching sky scraper heels. 'How about this?'

Kate gripped the arm of the sofa as if she were afraid she was in danger of falling off, so upside down had her world been turned. 'No. Really?'

'Really. It's yours.' She carefully folded the fabric and pushed it into a bag. 'I want the shoes back when you're done, mind you.'

'Of course. Oh my goodness, Ben is going to go mad with excitement.'

'Good. You'll have a great time. Go and tell him now.'

Kate gathered her things together, taking up the bagged dress and holding it to her chest like a most treasured possession before heading for the door. 'I will.'

'And, Kate,' Violet called after her in the hall. 'Stop at the off licence and get him a beer on the way home.'

Kate ran back and hugged her one last time before disappearing down the stairs, unable to wait for the lift in her agitation.

Violet closed the door and leaned against it, smiling. It was good to do nice things for other people. Her smile broadened. It was even better to receive a reward.

***

'Mmm, you have a complicated relationship with alcohol, don't you?'

Violet peered down her nose at him. 'I'm not even going to justify that with a comment.' She shook her head. 'Clearly this was a huge sacrifice on my part, turning down the opportunity to attend such a prestigious event, and I expected the reward to be equally impressive. I had visions of Niall arriving at my door in the small hours declaring his love…'

'I've already told you my opinion on that…'

She ignored his interruption, raising her voice to drown him out. 'Or a massive bunch of flowers delivered to my desk the next day. For some reason, I was convinced the payback would be connected to my love life, but I was completely wrong. I didn't expect to be kept waiting though. By the Sunday night I was giving up hope. I thought I'd given the tickets away for nothing.'

'You mean nothing apart from the knowledge of your doing something benevolent for your friend?'

She pursed her lips. 'Yes, obviously apart from that. To this day I haven't quite worked out the logistics of how sacrifice and reward tie up time wise in the deal. On a few occasions they were simultaneous, but more often than not there was a lag. I suppose it's not always possible to get an exact correlation.'

'Or there wasn't a deal?' The ombudsman mused.

'You can go off a person, you know?' She pointed at the screen. 'On this occasion, the reward came about at exactly the same time Kate and Ben were at the awards, as you will see.'

Mid-March

Violet stood in the supermarket, a basket over her arm, and studied the vast array of red wine. She heaved a sigh and glanced at her watch. By now, she should have been getting into the taxi, glammed up to the eyeballs, ready to party the night away, but instead she was concealing a onesie under the biggest coat she possessed, contemplating a night on her own, in front of the TV, with a microwave curry. She sidestepped to the spirits, but as she reached for the gin her phone rang.

'Hello?'

The number was one she didn't recognise, but she answered it anyway in the hope it was a nuisance call and she would at least have the satisfaction which came with letting off steam. No one spoke, but she could sense a presence at the other end of the line. That's all she needed, a heavy breather.

'I don't know who you are, but go get your jollies at somebody else's expense, pervert.'

She was about to cancel the call when a muffled sound broke the silence. It was crying or an attempt to restrain a sob. Surely Kate and Ben weren't at odds again. 'Who is that? Kate? Is that you?'

'No. No, it's me.' The voice was miniscule.

'Lu? What is it? What's wrong?'

'I didn't know who else to call. Kate's not at home and I know Issy's away with Martin.'

'What's happened?'

'Mum and Dad are in Brussels and I can't reach them. They thought they were safe to go.'

Violet sensed Lulu was evading the question and, if she was trying to reach her parents, then the answer was obvious. It was Rachael. 'Lu, where are you?' She kept her voice level and calm, a world away from how she was feeling.

'At the hospital.'

Violet dropped the basket on the floor and marched past the tills. 'I'll be there in ten minutes.'

She managed to hail a taxi and, for once, the traffic was on her side. True to her word she reached the hospital in minutes and swept into reception, where she was directed to Intensive Care. As she stood in the lift, waiting to be deposited on the correct floor, her heart thudded in her chest. If Rachael was in Intensive Care, her condition had clearly taken a dive. It made her angry. A young girl like that had no business suffering in the way she had; Lulu shouldn't have had to witness it.

She muttered under her breath. 'God, I know we have a deal, but sometimes I don't like the way you operate. They don't deserve this.' The lift doors swished open and she followed the signs to the end of the corridor.

Lulu was standing at a large window, wringing a cardigan in her hands, watching a host of gowned staff work around a bed, inside. It was impossible to identify the patient in the bed, buried under wires and tubes, but Violet guessed it was Rachael.

'Lu?'

Lulu turned and collapsed into her arms. All Violet could do was hold her, but that appeared to be sufficient, as after a few moments she gathered herself together enough to stand back and explain, eyes fixed on the activity beyond the glass. 'She was doing so well. Then, all of a sudden, her temperature went through the roof. There were no warning signs. One minute she was happy as Larry, the next she was like this.' Her hand shot to her mouth, as if trying to keep the words in. 'Vi, I don't think she's going to make it.'

Violet didn't know how to reassure her without sounding trite. She could see Lulu shaking, whether with fear or shock she couldn't tell, so in the end she simply slipped her arm around her shoulders, keeping her steady, trying to absorb some of the trauma with her own body.

One by one, the medical staff moved away, to a computer desk at the back of the room or to other beds, leaving only one doctor and a nurse hunched over Rachael's chart. The doctor made notes, before coming through the door towards them. He ushered them into seats and pulled another from the row to face them both, leaning, elbows on knees, a shock of scarlet socks showing in the gap between trouser hem and shoes.

'Ok, Louise, I don't need to tell you how serious the situation is. Have you managed to track down your parents yet?'

'No. They're not picking up. I'll keep trying.'

He was matter of fact. 'Yes, you should do that.' *A telling lack of reassurance was offered.*

'What is it? Is it the treatment? A reaction?'

Lulu's leg shook vigorously and Violet rested a hand on her knee, slowing the tremor.

'No, it's not the medication, it's sepsis. The treatment was going as well as we could possibly have hoped, but Rachael's immune system is seriously compromised. Infection was always the biggest risk at this stage. On our side is she was already here, so we got to it quickly. If she'd been anywhere else it would have been catastrophic. We're giving her broad spectrum antibiotics now and managing her temperature and fluids, but there is only so much we can do. The rest is down to her, I'm afraid, and whether she has the strength left to fight it.'

Lulu's hand crept down to grip Violet's. 'Is she going to die?'

The doctor frowned. 'I'd be lying if I told you it wasn't a possibility. You need to be prepared, but I always try to take the optimistic stance. The human body can cope with a great deal, and if I know Rachael, she's not the sort to give up without a battle.'

Lulu forced a weak smile. 'She's got attitude, that's for sure.'

'She has that alright. We should have a better idea by the morning.' *The doctor stood up and swung his chair back into line.* 'You can go in and sit with her. If we need room to work we might *have to kick you out, but there's no reason why you can't be with her right now.'*

Every hour of the night seemed like several. They sat by Rachael's side, making way for the nurses when they needed to, the machinery creating a melancholy rhythm to their vigil. They talked about the Rachael they knew and loved from times gone by, the annoying little sister who tried to gate crash their plans, who borrowed outfits without asking, who dyed her hair without parental consent with disastrous consequences, who was a major part of both their journeys into adulthood. They laughed quietly, ignoring the dread in their stomachs and the ache in their hearts, denying the possibility her own journey could be nearing its end. The counterfeit positivity was exhausting and, a little after four, Violet escaped to the ladies' loo.

The hall was surprisingly busy considering the hour, with uniformed staff carrying out their duties and pale, drawn visitors donning brave faces similar to Violet's own. She passed them all, avoiding eye contact, witnessing more suffering would have been the last straw and she needed to keep it together for Lulu. In the bathroom, she was pleased to be able to lock the cubicle and, for a few moments, gather her thoughts in uninterrupted space. As hard as this was for her, it was so much harder for her friend.

She looked at her watch. Kate and Ben were probably rolling into bed about now, after the party, high on excitement. No doubt, they had numerous colourful tales to tell. She hoped they'd had fun. The fragility and brevity of life suddenly weighed heavy on her, and she sat on the lid of the toilet, her legs too weary to hold her up.

'Please God. Let her be alright. Please make her better. If you do nothing else for me ever, please do this.' The plea came from way down in her chest and, as soon as it had left her body, she held herself stock still, listening for any kind of answer, but none came. She ran a comb through her hair, washed her face and returned to the bedside.

Lulu looked up. 'Mum and Dad are on their way back. They should be here in the morning.'

'Good. That's good news. I'll stay until then.'

'You don't have to. I'll be all right and they'll be here in a couple of hours.'

'No, I'll stay until then.' Violet knew Lulu was struggling to be brave. There was no way she would allow her to face this uncertainty on her own.

'Thank you.'

'Did you want anything from the machine? A coffee? Chocolate?' Anything to make the time pass more quickly.

'No, I couldn't right now. Maybe later.'

'Crisps.' A gravelly voice sounded from the bed and Violet and Lulu swivelled to face it. Rachael lay still, but her eyes were wide, if weary. 'Salt and vinegar.'

A half sob, half laugh erupted from Lulu's body and she dived at the bed.

'Get off me,' Rachael whined. 'What's the matter with you?'

She smacked a kiss on the girl's forehead. 'I've got a pain in the arse for a sister. That's what.'

A nurse appeared, at the bedside and a flurry of activity ensued. Violet backed off, an interloper to proceedings and retreated to purchase salt and vinegar crisps, the only useful thing she could think of doing. For one brief moment an image of her own sister crept into her consciousness. It occurred to her how long it was since she'd seen her and how she would feel if she was lying in the hospital bed. She pushed the thought away.

By the end of another hour, Rachael was declared through the worst, and Violet slipped away, feeling herself to be surplus to requirements. If she played her cards right, she could get back to the flat, change and still make it to the Monday meeting on time. A small dose of Niall de Havilland was sure to put some spring back into her step.

Unable to park directly outside, the taxi dropped her a little away from the flat and, as she turned into the entrance Peter launched a bucket of hot, soapy water down the path towards her and she was forced to hop out of the way.

'Sorry,' he yelled, far too cheery for this hour of the day.

She frowned at her soggy shoes. 'Don't you ever go home?'

'It doesn't feel like it sometimes. I had an extra early call today.' He shrugged. 'Some eejit allowed their dog to do its business right on the doorstep in the night, a great Dane if the size of the business is anything to go by, and an unsuspecting tenant walked it all the way to the lift. The life of a maintenance contractor is all glamour.'

She grimaced at the image and was thankful all she had on her shoes was soapy water.

Peter looked her up and down. 'Bold choice. Walk of shame, is it?'

Violet looked down at the tiger print onesie and sighed, her coat must still be in the waiting room. 'No, it's not.' She was disgruntled by his insinuation. 'I've been at the hospital.'

'Hey, I was only kidding. No offence, but it's not exactly walk of shame clobber. Are you ok?'

'I'm fine.' She was too tired to get into a debate and called the lift, then turned to face him. 'You believe in God, right?'

'Pretty much.'

'Do you ever wonder why he makes people go through the stuff we do? What it's all about? What it's all for?'

Peter stood his mop in the bucket and straightened up. 'From time to time, but it only gives me a headache. You sure you're alright?'

The lift door opened and she stepped in, a flat, unconvincing smile on her face. 'I will be.'

The doors closed and she was whisked away.

CHAPTER 16

It was a relief to pause the footage. In watching the events of that night Violet had experienced again a portion of the emotions, the frustration and helplessness of being an observer, unable to change what was taking place.

'So, are you trying to say Rachael's recovery was a response to your giving up your evening out? Or was it a response to your prayers in the bathroom? I'm not sure exactly where we are with this one.'

She collapsed back in her seat and shrugged. 'Oh, I don't know. This whole thing is exhausting.' Sighing audibly, she closed her eyes, temporarily shutting out the world.

The ombudsman waited as the silence stretched, but with no sign of Violet reengaging with the process, he cleared his throat to get her attention. 'I hate to rush you, but time is ticking away. If you want me to examine your case we need to be moving along.'

Her only movement was to open her eyes to glare at him. 'I don't think you're interested in my case at all. I think you've already made your mind up, so it doesn't matter what I show you.'

He shuffled around in his seat to face her. 'That's a little unfair. I've watched every scene closely, listened to your opinion. Granted I haven't always agreed with everything you've said, but that goes with the territory. I have to remain objective.'

'Objective. Right.'

'I did warn you an investigation is not a pleasant experience, but you were insistent.'

'Hmm.' Violet sneered. 'I was, wasn't I?'

'We can call it a day if you wish. I can arrange for you to be sent back.' He tipped his head to one side. 'But, I probably wouldn't advise it now.'

'You wouldn't?'

'No, I wouldn't. Whether justified or not, you clearly feel your case is valid and that doesn't bode well for your continued existence on earth. Bitter and twisted people do not make the best life choices. The outcome of the investigation could have serious implications on the rest of your life, whichever way it's settled.'

She mused over his comments. He was right. At the moment she felt neither vindicated nor proven wrong, and it wasn't a comfortable sensation.

'Is there much more evidence to view?'

'Yes, loads.' This was proving far harder work than she'd ever imagined, but there needed to be a definite outcome and she had to continue, for her own sanity's sake. 'Are you ready to carry on?'

The ombudsman scowled, his tone frosted with resignation. 'Yes, yes, as quick as you please. I'll try to keep up.'

'Good. Perhaps I should skip the more vague examples and stick to the obvious ones. Actually April was a quiet month. All the usuals, you know, giving up my seat for the elderly, helping Rhoda with shopping when the lift was broken again, doing Naomi's washing when her machine went kaput - who knew babies got through so many clothes - but there was no specific reward. Then, at the beginning of May, Maggie needed help again and I spotted an opportunity. Here we go.'

Early May

The meeting was in full swing. Niall had constructed a huge list of bullet points on the white board at the front and was busy underscoring words to emphasise their importance.

'Right guys. We need to hit the ground running. Ok. Anybody have anything else to add to the mix?'

There was silence as everyone looked at everyone else for a response. Only Maggie raised a timid hand. Violet saw it and was fairly convinced the rest of the room saw it, except for Niall, who cast his gaze everywhere except at Maggie, and continued.

'Nothing? Good. Get to it guys. Make me proud.' He swept up his briefcase and left ahead of the masses.

Maggie curled her hand back in. Violet was taken aback. It was almost as if Niall had ignored Maggie on purpose, but that clearly couldn't be right. He must have been distracted. He was always one step ahead of everyone else.

As people filtered away, Violet stepped in. 'You ok, Maggie?'

'Well, yes, but... No, I'm sure I'll find a way.' She shook her head as if trying to shake away the frown which had settled there.

Violet slipped into the seat next to her. 'Talk to me, Maggie.'

'Well, Niall sent me the details for the Mongolian Throat Singing shoot, which I'm more than happy to do, but he's scheduled it to coincide with the Acapella Gospel Choir shoot for the Daytime show, so the same production team can do both, to save money. But, the choir are only in the country for the weekend so we have no choice but to record it on Saturday. I wouldn't mind normally, but Mummy's carer has weekends off and the chances of finding a suitable alternative at such short notice is going to be very difficult. Mummy is so particular.'

Violet's stomach tied itself in a knot. She had tried babysitting, she had tried baking, but did she have it in her to become assistant to an elderly invalid? Was God really challenging her to step in?

She held her breath as she asked the question. 'Is there anything I can do to help?' Please say no, please say no, please say no.

Maggie chewed her bottom lip as she considered the predicament. 'I suppose you could, if you didn't mind doing the shoot instead.' She shook her head. 'But you've done enough for me recently, I couldn't ask you to give up your weekend.'

So relieved was she at this solution, Violet jumped right in. 'Of course I can. I've no other plans, or at least, none that can't be altered. I'm sure you'd stand in for me one day if I needed you to.' She rubbed her hands together, already contemplating a juicy reward. 'There, that's settled. Email me through the details.'

Violet pulled out her mobile phone as she headed back to her own desk. It would mean cancelling her Eurostar tickets, but then, she hadn't wanted to go anyway and now at least she had a valid excuse. Two problems solved for the price of one.

Violet recognised the church hall where recording was to take place. She was sure she had been here before. It was a lovely old building, a bit crumbly, but even from the outside she could tell the space inside would be cavernous and the acoustics amazing, not that that was her concern, she simply had to ensure everyone was in the right place at the right time and that everyone was happy. She could do that.

The woman who greeted her at the door was also familiar, but again, Violet couldn't quite place her.

"Hello. You must be here for the recording session. I'll show you around, then leave you to it, but I'll keep the office mobile telephone with me in case you need anything.' The woman squinted at her. 'Do I know you, dear?'

Violet felt uncomfortable under her intense gaze. 'No, I don't think so.' She looked around the hall. 'Can you show me the facilities?'

They conducted a quick tour together before returning to the entrance where the recording crew had arrived and were manhandling equipment from the van.

'Hi, Norm. Do you know where you're going?'

The overall'd man set down his box and held up a hand. 'All under control, doll. Straight into the church.'

Violet turned to her guide. 'Thanks for everything. It's a lovely building. It'll be great for the show.'

'It's been a bit of luck all round to be honest. The choir had been booked to appear here for months and when your producer people invited them on to the television it made sense to make use of this space rather than push the choir from pillar to post, and as I'm sure you'll appreciate, the hire fees are always welcome.'

'Well, your gain is our gain. This'll do nicely.'

'Ok, then, I'll be off.' She waved a phone. 'Don't forget, if you need anything. Oh, and a couple of our volunteers will be coming in with the singers later, as they're our guests, and I'm sure they'll be happy to help out if you need anything.'

'Thanks. Appreciated.'

Violet followed the woman out and got stuck in, lugging equipment. The place came alive with activity as lighting was adjusted, sound systems set up, camera angles checked and, by the time the guests were due to arrive, Violet had powered up the old water boiler in the kitchen and set to making drinks for the crew. With any luck they would manage to down a coffee before recording started.

An hour later, they were more than ready for action, everything in place, checked and double checked, but there was no sign of the Mongolian throat singers, and anxious glances were starting to pass face to face. Violet reviewed Maggie's notes and tried the contact numbers listed, but there was no reply.

'Don't worry, Norm, I'm sure they're on their way. Probably stuck in traffic or something. Is there anything else we can do in preparation?'

Norm tutted and drummed his fingers, impatience starting to show, though his Scottish burr gave nothing away. 'Not really, doll. We're raring to go, but the next lot'll be arriving before we've wrapped the first at this rate.'

Violet grimaced, what was supposed to have been an easy job was becoming complicated. 'I'll stick my head out and see if there's any sign of them. You never know, they may be circling for parking.'

She quick-stepped from the church, through the hall and out onto the steps, peering on tip toes in all directions. With no sign, she reached for the phone and hit redial. It immediately went to voicemail. Perhaps she should speak to Maggie for guidance, loathe though she was to disturb her weekend.

Maggie seemed distracted. 'I didn't speak to the group myself, the change of time and venue had already been arranged by Niall's Daytime team, and served to me as a fait accompli. As you know, I was none too pleased with the rearrangement, but... Yes, mum. I'll have a look in a minute.'

'They're not picking up on the numbers you've given me and there's no sign of them here. Norm's starting to look frazzled.'

'I could read the emails again, but otherwise I don't know what to suggest. It's always the same when you have too many fingers in the pie. I much prefer to handle things from start to finish, then you know exactly... No, mum, don't get up. I'll be right there.'

'Listen, Maggie. You've got your hands full. Will you forward the whole email thread to me and I'll check it through myself.'

'If you're sure.'

'Yes, sure. You sort your mum out.'

Ending the call, she changed app on her phone, waiting for the envelope symbol to appear. She didn't want to go back into the hall without something to offer the crew by way of explanation or expectation. As soon as it did, she scrolled to the first message and began to read. She was half-way through when a minibus pulled into the kerb and she heaved a sigh of relief. At last. This must be them.

She hurried to the foot of the steps to welcome them, hoping their English was better than her Mongolian, but was met with an unexpected American twang.

'Hey, there. Golden Voice Gospel Choir at your service.'

Oh no. They were early. Now what was she going to do? Not let them see there was an issue, for starters. 'Great to see you. Come on in and have some refreshments. Can I help with anything?'

A host of gowned people trooped from the bus and behind them came Peter. All at once the significance of the venue hit her. This was where he had rescued her months ago, drunk and shoeless. Violet raised her eyebrows. 'Fancy seeing you here.'

He carried a box under one arm and brandished keys to the minibus in the other hand. 'I got roped in to drive the bus for the big event. What are you doing here?'

She fell in beside him, following the group towards the hall, explaining through clenched teeth. 'Work. We're supposed to be recording another group first and then the choir, but for some reason they haven't arrived and we're running out of time. It's all becoming a bit of a disaster and I need to try and track the others down, but someone needs to look after these guys.'

'Alright, calm down. The choir are no trouble at all. They wanted to see the stage and so forth, so they know what they're doing later. Leave them to me and go do what you need to do.' He stepped inside and began to close the door. 'Go on. Do your stuff.'

Violet went back to the emails and read them one by one and, when she reached the end, the penny dropped. In all the to-ing and fro-ing no one had told the throat singers about the change of venue. She double checked to be certain, then dialled the number for the office. Although most desks weren't manned over the weekend, reception was always attended, by security staff if no one else. The voice which answered was one she recognised.

'Hi, Bob. Violet Harper. Tell me, do you have some singers waiting for the studio?'

'Your guess is as good as mine. I've got a group in bright costumes with pointy hats who don't speak a word of English. I tried to explain there was no one here, but they parked themselves in the waiting area. I've been trying to work out what to do with them.'

Violet swore under her breath. 'How many are there?'

'Umm, twenty? Twenty two, counting men, women and kids.'

'Ok, I'll get back to you.'

If the singers didn't speak any English, how on earth were they going to explain the change of venue to them, let alone give them directions to navigate the complicated city streets to the church? She would be lucky if they arrived at all, let alone before the choir's evening performance. Norm was going to go ape, and so would Niall when he heard his cost saving ideas had failed. She wished she'd never got involved. Even going to France and playing pretend happy families with her parents would have been less stressful, which was saying something. Better face the music.

She marched into the hall and was greeted by sweet harmonies filtering in from the church. Peter hovered by the door, peeking through at proceedings.

'What's going on?'

He turned at her low voice. 'Great, aren't they?' He pushed the door to, to cancel out any noise. 'Norm suggested they do a couple of takes while the choir rehearse, though as far as I can tell they're already pretty perfect. Any luck with the missing band?'

She shook her head. 'Yes and no. I've tracked them down, but they're at the studio and I've no idea how they're going to get here. I'd order a host of taxis, but they don't speak English and I've visions of the whole thing going badly wrong. Maybe it would be better to get the crew to go to them, but by the time they pack up here... Oh, it's a nightmare.'

'I've got the mini bus outside. I could be there and back in an hour.'

'Oh, I couldn't ask you to do that.'

'You don't have to, I'm offering. I either sit around here waiting for the choir to finish or I drive down the road and do you a favour. As long as you promise to keep these guys topped up with tea and biscuits until I get back, I can't see a problem.'

She carried out a quick risk assessment in her head. *'They don't speak a word of English.'*

'What do they speak?'

She shrugged. *'Mongolian, I assume.'*

'Well lucky for you I speak fluent Mongolian, or at least, I can speak English very loudly and slowly in the traditional British way with foreigners. We'll get along fine.'

Tense as she was, his stubborn optimism brought a smile to her face. *'Let me check that's ok with Norm. I don't want to create any more confusion.'*

'Go ahead. I'm in no hurry.'

She sneaked into the church, relayed the plan to Norm and returned.

'Am I away then?'

'Yes, please.' She waved Peter off at the door with a huge sense of relief.

The harmonised singing from the adjoining room crept into her consciousness and she settled in a pew at the back of the church to observe. Within minutes the hunch in her shoulders dropped, her furrowed brow relaxed and she closed her eyes to enjoy the wave of peace washing over her.

The tranquillity was short lived as toward the end of the recording Niall de Havilland crashed through the door into the church and Norm called a halt to proceedings with a shout. *'Cut. Sorry, we'll have to start that one again.'*

Niall held up a hand by way of apology and beat a hasty retreat, followed by Violet, into the hall. *'Bloody embarrassing. I thought you'd be between acts, according to the schedule, anyway.'*

Violet couldn't help wonder the sound of singing hadn't given him a clue before he barged in, but knowing him, he had probably been multi-tasking. 'The schedule's gone out the window, I'm afraid, but we're making progress.'

'You have carried out both recordings as per my instructions, I presume?'

'Not yet...' She made to explain, but he wasn't listening.

'I made it quite clear to Maggie. Costs have to be reined in. Where is she anyway? Why are you here?' He looked around, as if Maggie may be hiding under a table or behind a curtain.

'She had a prior commitment...'

'A commitment more important than her job?' He strutted around in a circle. 'I need staff who are prepared to give one hundred and ten per cent. I gave clear instructions how I wanted things done and I come here to find this shambles. It's absolutely not good enough...

A click by the front door made them both turn, to see Peter standing, staring in their direction. He held the door wide and ushered in a sea of confused, but contented Mongolians. 'This way. This way. There you go. Yes, that's right.'

They piled in, smiling and bowing, and Violet hurried to welcome them. Moments later the choir erupted from the other room and soon the hall was a mish-mash of the two groups.

Niall stood stony faced on the outskirts, watching, while Violet thanked the choir on one hand, while guiding the Mongolians in the right direction on the other. Norm stepped up too, shaking hands and bringing order to the chaos. Peter headed for the kitchen and began serving drinks through the hatch and, as soon as the throat singers were ensconced on stage, Violet returned to help him.

With everybody served, they stepped back into the quiet of the kitchen, Violet searching the crowd for Niall.

'If you're looking for your man, he's away.' Peter reached for a dishcloth and wiped down the worktop. 'Nice fella!' The compliment somehow didn't ring true.

'He was concerned things hadn't gone to plan. The budget's on his shoulders, you know. It's pressure.' Violet found herself making excuses for her stroppy, but gorgeous boss.

'He was lucky not to feel the pressure of my fist on the end of his stuck-up nose.'

She was surprised at the heat to Peter's tone and stared at him.

'What?' He realised she was looking at him. 'I can't stand a bully, that's all.'

She continued to watch, as he tidied. 'Thanks for today. You've been a life saver. I owe you one.'

Shaking a tea towel with a snap, he draped it over his shoulder. 'I know you do. Don't worry, it's all noted. I'll let you know when I'm ready to cash it in.' He winked and strode away into the crowd.

On Violet's count, she owed him more than one, what with retrieving shoes and burning cakes and now saving her bacon. More importantly though, whether things went to plan or not, thanks to her sacrifice for Maggie, God now owed her one too and she was seriously looking forward to receiving the reward.

CHAPTER 17

Violet glanced to her right, then did a double take. A young uniformed girl with a tray of snacks hung on a strap round her neck, hovered at the end of their aisle, while the ombudsman studied the contents, scratching his chin.

'Choc ice, Violet? Or something savoury?'

It felt slightly exposing, having a third party in the room and Violet couldn't help wonder how long she had been there and what she had seen. She frowned, but the lure of refreshments prevented her making a complaint. 'Just a drink please. Anything diet.'

He coughed a laugh. 'Yes, it's thirsty work watching yourself being lambasted by your boss.' He winked at the girl. 'Better make it a large one.'

Violet accepted a cardboard cup and took a long sip through the straw, watching as the waitress backed through the swing doors to the corridor beyond. 'It wasn't like that. You have to see it from his point of view. He was relying on us getting the job done and it looked as if we'd let him down. As soon as I explained at the Monday meeting, it was all forgotten.'

'I bet he tried to blame Maggie, didn't he?'

She gave a slow nod, as she thought back to that day. 'He did think Maggie bore some of the responsibility, but as soon as I pointed out the mistake in the emails, he moved on straight away.'

'I bet he did.'

'You're determined not to like him, aren't you?'

He dug the plastic spoon from his carton of ice cream and put it in his mouth before responding. 'I have no strong feelings either way. His character is not my business.' He winced as he swallowed. 'Ooh. Brain freeze!'

She watched him pinch his nose in pain, with a certain amount of satisfaction. She didn't much like his tone. 'Shame. Perhaps watching the next section will help you defrost.'

Early May

The air had a distinct chill to it and Violet saw her friends all huddled together for warmth out front of the pre-arranged address. This month's Culture Sunday involved visiting a backstreet art gallery with, according to Issy, whose tastes were often a little niche, a display of spiritually influenced modern art with dark, soul shifting undertones. As long as it ended with cocktails, no one really cared.

'Sorry. The bus was late.' She ran to greet them and temporarily disappeared inside a scrum.

'Come on. Before it gets too busy.' Issy rushed on ahead.

Ayesha muttered under her breath. 'Not much chance of that.'

Kate looked at her sideways.

'What? I checked it out on-line. A tenner says we're the only ones here.'

'You know the rules of Culture Sunday. No dissing other people's choices.' Kate reminded.

They paused at the glass front, from where they could see the artwork inside. Lulu giggled. 'I think the rules of Culture Sunday may need to be reviewed.' She pushed past and entered, setting an old-fashioned bell on the inside swinging, before Kate could tell her off.

Lulu followed Issy around, stopping to admire the works of art, nodding and making complimentary comments in agreement with her friend, then turning to make faces at the trailing group, despite Kate's warning glares. They made the circuit in super quick time, with no other viewers to hold them up. They gathered together again on the pavement outside.

Ayesha tapped her watch. 'That's got to be a record. We've never got to cocktails quite this early before. Woo Woos before three in the afternoon. Glad I don't have to get up for work in the morning.'

Issy was downhearted. 'I'm sorry. I thought it would be good. Perhaps I should have chosen something else. There are Mongolian Throat Singers at the Palace. We could probably still get in, if we're quick.'

Violet jumped in. 'No, you're alright. I saw them yesterday and once was enough. Woo Woos it is. Come on, first round's on me.'

The road to their favourite bar was a well-trodden path and they quick-marched through the damp to the front door. Inside was already busy, but they manoeuvred past a huddle in the doorway to a booth at the far end, leaving Violet at the bar placing their order. She swiftly followed and perched on the end.

Issy was still apologising. 'I promise I'll do more research next time.'

Kate was still as reassuring as ever. 'But you enjoyed it, Issy. That's the main thing. The whole point of culture Sunday is we all step out of our comfort zones and try something different.'

'It was certainly different.' Lulu and Ayesha were sat together, giggling and elbowing each other.

'You're worse than my Year twos. I'll separate you in a minute.' Kate couldn't help but smile, in spite of herself.

'Look, before we start drinking, I need to have a serious chat about something.' Issy waited until she had all their attention.

'Something happened yesterday, completely out of the blue, and I don't know what to do.'

Glances passed between the others, all wondering what Martin had been up to now.

'When I was leaving work yesterday, my boss called me into the office. She's decided to take early retirement and is selling the business.'

'Oh, Issy. I'm sorry, but you'll soon find another job. You're so good at what you do.' Violet patted Issy's shoulder.

Issy waved her hands in agitation. 'That's not it. She's selling the business as a going concern, so chances are my job would be ok anyway, at least for a while. The thing is, she's offered me first refusal.'

The table came alive with a wave of excited gasps.

Issy's shoulders dropped as the excitement seeped out of her. 'Do you think I could do it? It would be a major investment. I'd have to get funding and learn how to balance books and all sorts.'

Ayesha was quick to step in. 'Of course you could. Wow, what an opportunity. I could help you with accounts and tax and stuff. It's easy when you get your head around it.'

'And you've been saying for ages what potential the business has. You'd be able to make all those changes you've wanted to make. Go for it,' Lulu chipped in.

Violet couldn't help thinking the timing of the offer to Issy had coincided with her completion of the recording session the day before. When she had made the list months before, her request for Issy had been broad and non-specific. All Issy needed was some self-esteem. Running her own business was bound to show her what a capable person she was. Surely, this was Violet's reward.

A waiter arrived and conversation ceased for a minute as they poured drinks and settled back in their seats.

'Martin thinks it would be too much for me. He thinks I should carry on as I am and see what happens under the new owners. He doesn't think I'm management material.'

'What? That's complete and utter nonsense.' Lulu wasn't prepared to put up with her friend being disparaged. 'When are you going to kick that man into touch?'

Kate was more diplomatic. 'He's probably afraid you'll have less time to spend with him if you're running a business. You can so do it, Issy. You'd be great.'

Violet could read the doubt in Issy's eyes. If she wasn't careful this opportunity could evaporate and all her hard work with the shoot would be for nothing. It was time to put herself on the line and give her friend the encouragement she needed to follow her dreams. She gathered both Issy's hands up into her own. 'You know I'm not one for superstition or old wives tales and suchlike, but I have a gut feeling...'

'Ooh, er, the gut's back.' Lulu interrupted, laughing.

Violet ignored her. 'I have a gut feeling this is the right thing for you, Issy. You're more than capable, and if you turn the offer down, I think it would be a big mistake.'

'What's the gut thing?' Kate whispered to the whole table.

'Violet suddenly has this all-knowing digestive system, which can tell when something is right or not.'

Violet countered Lulu's mocking. 'I was right last time though, wasn't I? The treatment has worked out well for Rachael? She's doing ok?'

'Yes, she is. Actually she's more than ok. Things are looking really positive.'

'Good. So, I think you should be giving my gut the benefit of the doubt. Besides, it's more than that, I just know this is right.' She turned back to Issy. 'This is a good thing for you, Issy. Trust me.'

The tone had turned too serious for Ayesha's liking. She lifted her glass for a toast. 'Right, guys. Let's drink to new opportunities, exciting futures and accurate guts.'

All, except Violet, contributed to a chorus of "accurate guts", before drinking and collapsing in a heap of giggles. Violet drank, but didn't join in. Let them laugh. She knew there was more to it *than simply a good feeling, but she wasn't ready to share, quite yet.*

***

'The evidence is starting to stack up, isn't it?' Violet's eyes were wide with excitement. 'Are you starting to see a pattern?'

The ombudsman was frowning at the screen. 'I'm not sure...'

'Not sure? Look.' She counted examples off on her fingers. 'One, I babysit and Rachael gets her treatment. Two, I help Rhoda in the flats and Ben gets his promotion. Three, I help Maggie and meet the man of my dreams.'

'Are you sure...'

'Four, I do the cake sale and Ayesha's court case gets dropped and now, five, I stand in for Maggie at the recording session and Issy is offered a business. It's pretty conclusive, as far as I'm concerned.'

The ombudsman waited.

'Well, isn't it?'

'Oh, I'm allowed to get a word in edgeways now, am I?' He met her gaze. 'I think you're taking a certain amount of liberty with the data.'

'Meaning?'

'Meaning, it's by no means as clear cut as you'd like to think it is. Disregarding the Maggie episode, which we've already discussed, and good intention by the way side, you certainly did her no favours whatsoever, and it remains to be seen whether Niall de Havilland is the man of anyone's dreams, unless we're talking nightmares.'

'Harsh.'

'But fair. Which leaves us with your four remaining examples, and I have issues with some of those too.'

'Such as?'

He referred to his tablet. 'Example five, in the current climate, the question of starting or buying a business is a double edged sword. It may or may not be a good thing for Isobel in the long term. What was it supposed to achieve? What was it you requested for her?'

'I wanted her to have confidence, some self-respect. In all the time I've known her, she's allowed people to treat her like a doormat and it drives me potty. She's so much more than she thinks she is. New Year's Eve is the perfect example.' Violet began to scroll back.

The ombudsman rolled his eyes. 'Are we ever going to move past that one night?'

'Well, if you'd let me show you properly from the beginning, we wouldn't have had to keep going backwards and forwards.' She moved the footage to the point where he had cut her off earlier. Violet's glass was high in the air as she toasted her friends and thanked them for taking time out of their busy lives to fit the gathering in. 'Perhaps this time you'll let me finish.'

New Year's Eve – A Year Ago

'Actually, I didn't have anything else to do tonight at all.' Isobel butted in, her hands face down on the table, eyes darting from each of her friends in turn, as if this was a momentous announcement. 'I was waiting for you to get here, Vi, before I told everyone.'

They all stared in bewilderment and she laughed at their gawping faces. 'I finished with Martin. On Boxing Day. I told him I'd had enough of his antics and I am now officially a free agent.'

A moment of tense silence stretched out, as everyone tried to gauge the situation and come up with a suitable response. This bombshell, Violet had not been prepared for, but Lulu came quickly to the rescue.

'Thank goodness for that. I thought you'd never see sense.'

Isobel shook her head in self-deprecation. 'I know, I know. I'm too good for him. He's a letch. I should have more self-respect. All those things you've been telling me for eighteen months. I finally realised them for myself and, well, enough was enough, so I gave him the heave ho.'

Ayesha seemed astounded, her chocolate eyes round, her mouth opening and closing like a fish. 'Just like that? After all this time?'

'Yep. We were supposed to be going to the Boxing Day football bash. He went to the match in the afternoon and then came to pick me up. I had gone all out. My black dress, you know, the one with the silver beads around the neckline and low back, and those black patent sling backs I wore to the wedding do last summer.' Everyone nodded. 'Well, he came to the door, half an hour late, three sheets to the wind and said... You'll never guess what he said.'

Heads shook vigorously and Kate slapped one hand to her chest as she braced herself for something horrific. 'What?'

Isobel paused for effect. 'He said "is that what you're wearing?" and I just looked at him, like "what did you say?" and he said "only, Mickey's new bit of stuff is coming tonight and she's really fit so I want you to look your best, you know, not show me up or anything".'

Gasps of shock ricocheted around the table as she continued, her voice rising in consternation. 'Can you believe the nerve? He's standing there on my doorstep, half cut, his hair not brushed and a zit the size of a tangerine on his forehead. Well, I don't know what happened. I suppose I flipped. I didn't say a word; not a thing. I closed the door in his face, poured myself a bath and a vodka and turned up the volume on my stereo. That was the last I heard from him. Good riddance.' She punctuated the comment with a brusque nod of her head.

Violet was impressed, 'Well done, you,' she uttered, taking a quick swig from her glass. 'I'm proud of you.'

Lulu agreed. 'Absolutely.' She leaned in confidentially, lowering her voice. 'You know, he pinched my bum at Kate's barbecue last bank holiday? I didn't say anything before because I felt awkward, but he was lucky not to get a slap.'

Ayesha raised a sardonic eyebrow, as she slowly rotated her glass between both hands, watching the liquid rise and fall as it swirled. 'Get over yourself Lu. He pinched everyone's bum that day. He was slaughtered.'

Isobel frowned. 'He didn't pinch mine.' Then laughed abruptly, 'That says it all really, doesn't it?'

Violet called them all to attention. 'This is definitely cause for celebration. Come on, guys. Let's drink to Izzy being a free agent.'

Glasses were raised among a flurry of restrained cheers and congratulatory pats on Isobel's shoulders.

***

'You see? That's what you would have seen earlier, if you hadn't butted in.' Violet felt a little smug. 'Rather a vital piece of information.'

The ombudsman was frowning, concentrating on the film, ignoring her self-righteousness. 'It's the opposite of the point you were trying to make though, isn't it? Surely it's an example of Issy sticking up for herself, rather than being the doormat you profess her to be?'

Violet huffed. 'Oh yes. The evening started on a high, but it was a very different story come the end of the night. I hadn't finished yet.' She waved the controller at the screen. 'It went very seriously downhill later on. Here - Issy, New Year's eve, part two.'

Sharon Francis

New Year's Eve – A Year Ago

Violet surveyed her image in the mirror in the ladies' loo, between peeling stickers, crude lipstick messages and ugly splodges of discarded gum. In the bar the noise was a non-stop barrage on the eardrums and every time the door swung open and closed, giving entry and exit to a steady stream of staggering, scantily clad partygoers, she winced at the audio attack. Her hair was decidedly droopy after the trek from the restaurant, through the elements and her make-up was a little blurred around the edges, but her optimism had borne the brunt of the evening's events.

Why had she let herself have that last drink? She had felt pretty much in control until then, but now she had opened her mouth without thinking and really hurt Kate. Beautiful Kate, whose giving and thoughtful character was most susceptible and least deserving of damage. It didn't matter the slip up had been accidental, it had still happened and the sadness in Kate's eyes as she left them to head home had cut through Violet like a scalpel.

All her preplanning had failed miserably. First Ayesha had made an early exit, with Lulu in tow. Now Kate had disappeared into the night too, the trials and disappointments of the last couple of years rubbed in her face. So much for cheering everybody up. So much for reuniting their friendship group.

Now only she and Isobel were left and she didn't know how to proceed. She felt like going home and burying herself in her duvet with a sleeping pill until well into January, but then she would be letting Isobel down too, and this was her first New Year alone, post-Martin. Violet pursed her lips at the scowling image facing her. She should stay in spite of everything, though she probably wouldn't be the best company.

Reaching into her bag for a brush, she slowly went through the motions of touching up loose tendrils of hair, suddenly becoming aware of a drama behind her. The sound of vomiting in one of the stalls behind grabbed her attention and she felt a wave of sympathetic nausea rising within as the violent retching continued. The door was slightly ajar and, when the heaving finally paused, she honed-in carefully to ensure the occupant was ok. She was surprised to hear two voices from within.

'Sorry Kerry, did I get your shoes?' The voice was plaintive and apologetic.

'No, babe, you're all right. Are you finished?'

'Yea, I think so, but I might stay here a bit longer, just in case. Is it in my hair?'

'No, I held it out the way. A quick wash and brush up in a minute and no one would know.' The tone was calm, even and reassuring.

'Thanks Kerry, you're a gem'

'Ahh, what are friends for, eh?'

Violet caught her own eye in the reflection. Friends deserved better, they deserved the extra mile. Issy deserved the extra mile. Not only would she stay for Issy, she would stay and enjoy it, despite herself, and ensure she was the life and soul of the party into the package. There would be time to feel sorry for herself later, at home alone, with her feet up and a box of tissues at hand. She applied a fresh coat of lipstick, practiced a passable fake smile and marched back into the bar.

Issy was perched on a ridiculously high stool at the bar, another reserved alongside by warrant of her handbag, with a couple of wine glasses fizzing and popping like a Jacuzzi in front of her. She was waving to get Violet's attention. Violet locked eyes with her and waved back, grinning from ear to ear – operation Cheer Up Issy in top gear. She weaved through the crowds, dodging elbows and avoiding errant glasses of vividly coloured liquid ending up down her dress. When finally she reached the bar and mounted the threadbare stool uninjured she breathed a sigh of relief.

'Champagne, as requested.' Issy pushed the glass towards her haltingly as it snagged on sticky patches left by earlier occupants' drinks.

'Excellent, thanks,' She lifted the glass and sniffed the acrid bubbles, laughing as her nostrils tickled, then tapped it against Isobel's glass. 'Cheers, Issy! Here's to a fantastic year ahead.'

'Yes, you too.' Isobel sipped, before banging the glass down and pursing her lips, frowning. 'I'm sorry, Vi, I've got to come clean with you.'

Her face was so stricken Violet became quite concerned. 'Whatever's the matter?'

Issy smiled weakly, 'Nothing's wrong exactly, except, I've taken a call from Martin.'

Violet flinched, the grip on her flute becoming a fist, 'Whatever he said, don't take any notice. You're gorgeous and you don't need him.'

'Funnily enough, that is pretty much what he said. He said he realised I was probably better off without him, I could do much better than him, but he can't manage without me. He said he can't imagine next year without me, he's sorry and wants me back.' She spotted Violet's incredulous expression and shook her head, 'He really meant it, Vi, I could hear in his tone. I think he actually is sorry.'

Violet was beside herself with frustration. 'I was only in the loo five minutes and he managed to say all that? Don't fall for it. You know what he's like. Come tomorrow, his apology will all be forgotten and he'll be back to the same old bad behaviour. Be strong, Issy!' Where were the other girls when she needed them for back up?

Issy almost begged her, such was her desire to believe him. 'But he sounded so pitiful, Vi, like a little puppy. He needs me. He loves me.'

'Oh, Issy! What have you done?'

Isobel looked down at her hands, fidgeting restlessly in her lap, 'He's coming by in a taxi to pick me up, so we can see the New Year in at his local, with the rest of the lads. You don't mind, do you?'

The look on Violet's face told her exactly what she thought without the need for words. Isobel pleaded, 'It's New Year's Eve and I've got the chance to spend it with someone else, not on my own.'

'You aren't on your own.'

'I know, but you know what I mean.' A long drawn out pause indicated to Isobel she may be winning.

'It's a booty call. You know that, don't you?' Violet attempted to hold her gaze steady, but Isobel turned aside.

'Maybe, or maybe he does love me.'

Violet sighed, who was she to break her friend's heart and flamenco dance all over her dreams. 'OK. It's your call.'

There was no argument. 'You'll be all right on your own?'

'Me?' Violet was incredulous, 'I'll be fine. Come on then, best drink up and head out. His taxi won't be able to park and probably won't want to hang around too long waiting for him to find you.'

Isobel was already downing her drink, eyelids fluttering as the bubbles hit the back of her throat. She banged the empty glass down on the top, manoeuvred her handbag across her chest and hopped down from her perch, wobbling on her high heels, like a gymnast dismounting a pommel horse.

Violet watched her and glanced at her own half empty glass. Waste not, want not, she thought, closing her eyes and swallowing the contents in one gulp. She opened her eyes to see Isobel hopping from one foot to another in her impatience to be gone. Resigned, she slipped out of her own seat and squared her shoulders to make her way through the crowds, a space immediately opening as the couple to the rear saw the opportunity and pounced to refill the new gap at the bar. The journey to the door was far from a straight line, as they traversed tables overflowing with merrymakers and sidled past pockets of drinkers huddled in groups. By the time they emerged into fresh air, Violet was glad to have the space to breathe deeply, albeit damp and dank. At least the rain had paused. The line of taxis had shortened, while the queue of people waiting to hire them snaked along the pavement. As Violet attempted to find her bearings, Isobel was looking around, trying to assess the best place to spot Martin's arrival, but almost immediately a car swung in to the kerb, amid a flurry of beeping and squealing, as it cut up the front taxi, already indicating to pull away. The back window of the car was rolled three quarters of the way down and a dishevelled head, they both recognised as an inebriated Martin, poked halfway through.

'Issy! Issy, babe! Quick, before the natives turn ugly.' He guffawed at this own joke.

Isobel paused and threw a glance at Violet, torn between her own desire to drive off into the night with him and a last-minute sense of desertion of her friend.

Violet, unimpressed as she was with Martin's behaviour, refused to allow it to show. She grabbed Isobel for the briefest of hugs. 'Go on. Have fun.'

Isobel frowned, not quite letting go of her friend, 'Are you sure you'll be ok? Getting home on your own?'

'Yeah, yeah. I'm a big girl, and I'm right here at the taxi rank. What could go wrong? I'll speak to you soon. Go!'

A renewed flurry of horn blowing removed any possibility of further soul searching. 'Ok, ok!' Isobel shouted, as she dashed to the car and swung in beside Martin. Her head briefly reappeared through the window, yelling, 'Happy New Year, Vi!' before disappearing in the back seat with her man.

Violet waved into the distance, watching the car until it turned the corner, out of her view. She was surrounded by clusters of revellers, making their way in one direction or another, but suddenly felt very alone. She pulled herself together, checked she had everything she should about her person and made her way to the back of the queue to get a cab home.

***

'Ooh, watching that Martin makes my blood boil. He treats her like dirt and she puts up with it. She wouldn't do it if she had any self-respect whatsoever, but how do you tell her?' Violet seethed.

'I suppose it's a lesson she has to learn on her own. I'm not convinced buying a business is the way to do it though.' The ombudsman pinched his chin as he turned his attention from the screen back to his tablet.

'It's a start. If she has the confidence to run her own business, perhaps she'll have the confidence to be single for a while, not relying on some loser to give her life validation.'

He bobbed his head in acknowledgement of her point. 'Maybe. But anyway I have to discount that particular example because of the timing. The bakery owner had already decided to sell and discussed the offer to Isobel with her accountant before informing Isobel herself, which would mean the reward was planned before you'd actually carried out the relating task.' He scrolled down the page. 'Similarly, example two, although you only got to hear about Ben's promotion after helping Mrs Brent, Ben had already been told the day before, so again the timing is an issue. Then, if you make allowances for sheer coincidence, you're not leaving much actual evidence.'

Violet was astounded by his findings. 'Hang on, what about the party tickets and Rachael's recovery? Surely that's got to up the ante?'

He frowned, calculating in his head. 'But what about the recording session? Ok, it did help Maggie out of a hole, but on a deeper level it also suited you, as it meant you had an excuse not to visit your parents in France. It might have actually been a bigger sacrifice had you gone, considering your attitude toward your family.'

She opened her mouth to argue, but as his comments sunk in, in her heart she recognised the truth. Yes, that had played a part in her offer to help out. In retrospect, what she should have done was to arrange alternative cover for Maggie – Howard would probably have been happy to step up, and she could still have travelled down to meet her new niece. Her absence had no doubt caused upset to both her parents and sister and she had completely disregarded that result of her actions.

Glancing up, she caught him watching her, reading the expressions as they altered her face, and she closed them down. This was about her friends, not her family, and he had no business bringing them up. She certainly wasn't going to get into a debate with him about it. 'Right, well, if that's how you see it. It doesn't matter, there's plenty more evidence. I'd better get on with it.'

The ombudsman was aware of the abrupt change to her mood, but made no comment about it. 'Fine. Fire away. Let's see what you've got.'

CHAPTER 18

June

Early sunshine had encouraged Violet out of bed at an unusually reasonable hour for a Sunday and, with no pressing plans, she had decided on a gentle stroll to the newsagents for a newspaper and fresh croissants. She passed a couple of neighbours on the way back to the flat and the good-natured greetings they exchanged made her heart light. It was nice to be recognised and acknowledged. It made her feel like a whole person. Naomi was making her way down the front path and Violet paused to lean down to wiggle Arthur's bunny at him, which brought forth a pixie chuckle and, considering her previous experience with him, it was a real achievement.

Peter was hovering in the lobby. 'Sorry, the lift is playing up again. Enter at your own risk.'

'Is the door sticking again? Or am I likely to plummet to my death?'

'Just the door, as far as I know.' He lowered his voice. 'Don't give the contraption ideas, it might be listening, and it's given me enough problems this month already. Every time the engineer assures me it's sorted, lo and behold a few days later, it's at it again.'

'Oh well, it's good for the glutes. I might take the stairs anyway for the exercise.' The optimism she had woken up with was determined to stay put.

'It's not so good for the likes of Naomi, or Mrs B though. They ought to sort it once and for all. Actually, I'm glad I bumped into you. You're close with Naomi, aren't you?'

'Not really. We've had a couple of chats recently, but... Why?'

His face gurned as he considered whether to say anything or not. 'Well. She seems a bit low, you know? I thought maybe she's lonely, stuck in the flat all day with only the little one for company, and I don't think she has anyone else. I suggested she popped along to the playgroup for young mums down at the church hall on a Tuesday morning, make some friends, but she doesn't seem keen. But then, it's none of my business when all's said and done. I'm probably sticking my nose in where it doesn't belong.'

Violet gave the matter some thought. She had wondered at the link between Peter and Naomi, if there wasn't a relationship brewing, but his tone now seemed totally fatherly. Perhaps she should try to help. On one hand, Naomi wasn't her problem. Their paths crossed more often than they once had, but they weren't friends as such. On the other hand, this was an opportunity to do good, and they weren't always easy to find, particularly when you were really trying.

'Did you want me to have a word with her? I could go round and see her later.'

'You could do.' He narrowed his eyes. 'Or, if you weren't too busy now, I happen to know she's taken little Arthur to the swings behind the caff at the end of the road.'

She pursed her lips. She couldn't help thinking this had been his plan all along.

'The walk would be good for those glutes.' His smile was disarming.

'All right. Tuesdays, you say? At the church hall?'

'Ten 'til twelve. I have it on good authority, they're a friendly bunch.' He called after her, as she backtracked out of the front door.

For the first part of the walk it seemed like a good idea, but as she got closer to the park a seed of doubt kicked off. What if Naomi told her to mind her own business? It was, after all, nothing to do with her. She knew zilch about Naomi's life. How dare she wade in and start telling her how to live? The voice quietened as soon as she turned the corner and saw the young woman perched on a bench, staring into space, a single tear coursing down her cheek. Peter's perception appeared to be spot on.

'I thought I'd indulge in a proper coffee to go with my croissant.' She pointed at the café. *'Did you want one?'*

Naomi scrabbled for her purse, surreptitiously wiping away the tear in the process.

Violet kept walking. *'My treat. Save me a seat.'*

As she queued in the shop, she tried to devise a plan. How could she drop the playgroup into conversation without letting on she and Peter had been talking about her? Maybe she didn't need to. Maybe it was enough to give Naomi some of her time, and the future would sort itself out. Who knew? She was going to have to wing it.

Naomi was watching for her as she exited and shuffled along the bench to make room, although the park was all but empty, only a few early risers having made it out as yet.

'Here you go.' Violet handed over the cup, then rifled in her pocket for sachets of sugar, before sitting down. *'I didn't know how you liked it.'*

Naomi accepted a single sachet and tore off the end. *'Thanks.'*

'Arthur didn't make it to the swings then.' She nodded at the slumbering boy in his buggy.

'No. I guess it's the fresh air. It's nice to sit here and watch the world go by though. At least it's a change of scenery.'

Violet sipped her coffee, buying time. 'I suppose it's hard being a single mum. I mean, you are a single mum, aren't you?' *She had made assumptions, but there may be a man somewhere on the scene, there must have been at some point.*

'Mmm.' *Naomi nodded briefly in agreement. She didn't seem in a chatty mood.*

'And Arthur's dad...?' *Prying went against Violet's nature, but somehow it seemed important to show an interest.*

'Long gone.'

'Aah.' *There was a pause as Violet tried to think of something to say.*

'To be honest, I didn't really know him. A drunken night out with my mates. I've never seen him since, so he doesn't even know he's got a little boy.'

'Oh.' *She tried to come up with reassurance, but Naomi was on a roll.*

'Stupid, isn't it. Getting caught like that in this day and age, and I'm twenty. It's not like I'm a kid who didn't know better. Mum and dad brought me up better than that. Not that they've disowned me or anything. They've been there for me right from the word go, but it's my mistake, you know? I couldn't let them bear the brunt. That's why I moved out. I needed to take responsibility for my own actions.'

'That's very brave.'

'That's one word for it.' *She played with the cup.* 'Don't get me wrong. I knew it would be hard, but... I didn't realise all my friends would disappear. They loved it to start with. I felt like a celebrity with all the attention. Then, all of a sudden they're gone, carrying on with their lives, as if nothing's happened. Partying every weekend. Weeks in Ibiza. Concerts at Wembley. They don't have time for any of this, and even if they did, we've got nothing in common any more. I've got nothing interesting to say.'

'Perhaps you need to give them a bit of time to catch up. In another year or two they'll have grown up a lot and maybe you won't be the only one settling down,' Violet offered.

'In another year or two I'll have gone stark, raving mad.'

This was her moment. *'Perhaps you need to find new friends, to bridge the gap. Peter was talking about a playgroup he's involved with. He thought you might be interested.'*

Naomi shook her head with vigour. *'Oh no. I don't think I could cope with that. All those strangers, staring at the new girl, judging me. It would be like going back to school.'*

'I bet they're all in the same boat, or at least, some of them will be. You're not the first single mother on the planet, you know?'

She shivered. *'The thought of walking in there on my own though. I couldn't'*

Violet sensed she was losing ground and panicked. *'Oh, but you wouldn't be on your own. I understood Peter was going to go with you and introduce you to some of the regulars, help you break the ice.'*

Naomi chewed on her bottom lip, seemingly thinking about it.

'I bet there are other girls there desperate to meet people like you. You could arrange play dates and meet ups at the park, and maybe even share babysitting for the odd night off.'

Arthur shuffled in his seat and whimpered and Naomi instantly reached to take him into her arms. *'Do you think so?'*

'More than likely. Why don't you give it a go this week and if you hate it, knock it on the head. You never have to go again, if you don't want to.'

'Well...'

'Go on. You can come round to mine on Tuesday evening and tell me all about it. I'll get a bottle of wine in.'

The girl was clearly perkier. *'Ok. I'll try it.'*

'Good. That's settled then.' Violet rose to her feet. *'I'm heading back. Are you coming?'*

'No. I'll let Arthur have a few minutes on the swings and then go feed the ducks. Thanks though, for the coffee and everything.'

'No worries.'

Violet marched back to her apartment satisfied her mission had been accomplished. She had gone with the flow, rolled with the punches and come out on top. It felt good.

Peter was still in the lobby.

Violet stopped to brag. 'Thanks to moi, Naomi will be happy to attend the young mothers' playgroup on Tuesday morning.'

'Really? That's fantastic. It'll do her the world of good, and it won't do the wee chap any harm either to be in the same room as other whippersnappers.'

She turned to take the stairs. 'I'm glad you're pleased. I told her you'd go along as support for the first session.'

'What?'

'She was too nervous to go on her own and as it was your idea…'

His mouth was open. 'Me in a room full of young mothers. I'll be lucky to make it out alive.'

She took the stairs two at a time, laughing. 'You're a big boy, I'm sure you'll be fine.'

***

Violet's face carried a smile at the images. She had forgotten how good it had felt to connect with her neighbour. 'It's funny you know. On that occasion I forgot all about getting a reward for doing something nice, I just wanted to cheer Naomi up. I know what it's like to feel lonely from time to time.'

'Do you? I thought you had it all worked out, with your friends and all.' The ombudsman seemed genuinely interested.

'Yes, but everyone feels alone sometimes, don't they? I mean, like, Naomi still had her family, but no friends and I have friends, but no...'

'But you do have family, Violet.'

She shut down, her smile fading. 'Yes, of a kind, but they're not here when I need them, and this has nothing to do with them anyway. This is about me and God and our agreement. Let's stick to topic. You'll want to see what happened next.'

His eyes narrowed as he watched her. 'I suppose I will, won't I.'

CHAPTER 19

July

Violet stared at the vibrating phone on her desk and deliberated whether to answer it or not. She was pretty sure it would be Maggie as she had already missed four calls from her during an early morning meeting, but those calls usually meant trouble, and she was not in the mood for complications pre caffeine. On the other hand, it may mean the opportunity to do a good deed and, with quite a bit still outstanding on her list, not to mention the continuing lack of progress with regard to Niall, she could probably do with momentum cranking up. She snatched it up.

'Hi, Mags. What's up?'

'Oh Violet, thank goodness. I was hoping you could do me an enormous favour.'

Fantastic. That was exactly what she wanted to hear. 'Really? What's that then?' Maggie sounded excited rather than stressed, which was a good sign. Hopefully that meant a favour of a simple nature, like covering a shift, rather than skydiving from a high rise in her pyjamas.

'Do you remember Saffron Headland? You know from Daytime? You met her at the cake sale?'

Violet was intrigued. 'Yes, of course I remember.'

'Well, she has a major problem and was hoping you may be able to help, but it is extremely urgent. Apparently the cakes made quite an impression.'

Violet was flattered. She had been pretty pleased with how the brownies had turned out, in the end, but for them to be remembered weeks later was gratifying indeed. 'It was only a standard brownie recipe I found online. I could email it to you if you like.'

'The brownies?' There was a pause as Maggie formed a response at the other end of the line. 'Yes, they were lovely, but it was actually those amazing muffins your friend supplied she was thinking of. You see, she's looking to put together a new panel of professional chefs for Daytime and wondered if your friend might fit the bill.'

'Issy? I guess I could ask her.'

'Mmm, the thing is, she needs to sort something this week, for Monday's episode. Do you think you could get her into the studio today or tomorrow for a trial? Apart from her cooking ability, obviously Saffron wants to be sure she's camera friendly, etc. As you know, it's not for everyone. Some people are clearly better suited to radio.'

Violet was confused. This sort of team building was usually weeks, if not months, in the preparation. There were usually interviews, auditions, negotiations with managers and no end of bureaucracy before the dotted line saw a sniff of a signature. 'Isn't it all bit rushed?'

Maggie sighed. 'Between you and me, there's been a bit of a falling out. The current chef, what's his name, you know the one with the accent, anyway, he's walked out and refuses any attempt at reconciliation. She's a lovely woman, but Saffron does have her idiosyncrasies and not everyone is prepared to bend sufficiently to facilitate them. Call it "a clash of personalities". Basically, they either have to drop the cookery slot and fill it some other way or find someone new to do the cooking.' She took a deep breath. 'So, *do you think your friend would be a suitable candidate? And would she consider it?'*

'It's worth a shot.' As the situation cleared in her mind, Violet realised what a boost this would be for Issy and her new business. It could, in fact, be precisely what she needed to take it to the next level. *'Where and when would you need her?'*

Maggie provided the details and Violet got straight onto the job of persuading her normally self-deprecating friend that baking cakes on live television, in front of millions of viewers, was within her capabilities.

'Are you sure this is a good idea? I've only been running the business a fortnight. What if I stuff it up? I may lose all my customers before I've even got going properly.' Issy was harbouring last minute nerves, despite the roaring success of her interview and rehearsal. Saffron had instantly become a huge fan, thanks to Issy's complete lack of ego, her simplistic style and fawning deference to someone she considered a massive media star.

Violet had arranged to be at the first recording for this very reason and together they stood, whispering, at the edge of the set. *'No publicity is bad publicity and besides, you'll be amazing. You know you will.'*

'I don't know about that.' She straightened her crisp, white chef's coat for the umpteenth time. *'What if I forget what to do?'*

'Issy, you know you could bake with your eyes closed and your hands tied behind your back. You're a natural.'

She frowned at Violet's encouragement. *'Even I couldn't bake like that. How would I stir the mixture?'*

A runner informed them Issy's introduction was imminent and Issy let out a frightened whimper. *'You will stay here, won't you? In case I need you.'*

'I will, but you won't.'

Girl Plans, God Laughs

They watched as Saffron and her co-host, Robert Harrison, rose from the sofas at one end of the set and gradually stepped around the corner to the free-standing kitchen area. The camera was on Saffron, who was building up Issy's entrance enthusiastically, while Robert picked lint from his sleeve out of shot. On cue, her name was mentioned and the runner nudged Issy toward the spot marked on the floor behind the worktop where she was to carry out her demonstration. With one final look of terror over her shoulder at Violet, she stepped forward and took her place.

Violet relaxed back. This was nothing new to her. She had seen it a thousand times before and, nerves or not, she knew Issy would be amazing. It was meant to be.

Since the initial call from Maggie, Violet had considered the situation carefully. It was a new state of affairs, but it still worked with the deal and her list. In fact, as far as she was concerned, she would be happy if all the future instalments worked like this. Her good work, sorting out the introductions between Issy and Saffron, had led to an instant reward, in that Issy got an immediate boost to her self-esteem and her business. It was cutting out the middleman, or the tedious waiting around to see if and what her reward would be. This was so much better.

As expected, as soon as Issy started cooking, she forgot the camera and carefully and patiently explained to Saffron what she was doing and why. Saffron looked as if she were rapt in the process and even Robert had slid into shot when he realised Issy was new, young blood to the show. He hadn't bothered attending the earlier meetings and from what Violet could understand, he saw his role purely as front man and gave any involvement with planning and organising a wide berth. Although, she also understood he liked to welcome new females on the crew to the show personally, given half a chance. Violet could handle his sort.

The section drew to a close and Saffron and Robert sidled back to their sofas to introduce the items due to follow. A display plate holding an array of cakes was thrust into Issy's hands and she was shoved forward to join them. Suddenly, without the protection of a work surface in front of her she was a fish out of water. She shuffled forward and set the tray down on the coffee table strategically placed centre stage, but in her urgency, half the cakes flew off, onto the floor behind the sofa. Saffron, ever the professional, carried on with a generous portion of oohing and aahing at the remaining confectionary. Issy, eager to put things right, dived across the scene to pick the cakes up.

The camera closed in on the couple so Robert could sign off for the break. He smiled, a mischievous glint in his eye as he glanced sideways. 'Thank you, Issy. As far as I'm concerned, we can never have too many delicious buns on the show.'

The camera panned to the side, following his gaze, to where Issy's bottom was stuck up in the air, then swiftly panned back. Robert winked and reached for a cake. 'We'll see you after the break.'

A host of crew swarmed onto set as soon as shooting ceased, removing, replacing and plumping. Saffron had already taken an enormous bite from a shocking pink muffin and an assistant stepped in with a napkin for her to spit it into.

Issy watched bemused. She had completely missed the reference to her rear.

Saffron saw her watching. 'No offence, my darling, but if I start on refined sugars at this time in the morning, goodness knows where we'll be by supper. The camera adds ten pounds, you know.'

Issy was too in awe to disagree and anyway, before she had time to speak, Saffron had turned to her co-host in disgust.

'Robert, darling, I have told you before, I will not have smut on my show.'

'Smut, Saffron, I don't know what you mean.'

'You know exactly what I mean. Innuendo, Robert. Innuendo. It's beneath us. Our show is better than that. We don't do tacky.'

Robert rolled his eyes. *'Don't be such a prude, Saffron. The audience love it.'*

'But what about the young ladies, Robert. In this day and age that sort of thing isn't acceptable.'

His face straightened as if he were taking her comments to heart. *'I'm sorry, Saffron. In future I will make no such comments to young ladies.'* He turned to one side to allow a make-up artist to pat his cheeks, and muttered quietly. *'I'll save it for all the old, unattractive ones. They don't seem to mind.'*

Violet grabbed an open mouthed Issy and ushered her towards the dressing room before things properly kicked off. *'Never mind them. Artistic temperaments. Best to keep out of it.'*

Issy sat in a swivel chair and twisted to face Violet. *'Is it true? Does the camera really add ten pounds?'*

'I don't know. You don't need to worry anyway. You're gorgeous either way.'

She leaned toward the mirror and grasped her chin with both hands. *'Martin said it did and I told him to mind his own business. I thought he was just jealous.'*

'Issy. You don't need to worry about adding a few pounds. Honestly. I can't believe that boyfriend of yours. He's supposed to be supportive, not filling your head with nonsense.'

'He's not.'

'Well, it sounds to me like he is. You can do without people bringing you down.'

'I mean, he's not my boyfriend,' Issy clarified.

The make-up artist swept into the room and Issy swung to face him so Violet couldn't see her expression. Violet grabbed the arm of the chair and swung her back. *'What did you say?'*

Issy sighed. *'He's not my boyfriend. I told him it was over.'* She shrugged. *'What with the business and everything, I don't have time for it. He's so needy, and I'm too busy for all that. I can't be constantly reassuring him and, to be honest, he's not really worth the effort.'* She raised her eyebrows. *'If you know what I mean.'*

Violet grimaced. 'I don't and neither do I want to.'
'Look at you all prim and proper in broad daylight, but once you've had a couple, back in the day it was all, Ryan did this and Ryan did that. No holds barred.'
'Note to self. Drink less.' She drew her thoughts back to the main point. 'But, Issy. Have you actually finished with him? For good this time?'
She rolled her eyes. 'Yes, for good. Let's face it, it was long overdue.' Her brow contracted. 'But there's no need to start with your "I told you so's".'
Violet's tone was subdued. 'I wouldn't dream of it. But I can't pretend I'm not happy. There are big things ahead for you.'
'That remains to be seen.'
'Listen, I should get back to the office. Will you be alright?'
Issy waved her hand. 'Yea, yea. I'm a big girl. Go do your thing.'
Violet headed off, but couldn't help a quick glance over her shoulder. Things were happening so quickly for her friend, and she deserved every bit of it, but Violet knew it wasn't all roses. She hoped her support would be enough to help Issy through the tough times.

***

The ombudsman squinted at the screen, nodding in agreement. 'Great decision.'

'Yes, and I know it wasn't easy for her to finally give him the boot, but it needed to happen.'

'Sorry? Oh, you mean the Martin thing. Yes, that was probably good too, but I meant the giving up alcohol thing. You know? The "note to self"? I didn't want to say anything, but you and the booze... well.' He drew the word out like it had a dozen vowels.

Violet slapped his arm. 'I do not have a drinking problem. I occasionally over imbibe, or at least, I did. As you'll find out later,

I had pretty good reason to knock it on the head. These days I barely touch a drop. So, can we get back on topic?'

'Which is?'

'Well, obviously, the fact the deal had moved into a new phase – direct results to my good deeds, instead of the previous lags. The connection was so plain to see, even you couldn't miss it. I figured I'd worked through like a trial period and now God was moving it up a notch. It was a very exciting turn of events.'

He pursed his lips. 'Exciting events, yes, but I fail to see God's involvement. Surely it was simply a matter of action and reaction. You did certain things and the results were a direct consequence.'

'No, no, no.' She wasn't having any of his denial.

'Yes, Violet. It's like saying you breathed the air and as a result God rewarded you with life, or saying, a bumble bee flaps its wings and God rewards it with flight. Actually cut that illustration. To this day I have no idea how a bumble bee gets off the ground without divine intervention. But you see what I mean? There was nothing Godly about the interaction whatsoever. It was purely mechanical.'

'What? Really? That's your take on it?' Her mind was blown as she absorbed his opinion.

'I can't see any other possible stance. You stand in the rain, you get wet. You get your friend a spot on a show, they get publicity for their business. Nothing supernatural there.'

Silence stretched as Violet tried to make sense of it and the ombudsman gave her the space to do so.

'You see Violet. One of the problems with this "deal" of yours is, there's no certainty of terms, vital to the cementing of a contract. There is no, if A happens then B will be the result. It's a moving target. And without that certainty it's too easy to manipulate facts to fit inside the framework of your idea. But that doesn't make it real.' He paused again for the information to sink in. 'If I'm to accept such a contract existed, you're going to have so show me something far more compelling. Something phenomenal which cannot be explained away by any other means. I'm aware it's a big ask, but it's the only way.'

Violet shot up right in her seat, suddenly alert, a boost of positivity reviving her flagging mood. 'Yes. I can do it.'

The ombudsman was doubtful. 'You can?'

'Yes, yes, I have just the thing.' She pointed the remote control with renewed purpose.

'Great.' He gave a single, sharp nod. 'Let's see it.'

CHAPTER 20

August

'What the hell am I going to do?' Issy was verging on the hysterical.

Violet tried to be the voice of reason. 'Issy, I'm sure we can sort it out between us. It'll be fine.'

In only five hours the building was due to be inundated with prestigious guests, all specifically invited to celebrate the relaunch of Issy's shop, but her plans to rearrange the interior and dress it for the party had ground to a halt, when some of the fixtures proved too heavy for her to move.

'Where is Martin when I need him? He was supposed to be helping me. His footie mates were going to come in and do the shifting, but now what?' She ran one hand through already tousled hair and grabbed her forehead in despair. 'I should never have finished with him.'

Violet detected the stench of backsliding and jumped in quickly. 'Don't be ridiculous. You can't go out with a guy purely because he's handy when you need furniture moving and, let's face it, you haven't missed him in the slightest otherwise.'

'I know, but it's only been a fortnight.'

'No it hasn't. It's been six weeks and you're far better off without him.'

Issy's head flipped around to face her. 'Six weeks? No!' She did a tally on her fingers. 'Gosh it has. I'd completely lost count.'

'No, you've been too busy and too happy to count, so don't start now. So.' She glanced around at the chaos. 'What needs to be moved?'

Issy pointed out the offending articles and explained what was to happen. Together, and with the aid of two of Issy's colleagues, they approached the first and, Violet had to agree, there was no way they were going to manage it.

Violet stood back to consider the issue, and spotted Issy retrieving her phone from her back pocket and staring at her contacts.

'Perhaps I should ring him.'

'Stop right there.' There was no way Martin was going to get his foot back in the door. There had to be another, less abhorrent, option. She studied her own contact list and a single name stood out. Yes. Problem solved. 'You go and get on with the preparations in the kitchen. Leave this to me.'

Violet dialled and waited, stock still, willing for it to be picked up. Only when it was did she allow the breath out of her lungs. 'Oh Peter. Thank goodness you're there.'

'Violet, is it? What can I be doing for you? If it's the bulb in the hall again I'm going to have to get the electrics checked...'

'No, no. All's good at the flats. Is there any chance I could talk you into a big favour?'

There was a pause. 'That rather depends on the favour.'

She explained the situation, lip held between her teeth as she waited for a response.

'And you'll owe me one, you say?' There was mirth in his voice.

'Absolutely.'

'The debt's starting to pile up, you know? I'll be looking to cash in any day now.'

What could he possibly demand in return? She decided he was all talk. 'No worries. So, will you do it?'

'I'll be there in twenty minutes. Get the kettle on.'

Peter arrived with a van full of muscled young men in tracksuits. They tumbled out, raring to go and the task was achieved in next to no time. Issy had popped in and out, agog at the influx of testosterone, checking on progress and, when they had finished, provided refreshments, only disappearing back to her post because a timer sounded in the pocket of her overalls.

'Thank you so much.' The transformation was taking shape and Violet could now picture the blank canvas becoming an exciting venue.

Peter stood apart from the rest of his group, all tucking into pink iced cupcakes, topped with glittery confetti. 'No bother. I was going to drop these guys off for a charity five a side tournament so it's no hardship to stop by for a few minutes. I'm not sure they'll be on their best form with a bellyful of buttercream, mind you. Eh, lads?'

There was a rumble of mumbled chuckles and grunts, but none of them stopped eating.

He rattled his keys. 'What's this all in aid of any way? Paint job, is it?'

'No, tonight is the big launch. It's massively important to my friend, the owner. There's a big list of VIPs coming along and she needs to make a good impression. Personally, I don't think she's got a thing to worry about, but, you know, she wants it to be perfect.' She began to wipe the surfaces with a damp cloth as she spoke. 'Create the wow factor.'

Peter glanced around at the bare bones of the interior. 'You've a long way to go. Do you want me to nip back after I've delivered these louts to give you a hand? I'm at a loose end this afternoon.'

Violet grinned. It was a tempting offer. 'I don't know if I can afford it. I already owe you for today, and the Mongolian Throat Singers. What are your rates like?'

'This'll be a freebie, like buy two get one free. Then if you need someone to test the catering later I'll be at the front of the queue, maybe?' He finished his cake and crushed the wrapper into a ball, launching it into a bin on the floor. 'Come on, lads. Back to the wagon.'

Looking around the room, you would never have guessed tea shop was its day job. The walls were draped with garlands and colourful arty posters of show-stopper cakes and pastries. Countertops were laden with trays of champagne flutes and fruit juice and various impressive nibbles. Issy and Violet had both changed into their best party frocks in honour of the event, and Ayesha, as Issy's manager, had arrived as back up. Between them, they issued the hired help with instructions for the order of the night. Issy was a nervous wreck, having convinced herself no one was going to turn up, whereas Ayesha was calm, collected and ready to take on the world.

'I told you, you've had forty five RSVPs so there's nothing to worry about. Even if a couple back out last minute it'll be a good showing. We've just got to hope the journalists and bigger names put in an appearance. Then you'll be sure of getting some coverage locally, if not in one of the magazines. Otherwise, networking is the name of the game. Daytime is a good slot for you, but it wouldn't do any harm to guest on a couple of other shows, get your name out there.'

Issy shuffled from foot to foot. 'My stomach hurts. Why didn't I stick to baking? My stomach doesn't hurt when I'm baking. I'm not cut out for all this TV palaver.'

'Nonsense. You're a natural.' Violet was quick to reassure. 'Everyone at the studio says so and the feedback from your

appearances has been fantastic.' She did a final visual check of the surroundings. 'Look. I know nobody turns up to these things on time, but we should bring the centrepiece in and get it set up so we're completely ready. Oh, and Ayesha, can you set the music going?'

Violet and Issy moved through to the back to collect an enormous polka dot tea set, complete with teapot and cups made entirely of cake. Carefully carrying it to its final resting place, they were surprised to see Ayesha already welcoming guests. Issy whimpered in fear and the display wobbled.

'Hold it tight. Don't worry. They're here to wish you well,' *Violet dispelled Issy's fears.* 'If you act confident, you'll appear confident. Remember, smile and be nice and let the cake do the rest of the talking for you. No problem.'

They turned in time to see Ayesha striding across the room toward them. 'Issy. This is Nigel from the Gazette. Come and say hello.'

Violet winked at Issy, who took a deep breath, straightened her skirt and plastered on a smile. 'Nigel, lovely to meet you. You haven't got a glass in your hand. What can I get you?'

Violet watched from the wings, chest expanding with pride. She had always known Issy could achieve big things and she was so pleased her moment had arrived.

Ayesha fell in beside her. 'She has so got this.'

'She has.'

Ayesha glanced across at her. 'Are you blubbing?'

Violet shook her face and patted her eyes, smiling. 'Absolutely not. When have you ever known me to be sentimental?' *The door opened and a small stream of people trickled in, among them faces she recognised, and she felt her breath catch in her throat.* 'You didn't tell me he was coming.'

'Who's he?'

'My boss.' *She whispered out of the corner of her mouth.* 'Niall de Havilland.'

'*Not* the *Niall?*'

Violet raced forward, away from Ayesha's probing, to carry out her assistant hostess duties. 'Saffron, Niall, hello guys. It's good of you to come.'

Saffron acted as spokesperson for the group and delivered ostentatious fake kisses to Violet's cheeks. 'My pleasure, darling. If Isobel's going to become a permanent part of the team we must make her feel welcome.'

Niall butted in, in agreement of sorts. 'There's no I in team and it's mission critical we're all fully on board.'

'Yes.' Violet frowned, trying to convert his sentence to English and failing. She turned to Saffron. 'No Robert this evening?'

Saffron rolled her eyes and lowered her voice. 'No, darling, he's confined to barracks until he learns how to behave. It could be a long year.' She cast her eyes over the room. 'Oh good, there are treats and I'm in my half hour window.'

'Sorry?'

'My half hour wind...' She shook her head at Violet's ignorance. 'No carbs before supper, or within three hours of going to bed. Gives me a small window of indulgence. Tough regime.' She ran her hands down her angular flanks. 'But I think you'll agree it's worth it.' Spotting Issy across the way, she abandoned Violet and headed towards the buffet.

Violet was left with Niall, as the rest of their group dissipated, allowing space for others to enter behind them. 'Issy will be pleased you've all made the effort. This is such a big deal for her.'

'Going forward, if we can move the needle on Isobel's business, it'll only help to up her media profile, and any increase in exposure will feedback to Daytime and Prime. It's low hanging fruit, so it's a no brainer in the long run. Do you hear what I'm saying?'

'Mmm, I think so.' She hadn't a clue, but didn't want to look stupid.

He leaned in, having checked over his shoulder for eavesdroppers. 'Talking of effort, may I say, you brush up rather well?' He indicated her outfit and winked. 'Sharp.'

The unprompted compliment took her by surprise. She glanced down at herself and by the time she looked back he had moved across the room to join Saffron. A blush filled her cheeks. Had he finally made a move? Was he showing his hand? Or, was it merely an observation, one colleague to another? Whatever, the blood in her veins had turned molten and it took all her strength to prevent the sudden tremor in her knees. The door swung open and she stepped forward to welcome another influx of guests.

By the end of the first hour, the room was buzzing, with guests overflowing onto the patio outside. It was a balmy evening and even though the sun was beginning to fade, fairy lights strung around the edges and candles lit on the tables, made it seem warm and welcoming. Issy had made a fantastic impression, greeting everyone personally, albeit with the odd prompt from Ayesha, and chatting easily with them.

When pretty much everyone expected had arrived, particularly those it was most important to impress, Ayesha gave Issy a nudge and together they moved to the back of the room, ready to carry out the grand unveiling of the centrepiece, hidden until now under a red and white checked cloth. Ayesha tapped a knife against her glass to get everyone's attention and Issy waited for quiet, clenching and unclenching her hands, hating the attention, but determined to make her speech.

'Hi, everyone. Hi. Hello.' The noise dropped away. 'First, can I say thank you for coming out to celebrate with me tonight. I hope you've enjoyed the wine and the company. I know I have.' She laughed, slightly breathless with nerves. 'But now it's down to business…'

Violet was watching from the rear of the crowd, taking in the relaxed and rapt expressions of those around her, as they tuned in to Issy's natural and easy style, when she sensed a presence behind her.

'Hey, Violet.' Niall's lips were only inches from her ear, his chest pressed against her back. 'There seems to be a rather pretty little terrace outside. Do you fancy tasting the night air with me?'

Without moving, she glanced sideways. He lifted two glasses of sparkling liquid and nodded his head toward the side door in encouragement. His closeness and the directness of his gaze was a challenge, and a suggestion of more than fresh air, and she felt her tongue run across suddenly dry lips, as realisation struck that the moment she had been waiting for may have arrived.

She allowed a smile to form as she met his gaze and reached out to take one of the glasses from him. He took one step away and she made to follow, but out of the corner of her eye she saw the front door swing open and a sense of duty to her otherwise occupied friend stepped in. She rested one hand on his arm to stall him, enjoying the firm bulge of muscle beneath the fabric of his shirt, and then pointed to the door. 'Give me two minutes. I'll see you out there.'

He took the time to sweep his eyes from the top of her head to her toes and back, before winking. 'Don't be long.'

She had no intention of being any longer than she absolutely had to be. She skipped away from the crowd to the front door, confused that it stood wide open, but no one had walked through, but as she got closer all became clear. Holding onto the door frame for balance, but swinging onto the pavement on his heels was a red faced and extremely inebriated Martin.

Violet swore under her breath. 'Not now,' she whispered. Issy was doing so well. All the VIPs were still in attendance, as were the small press and if there was one thing Issy didn't need it was a bigger, juicier story than the launch to unfold right in front of them. Her profile could be tarnished for good.

Violet sneaked out and pulled the door closed behind her, slipping one arm around Martin's back in an attempt to prevent *him falling into oncoming traffic, or through the tea shop window. 'For goodness sake, Martin. What the hell do you think you're doing?'*

'Where's Issy? I need my Issy.' His voice rose. 'Where's my snuggle muffin?' He stepped away from her, wobbling back and forth on the edge of the kerb and shouted at the shop front. 'Issy Whizzy, let's get busy. Come on babe. Marty needs his muffin.'

Violet grabbed him, tucking one arm under his, and attempted to steer him away. 'Not now, Martin. You don't want Issy to see you like this. Come away.'

Whipping his arm away, he turned back. 'I do want her to see me. She's broken my heart and I neeeeed her.' His vowels stretched, like a child trying to persuade its mother.

She blocked him and spun him around again. 'No, you don't. Martin, you need to go home. Come on.'

He was like an octopus. Every time she felt she was winning, he somehow managed to extricate himself from her clutches and dodge around her. She felt her last remnants of cool slowly trickle away and one of the pins, which had been holding her impressive up do in place, drop down the back of her dress, at the same time as a big lock of hair fell across her eyes. She blew it away and continued to wrestle with the man, six inches taller and easily thirty pounds heavier. It was a David and Goliath battle she was destined to lose, if left to her own devices.

Martin, losing patience with her interference, shoved her away and she smacked back against the wall, her breath escaping in a poof. Her strength was gone and he had the upper hand. He launched himself back toward the door, but came upon a solid object first. A grim-faced Peter.

'What do we have here then?' He got Martin in a half nelson and held him firm, waiting for Violet to regain her voice.

She pushed herself away from the wall but held onto it with one hand, leaning forward to catch her breath. 'This is Issy's ex. If he gets inside he's going to make a complete nuisance of himself.'

'Is that so?' He applied his question to Martin, who semi collapsed in his grip.

'I just want my Issy.'

'Well, apparently she doesn't want you. And she definitely won't want you if she sees you in this state, pal.' He turned to Violet, without releasing his grip. 'What do you want me to do with him? Do the police need to be involved?'

Violet shook her head. 'No, we definitely don't want the law turning up. We need to keep it as low profile as we can.' She considered the options. 'Could we find a taxi, do you think? Send him home?'

Leaning back, he scanned the street. 'You'll not get a taxi around here unless you want to order one, and I'd recommend removing him from the area ASAP if I were you.' He studied Martin's demeanour. 'Listen, I've had to park a way down the road, but if you give me a hand getting him in the van, I'll take him home.'

'Would you?' Violet heaved a sigh of relief. 'You're such a hero, Peter. Sometimes I wonder what I'd do without you.'

Together they manhandled the drunkard to the end of the road.

'What are you doing here, anyway?' Peter had disappeared in the middle of the afternoon, but Violet had been so caught up with the preparations, she hadn't noticed him leave.

'Oh, Issy asked me to come along. More the merrier, she said, so I thought I'd pop my head in the door.'

'And instead you've ended up acting as security.'

He laughed and unlocked the double doors on the back of his van and hefted a subdued Martin inside, then closed and locked them securely. 'I take it you've got an address?'

Violet gave him the information, he climbed into the driving seat and pulled out into traffic. She watched him go then strolled back towards the tea shop, musing over Martin and Peter and the events of the last few minutes. It had been a lucky escape. If Martin *had managed to crash the event, Issy's reputation would have been in tatters.*

Violet's dress was crumpled, her hair half up and half down. She pulled out the last few grips and shook it all free. In all honesty, if it wasn't for the sake of Issy, she would have gone home there and then, called for a taxi and disappeared back to the comfort of her flat. But, as it was, Issy still needed her, so she had to go back and join the party, make sure everyone had a drink in their hands, schmooze the press and make sure celebs like Saffron were getting enough attention to keep their egos nourished. Issy's future career depended on her being on good terms with as many people in the business as possible, those in front of the camera, those behind it, the managers... Niall!

She had completely forgotten about her conversation with Niall and that he was waiting for her on the terrace. She had been waiting for this opportunity for months, had imagined it, dreamt about it, and somehow it had slipped her mind. What were the chances he would still be there? Someone like Niall didn't hang around. She slipped off her high heels, hitched her skirt up around her thighs and ran like the clappers.

***

'And was he there? Waiting for you?'

Violet huffed at the ombudsman. 'You know very well he wasn't. I saw you reading ahead on your gadget thing. He'd left before I got back. I guess he got fed up waiting, or thought I wasn't coming.'

'Or had a better offer.' His tone was cynical.

'What?' The idea hadn't crossed her mind. She had assumed she had blown her chance with Niall, leaving him disappointed, not that he had moved on to someone else. It wasn't a comfortable thought, not painful, but not comfortable either. 'Do you know something? Should I ...know something?'

He shrugged. 'Who, me? No, no. I'm only accessing your information, nobody else's.'

Eyes narrowed, she stared at him unconvinced, but his face was carefully blank. 'Though, I guess, considering what happened later, I shouldn't be surprised. Hmm. Alright. Moving on.' She jumped the footage forward. 'You wanted something phenomenal, something which couldn't be explained away, a reward completely unconnected to my actions. What happened the next day, my reward for giving up my Saturday to help Issy and for preventing Martin from ruining her night, was something completely unrelated and most unexpected.' She shook her head. 'Just the thought of it still blows me away.'

'Fire away. I'm ready to be impressed.'

CHAPTER 21

August

'Do you know what this is all about?' Violet had bumped into Issy on the pavement outside Kate and Ben's house, both answering an urgent call to be in attendance, with no explanation.

'No clue, but I wish it could have waited. I'm still hanging from last night. I'm sure somebody slipped something in my drink.'

Violet laughed. 'Yeah, right. It had nothing to do with the six glasses of champagne.'

'Hey, I was celebrating. What can I say?' Issy shrugged.

'I'm not judging, babe. It was a great success. I think you're entitled to let your hair down.' Violet thought it best not to mention her encounter with Martin. 'So Kate didn't let on what was going on? I take it her and Ben are ok?'

They marched up the front steps and rang the doorbell. 'Kate and Ben? Permanently joined at the hip, and I can't imagine it any other way. She did mention the other day they were hoping to start the IVF roller coaster again pretty soon. I was hoping it would be a few months yet. I'm not sure I'm ready for that ride again already.'

The door began to open and Violet nudged Issy to keep quiet.

Ben let them in. 'Go on through guys. Ayesha and Lu are already there.' He headed toward the kitchen. 'I'm on kettle duty. Coffee? Tea?'

They gave their orders and joined the others in the lounge. Kate was nowhere to be seen. Sitting on opposite sofas, they all exchanged noisy greetings then dropped their voices.

Violet pointed at the door. 'What's going on? Has Ben said anything?'

Lulu shook her head. 'No, and no sign of Kate either.'

'Didn't you have lunch with her Wednesday? Didn't she say anything then?'

'Not a saus...'

Ben walked in with a tray of steaming mugs. 'Sorry, I forgot to ask who took sugar so you're going to have to help yourself.' He dropped the tray down on a pouffe.

'So where's Kate then, Ben? Why all the cloak and dagger?'

He dodged the question. 'Hang on, I forgot the teaspoons. Back in a minute.'

Ayesha leaned in. 'There is definitely something going on.'

The sound of Kate and Ben's hushed voices could be heard from the hall and Violet shrugged. 'Well, I guess we're about to find out.'

The hosts walked in. Ben dropped spoons on to the tray then quickly stood back and, having spotted a pile of paperwork left on the seat of the armchair, rushed to clear it to make room for his wife to sit down, plumping and straightening the cushions. 'There you go, Hun.' He stood back and looked around as if he was sniffing the air. 'Are you warm enough? Do you want me put the heating on?'

Kate tutted. 'Ben, I'm fine. Sit down.'

'Oh, ok. Sorry.' He perched on the arm of the chair next to Kate and crossed his hands on his knee.

The silence stretched, everyone waiting, but not knowing what for. Lulu's patience ran out first. 'Come on then, Kate. Put us out of our misery. What's going on?'

Kate and Ben shared a look, then she faced the group, shuffling forward in her seat and swallowing hard. 'We went to the clinic on Friday to start the ball rolling for the next lot of IVF.'

Ben slipped his arm around his wife's shoulders, while the others looked at each other. They all wanted to be pleased for the couple, but the process had been a rough experience for all of them in the past.

Ayesha was first to find something to say. 'I knew it was the plan, at some point. I didn't know you were there already. Why didn't you say anything before?'

'I don't know. I guess I had mixed feelings about it and...' *She shrugged, then rested her head against Ben's arm.* 'I know what a pain in the arse I've been in the past and I didn't know how you guys would feel about it either. I mean, I know you only want the best for me, but I'm not sure we're always on the same page with regard to what that best actually is.'

Violet couldn't help remembering their exchange after the New Years' dinner the previous year and a prickle of guilt set her chewing on her bottom lip. 'Kate, we're all for whatever you want. And, you weren't a pain, it was the hormones and...'

Kate held her hands up, palms outward in denial. 'Yeah, yeah, hormones. Blah, blah. Anyway it doesn't matter. We're going off topic.'

Issy was frowning. 'We're listening.'

Kate took another deep breath and Ben squeezed her shoulder. 'Well, we went to the consultation and the first thing they do is a medical. You know, check us both out to make sure there are no contraindications or reasons why treatment shouldn't go ahead and, well, they found a reason.'

'What?' *Issy's mouth fell open and Ayesha clutched her hand, whether for Issy's or her own benefit was unclear. The others looked at each other, unsure what to say. It seemed Kate's dreams had been smashed to pieces.*

'No. No, it's ok.' She let out a half sob, half laugh. 'It was a good thing.' Her emotions took over and she was unable to speak. She nudged Ben in the side.

Ben coughed. 'Right, yes.' He looked like a rabbit in the headlights, his gaze flitting from face to face and back as he searched for the right words, then his shoulders collapsed as he accepted he wasn't able to find them. He shrugged. 'She's pregnant. Almost five months.'

'What?' Violet's bottom actually left her seat.

Kate had pulled herself together. 'I know. They had told me the chances of me getting pregnant naturally were zero, but somehow...' She gestured at her belly.

The whole group dived to hug her, but were intercepted by Ben. 'Take it easy, take it easy. Pregnant woman here.'

Lulu patted his cheek. 'Ben.' She winked. 'Clever boy.'

He chuckled and stepped aside, but remained watchful as they took turns to embrace their friend.

***

Violet wiped a tear from her eye and saw the ombudsman watching. She waved him away. 'They're happy tears. You know, when I wrote my list and requested a baby for Kate, this was exactly what I wanted. Not IVF. Not months of wondering if it would work or if it did work, whether it would last. Not only was she pregnant, but she was past the most dangerous part. She'd had a scan and seen her baby and it was a proper baby, not just a clump of cells, and all its bits were there and in the right place and... and it was perfect.' She shrugged. 'It had to be God.'

The ombudsman pursed his lips. 'Well, I'm not going to argue with you there. New life, creation, I can accept God had a hand in that one.'

Violet released a small fist pump in satisfaction. 'At last.'

He held up one palm. 'Hold your horses. I'm saying I accept God had a hand in the existence of the child. I'm not saying it had anything to do with you or your actions.'

'Come on.'

'Sorry, but the same arguments stand as before. You said yourself, Kate was five months pregnant. That didn't happen overnight because you went the extra mile for Issy. And Kate and Ben found out on Friday, they simply didn't tell you until Sunday, so again, it couldn't possibly be because of you.'

'Ok, so it must have been in response to something I did five months ago. I told you I was doing lots of little good deeds. Perhaps there was something in the mix that qualified for Kate to get pregnant.'

'I wonder what it could have been. The day you resorted some of the office recycling into the correct bins? Or, perhaps when you removed the lid from a particularly tricky jar of pickles, for Mrs Brent.'

She let out a huff. 'There's no way I'm ever going to win this, is there? And to think I missed out on a liaison with Niall to sort Martin out. I shouldn't have bothered.'

'Now then, don't sulk. You wouldn't have wanted to let Isobel down, regardless. You're better than that.'

She picked at lint on her sleeve. 'I guess.' It seemed everything was working against her, but there must be some way to prove her point. She sighed. 'At least something good came out of the opening night. It was only looking back at that event I had the great idea to get Issy and Peter together. I suddenly realised how perfect they would be for each other. She's young, but mature, pretty and funny and passionate. And he's, well, he's Peter. Handsome and kind and gentle and the sort of guy you can turn to when you're in a jam. Perfect.'

The ombudsman failed to contain a chortle and Violet stared at him, confused. 'What?'

'You thought it was a good idea to get Isobel and Peter together? The perfect man for your friend?'

'Yes. What's wrong with that?'

He pursed his lips, choosing his words carefully. 'Did it ever occur to you, if Peter seems perfect to you, it may be you he's perfect for, and not Isobel?'

She stared into the mid distance, piecing together the meaning behind his words. 'Peter? And me?' She shook the idea away. 'No. Clearly Niall is the man for me. I mean... Nooo, you're way off course on that one.'

'I am?'

'Way off. Although, as it happens, I couldn't do anything about my idea straight away anyway. There was too much other stuff going on, but the seed was sown, I just had to wait for the timing to be right.'

He nodded as if taking her comments on board. 'Ok. I'm guessing you have something else to show me then? To back up your case?'

She tutted. 'I suppose, though I'm beginning to think it's barely worth the effort. Everything looks different from this angle. When it was happening, when I was living it, it all seemed very straight forward. It all seemed to make sense then. Now?' She shrugged. 'I don't know anymore.'

'It is possible to be too close to something to see it clearly. That's when we have to take a step back, or rely on others around us to give us perspective. Friends, colleagues... family.'

'Huh. Chance would be a fine thing. My friends and colleagues were all part of the mess and my family are in another country. I know a bit of distance can be helpful, but almost a thousand miles is probably beyond practical.'

'A conversation on the phone would bring them closer. A visit to them would buy you some space.'

'Here we go again.' She rolled her eyes. 'Look, they didn't have time for me and my problems, and, besides, I was building a new network with my neighbours. Naomi was great fun, like a cheeky baby sister, and Rhoda, she was like the grandma I never had. They both enjoyed spending time with me and we helped each other out. In fact, that's the next example I want to show you. Rhoda had some real issues, but between us we found solutions, and everyone was happy. Sometimes it's like things are meant to be. Have a look at this.'

CHAPTER 22

Mid-September

The face opposite her on the underground was vaguely familiar, but for the life of her, Violet couldn't remember who it was. They had made awkward eye contact a couple of times and she had forced herself to look at the floor to avoid further incidents, but as soon as her mind wandered, her gaze flicked back and she simply couldn't draw her attention away. The middle-aged man was now otherwise engaged, studying something on his phone with a deep frown. It began to vibrate and he put it to his ear. Glancing up and catching her watching, he half smiled and, blushing, she pretended to be interested in something further down the carriage.

'Hi. Mm... Mm... Mm... Uh huh...'

It would appear the person at the other end was doing all the talking.

'Yeah... Mm... Friday... Yeah, the removals are sorted. Yeah... Arm and a leg, you know how it is. No, no, no. That won't be necessary.' *He put a second hand up to the handset as if waiting for the other person to stop talking so he could end the call.* 'Yeah, thanks for the offer though. Great... Yeah... Bye... Bye... Yeah, bye.'

He sighed and slipped the phone in his jacket pocket and made eye contact with Violet again. 'Burnt the place down recently?'

She had been caught again, and this time couldn't avoid responding without being offensive. 'Sorry?'

'Cakes, wasn't it? The gathering on the lawn.' He waved his hand at his front. 'Hula girl apron? It is you, isn't it?'

The penny dropped. He must be a resident at her apartment building, but she didn't remember ever bumping into him in the lift. He must be from a lower floor. 'Oh, yes.' She laughed in embarrassment. 'Sorry, I knew I knew you from somewhere. Yes, the cakes. Sorry about that. Shan't give up the day job. It won't happen again, I promise.'

He waved her apology away. 'Wouldn't bother me if it did. I'm off at the end of the week. Moving up North.' He shrugged. 'Transfer.'

'Oh, well.' She wasn't sure whether to congratulate or commiserate. 'A change is as good as a rest.'

His phone vibrated again and he retrieved it from his pocket, tutting. 'No rest for the wicked.'

An influx of passengers filtered into the carriage between them, making communication impossible for the rest of the journey.

As she got off one stop earlier than usual, to facilitate a quick trip to the off licence, she leaned around the pole by the door to take her leave. 'Good luck with the move.'

He simply nodded, phone still glued to his ear.

It had become a common occurrence for Naomi to pop into Violet's flat for a few minutes in the evening, either with Arthur in tow, or with his baby monitor in her pocket, if she'd already settled him in bed. Naomi seemed to like the company and it gave Violet the opportunity to vent about whatever crisis had taken place at work on that particular day. In fact, Naomi listened with relish to the tales of egotistical celebrities and the weird and wonderful random segments Violet had to handle, from embarrassing health issues to psychic squid.

This particular evening Naomi had a despondent air and even Violet's story about ultra-competitive hand bell ringers attempting to tamper with opponents' clangers backstage didn't raise a smile. Naomi turned the baby monitor over and over in her hands, concentration elsewhere.

'Go on then. What's the problem?' Violet wasn't used to such an unappreciative audience.

'Oh, nothing.' She shook her head, but immediately changed her mind. 'The lift broke down again today.'

That hardly seemed to warrant the doldrums. 'And? That's nothing new.'

'I think Rhoda's going to move out. I nipped up to see her because I hadn't seen her for a few days and she was really upset. It was a stupid idea moving her into a flat on the fifth floor, but I suppose her daughter was doing the best she could at short notice, but every time the lift breaks down, she's completely cut off.'

They were both rather unimpressed with Rhoda's daughter. She had arranged to move her mother closer to her own home, but her visits seemed few and far between, though the way Rhoda talked about her, you would think she was overdue a sainthood. Violet and Naomi had taken it upon themselves to check on her every couple of days and were always welcomed with tea, biscuits and a smile, and they had come to enjoy the interaction as much as she did.

'It is a nuisance, that lift. Was she all right though?'

'She was, but she'd got herself right upset. Apparently she ran out of teabags yesterday and was down to her last loo roll. I've told her, in future she's to ring me. I pop to the shops most days for an excuse to get Arthur out in the fresh air, so it's no hardship for me to pick her up a few bits. But you know what she's like. Mrs Independent.'

Violet frowned. 'You can't blame her. It must be hard to not be able to do things you've always been able to do.'

'She said she's thinking about a care home. Actually, she said she was thinking about the knackers' yard, but I'm guessing a home is what she meant. It would be a shame for her to go. I'd miss her. I haven't got many friends around here as it is. And she could get by on her own if it wasn't for all those stairs.'

A gurgle at the other end of the baby monitor sent Naomi to her feet before Violet could respond.

'Here we go again.' Naomi rolled her eyes. 'Bless him, he's got more teeth coming. You know, Rhoda said, in her day, they put a spoonful of brandy in the kids' bottles to get them to settle.'

She retrieved her keys from Violet's table. 'Don't worry. I'm not going to try it. I might have a little snifter myself later though.'

Violet leaned against the doorjamb, watching Naomi cross to her own flat. 'Listen. If you need a hand, or a break, you know where I am.'

Naomi's chuckle had a weary undertone. 'We're alright.'

'And don't worry about Rhoda. We'll sort something out. Perhaps I could have a word with Peter about the lift situation. It's about time it was fixed once and for all.'

'Good luck with that.'

Violet closed the door, strolled to the bathroom and set the bath running. She sat on the side and poured a generous portion of scented oil into the middle, swirling it with her hand as she considered the situation. Naomi had seemed so much more settled recently, having created a routine for herself and little Arthur, and Rhoda was a big part of that. In fact, she had become a grandmother figure to them both, with her wise words and hilarious old wives' tales. It would be a shame for anything to have to change right now.

She undressed absentmindedly, dropping her clothes into a wicker hamper in the hall. There must be something she could do.

Hopefully she would run into Peter over the next day or two and tackle him on the subject.

She didn't have long to wait. The next morning, rushing from her flat, keys gripped in her teeth as she pulled her jacket over her shoulders, she was brought up short by a makeshift sign on the lift doors, declaring them out of use. She huffed and trotted down the stairs. Peter was stationed at the bottom with a large metal tool chest and a clipboard.

Violet nodded at the chest. 'You finally having a go at it yourself?'

'Not likely. If I lay a finger on the thing, it invalidates the contract. I was on my way to patch up some woodwork on the top landing, when I got a call saying it had broken down again. Blooming thing. It's the bane of my life.'

'Not only yours. Poor Rhoda…'

A door leading into the left-hand ground floor apartment opened and the man from the train emerged, nodded at both of them and passed through onto the street.

A thought suddenly occurred to Violet. 'He's moving out on Friday.'

'Who's that? Rufus?'

Violet shook her head. 'I don't know his name, but the guy who just left.'

'That'll be why his flat's on the list for a paint job next week. They'll be tarting it up for potential tenants.'

She rubbed her chin. 'Peter, you've been into all the flats, haven't you? Are they all the same size and stuff? The same amount of rooms?'

'More or less. It's a purpose built block so they're all pretty much identical.'

'So, is there any reason why Rhoda couldn't do a flat swap? Move from the top floor to the bottom? I mean, that would solve

her access problems. The broken lift wouldn't be an issue any more.'

'It would still be an issue for me, let me tell you, but no, I don't suppose there's any reason why Mrs B couldn't move. She should talk to the Landlord. The only spanner I can think of would be arranging removal men at short notice. It's not like she could pop the sofa on her Zimmer frame and walk it down, is it?'

Violet's eyes narrowed. 'It's not like she could send it all down in the lift either, is it? I bet we could get a team together and help her out if we put our heads together.'

'We, is it now?'

A smile lit up her face and she peered at him through her lashes. 'You know you can't resist a damsel in distress, and Rhoda would be eternally grateful, I'm sure. You'd never run short of tea and biscuits.' She pulled out her phone and dialled the office. 'I'll go and have a quick chat with her now.'

Backtracking, she began the long walk to the top floor. 'Hi, Maggie. I'm going to be a little late. Cover for me will you? If anyone asks, I'm seeing a man about a dog... No, the dancing Chihuahua was last month... I don't know, any dog... Thanks. See you in an hour.'

Finishing her call, she leaned over the banister to Peter. 'Can I tell Rhoda you're on board?'

'Aye, go on then, but you owe me one.'

'I hope you're keeping a tally. I've lost count.'

He tapped his head. 'Don't you worry, it's all up here.'

***

'Were you flirting with him?'

'What? No. It was friendly banter, that's all.' Violet pursed her lips, detecting a hint of teasing in the ombudsman's tone. 'Don't start with that again, I've already told you my thoughts on the matter.'

He held his hands up in mock defence. 'Ok, point taken.' He slipped his pen from behind his ear and tapped the top of the tablet. 'So what are we calling this? A good deed, I suppose?'

'It's good deed part one. Rhoda went for my idea. I think she was at the end of her tether. She didn't want to go into a home, but couldn't stay trapped on the fifth floor either and, to be frank, you've got to be on the ball if you're looking for affordable accommodation in the city. As soon as something becomes available it's snapped up. And it worked for the Landlord too, because otherwise he was going to have to market both flats, if Rhoda decided to move out, and there's all the paperwork too, references, etc. So, he was happy to go for it provided Rhoda could move quickly.'

Hopping the footage forward, she continued to explain. 'As it turned out, Rhoda's daughter was going to Greece for a fortnight, and her grandson's at Uni somewhere on the other side of the country, so it did come down to me and Peter, and a few other friends, of course.' She nodded at the screen, ready to press play. 'I had thought it was merely a case of giving up my spare time to do the move, but it cost me rather more in the end.'

CHAPTER 23

Mid-September

Violet's desk was piled high with files. She had worked through her lunch to make up for arriving late first thing, but the heap didn't seem to be getting any smaller and she had meetings pencilled in for most of the afternoon. So, when a curt knock at the door interrupted her thought processes she was none too pleased, but that speedily changed when Niall's head appeared around the door.

'Now then, Violet, hard at it I see.'

It was the first time she had seen him alone since Issy's grand opening and their aborted tete-a-tete and her heart skipped a beat at the thought he was about to suggest another tryst.

'Can you spare a minute for something non work related?'

She dropped her pen and sat up straight, concentrating on not embarrassing herself by squealing in delight or throwing herself across the desk at him. 'Non work?' *Play it cool.* 'Of course. Fire away.'

He slouched onto the sofa against the wall. 'A group of us front liners have arranged a social for the nineteenth. Nothing fancy. A little adventure away day. A chance to lay the shackles of responsibility aside and let off some steam.'

She wasn't sure why he was telling her. Was he wanting her to fill in for someone who was supposed to be working that day, or was he inviting her along. She decided to hedge her bets. 'An adventure day?'

He placed one ankle on the opposite knee, relaxing further into the cushions. 'You know the type of thing, climbing wall, high ropes, zip wires.'

'Sounds exciting.' Sounded horrific and not Violet's thing at all, but if it was an opportunity to spend time with Niall perhaps it would be worth it. She imagined his muscled frame in overalls and climbing gear, rather than his usual tailored suit, and weighed up whether the image would be sufficient to help her overcome her horrific fear of heights. Heights? What heights?

'Yes. It's a team event, and we're trying to make up the second team. Up for it?'

Aah, so this wasn't a personal invitation. It was about making up a team. Even so... The image of Niall dressed Top Gun fashion resurfaced. 'Definitely sounds fun.' She reached for her diary. 'When did you say? The nineteenth was it?'

As she flicked the pages over, the date rattled around her brain. Nineteenth, nineteenth, nineteenth. And there it was, in black and white. The nineteenth. The day she had just agreed to help Rhoda with her move. She tapped her teeth with the end of her pen as she tried to shift things around in her head.

'Well? What's the verdict? Are you in? Or are you yellow?'

There was a challenge in his tone and she didn't want to let him down, but...

'We'll be stopping at a quaint little pub after for a swift couple.'

The images of being squished up with him in a cosy bar, with a glass of red, in front of an open fire, almost outdid that of the climbing clobber, and she desperately wanted to say yes, but the idea of poor Rhoda being let down won out. 'Oh, I can't.' She underlined the note in the diary three times, each score emphasising how important it was to be there for her friend. 'I'm helping out a friend that day.'

'Surely it's nothing you can't rearrange, is it?'

Could they make it another day? The flat would be empty for several days before that weekend, but, no. It wouldn't only mean messing Rhoda around, it would be Peter and Issy and Ben, all of whom she'd strong armed into getting involved. There was nothing for it. It would have to go ahead as planned. 'Sorry. No can do.'

He pouted like a spoilt little boy.

'I hope you're not too disappointed.'

'Not a problem, though I did have you down as a girl with a can do attitude.' He jumped to his feet. 'I'm sure I'll find a suitable substitute, don't you worry.'

He let himself out of the office and closed the door and, as Violet swore under her breath at such appalling luck, she heard him call across the room to Khalid. Clearly she was easily replaceable. Not so in the case of Rhoda though. There, Violet knew, she was pretty much essential.

Violet had tried to approach the day with good grace, but as she dressed in her oldest, scruffiest clothes, ready for several hours of hard work, she couldn't help but wonder what Niall and his crew were doing right then. Were they already on a minibus heading for adventure? Or even already there, testing their courage against the obstacles ahead of them? To add insult to injury, she had had to listen to Khalid for the last few days, venting his excitement at being included in the escapade, while she simmered quietly at not being able to go.

Issy was first to arrive, and Violet answered her knock with keys in hand, ready to go up to Rhoda's floor. Peter was there, as was Naomi and Arthur, who had been set up in a play pen in a corner for Rhoda to oversee, while Naomi joined in with the rest of the team. Naomi had been an eager assistant and spent most of the last few days helping with preparations. Rhoda, smart in a freshly laundered apron, perched on a stool, the better to supervise events.

'Ben will be here in about half an hour to provide more muscle, so perhaps we could start with some of the smaller boxes to clear some space up here.' Violet suggested.

'I've brought some trolleys to make life easier, but for goodness sake don't be overloading them. I can't stand the sight of blood. And for once, the lift is actually working, so we can make as many trips as we need.'

Between them they made good progress and the rooms gradually cleared of clutter. Ben arrived, with Kate in tow, although she was under strict instructions to do nothing but make tea and keep an additional eye on the baby. She pulled up a stool and perched alongside Rhoda, an unusual set of bookends.

They separated into teams, Violet and Naomi tackling the smaller loads while Ben and Peter took on the bulky items and Issy started to dismantle furniture. The ground floor flat had had a fresh lick of paint and smelt clean and new and Peter had set a radio up in one corner of the bare lounge, to jolly up the workers.

Violet and Naomi arrived back on the top floor at lunchtime, to find Rhoda arranging sandwiches on a tray, Kate busy with a bubbling kettle in the background.

'Alright girls, time for a breather. Quick, park it, before there's nothing left to sit on.' Rhoda pointed at the sofa. 'Issy!' She yelled through to the bedroom as if it were half a mile away, not a few feet.

Issy emerged, cheeks red with exertion, her hair askew.

'Good grief girl, you got a man in there?' Rhoda chuckled.

Issy puffed and collapsed on the seat next to Violet. 'Rhoda, you are naughty. I just wish I had the energy.'

'You youngsters have got no stamina these days.' She stretched her neck to see what Naomi was doing, fussing over Arthur in the corner. 'The young'un's fine. He had a little grizzle half hour ago so I gave him a wooden spoon and an old saucepan and we

haven't heard a peep since. Apart from the banging of course, but I don't mind that. Come and have a bite to eat. Come on, you've earned it.'

Naomi did as she was told, and when Peter and Ben returned, they found the three women lined up on the sofa eating and drinking merrily.

'So this is how it is, is it? Filling your faces as soon as a man's back is turned.' Peter laughed.

'Listen to him, hard done by.' Rhoda was enjoying being Queen for the day. 'There's plenty left for you. Come on, find somewhere to plant yourself.'

The atmosphere was light, good natured banter filling the air as they recharged their batteries. Ben and Peter seemed to have bonded already and Naomi fitted right in with the rest of the girls. As the mealtime came to an end, the party relocated to the new flat, Rhoda, Kate and Violet travelling down in the lift with the kitchen stools and the kettle, while Issy guided the men down the stairs with the bulky bed frame.

The afternoon flew past and, with the end of the task in sight, moods became buoyant, the halls filled with laughter. Violet waited on the ground floor for the elevator with Naomi and Arthur, the only one whose patience had finally run out.

'I think I'm going to have to put him to bed.' Naomi bounced him on her hip in an attempt to stop him whinging. 'I don't like to desert you though.'

'We'll be fine. It's almost done, and you've been hard at it all week. You've done your bit.'

'It's been worth it to know Rhoda will be able to stay put, and I'll help her put the knick knacks away tomorrow. She'll be so tired.'

'Yes, it's exhausting watching everybody else work.' Violet laughed as the doors swished open to reveal Peter, Ben and a gigantic wardrobe. She stepped forward to keep her foot in the gap while they manoeuvred the bulk out.

'Mrs B must have lived in a mansion before she moved here.' Peter huffed. 'This stuff was not built for small spaces.'

'Lean it forward.' Ben heaved from behind and Peter staggered back under the weight.

Violet dived in to help support the corner and between them they edged it into the hall, the men pausing for breath before forging on. A group of other residents had gathered to use the lift and Violet waved them ahead with Naomi and Arthur, happy to wait for the next trip. She watched the digital numbers count up to the top and back down, then stepped in.

'Hold it.' Peter jumped in behind. He rolled his shoulders and stretched his back to relieve the tension, then slipped his track top off and tied it round his waist. 'Who needs a gym? Best workout I've had all year.'

Violet nodded and looked away, suddenly aware of the curve of his pecs, solid beneath his t-shirt. 'Tell me about it. I've spent too many hours stuck behind a desk. I'm not used to this.'

'Never mind. The end is nigh. Mind you, Ben's using his pregnant wife as an excuse to sneak an extra break.' They reached the top floor and he held his hand out to allow her to exit ahead of him. 'I don't suppose you fancy grabbing the other end of the sofa, do you? I don't want to start slowing down quite yet.'

'I'll give it a go.' She took one look at the settee and grimaced. 'Do you honestly think we can move that?'

'What? Are you chicken?'

It was the second time she had been accused of lacking courage in under a week. She leaned down and grabbed the underside of one corner, eyebrow raised in challenge. 'Who's chicken?'

He held his palms up. 'Hey, I'm right there. Let's do this.'

It took all their efforts to get it into the hall.

'Chicken or not, there's no way I'm doing five flights of stairs with this. Will it go in the lift?'

They tried it lengthways, front to back and diagonally, but it wasn't even close. In the end, the only way it would fit was *standing on one end. Violet wrapped her arms around it to prevent it toppling over and Peter gripped it higher up to keep it steady, but as the downward journey started the bottom slipped out, sending Violet backwards. Landing hard against Peter's chest, his muscles bulging as he took all of the weight, Violet struggled to find her feet.*

'Are you alright?' His voice was gruff with effort.

She had nothing but his body to hand to assist her balance and felt herself slipping down. 'I can't get up...'

'It's alright. Hold on to me.'

The weight of the sofa was against her and she shuffled around so her rear was to it, enabling her to push back up. When finally upright, she found herself face to face with Peter, his arms either side of her, her own arms now bracing on the wall of the lift behind him.

'Well, hello.' Peter laughed. He obviously found their new situation amusing.

She smiled back, temporarily enjoying the experience of being within his embrace, but after a few moments the extended eye contact became unbearable and she shifted her gaze to the side of his face. The shared body heat brought a deep blush to her cheeks and, try as she might, she could not make the breath flow smoothly in and out of her lungs. An elevator journey had never seemed so long.

When the door finally opened on the ground floor, Ben was waiting and jumped straight in to help.

'Here, let me get this.' His added strength lifted the offending item from her and she slid out to give them space.

Amid much huffing and puffing they carried the article away.

Alone in the hall, Violet took a deep breath and supported herself against the wall with one arm, taking the opportunity to adjust her thoughts. In the last few minutes something very important had become clear in her mind. Peter was not only a kind and thoughtful man, a heroic figure who appeared whenever help was needed, he was also incredibly sexy. Exactly what Issy needed in her life.

CHAPTER 24

Violet was still feeling warm under the collar as she stopped the film.

The ombudsman seemed bemused. 'I'm not sure I get how this works. You find the perfect man for you and push him in the direction of another woman?'

'The perfect man for someone else.' She shrugged, shaking her head. 'What? I'm not blind. I can recognise a good thing when I see it, but that doesn't mean I'm suddenly going to forget about Niall. I had a clear plan set out for me. I wasn't going to ruin that, sexy bod or no sexy bod. But Issy...'

'So you went straight out and fixed them up?'

'Oh no, you can't go at things like this gung ho. It requires thought and organisation and a clear plan of attack. People can be so blind to opportunity. You wouldn't believe it.'

He bobbed his head to one side in acknowledgement, but refrained from replying.

'I had to mull things over for a bit, work out how to go about it. You've got to remember, if you're involved in a couple getting together, you're going to be part of their story forever. They're going to tell their kids and grandkids about you, so it's got to be good. Nothing haphazard.'

'I see. You've obviously given this a lot of thought.'

'Absolutely. So, I decided to make some notes about what they had in common; what they both enjoyed; what they didn't like, that sort of thing. Of course, for Issy it was easy. I've known her a lifetime. For Peter, not so straightforward.' She pointed at the ombudsman's tablet. 'And I don't have the benefit of insider information like you have there.'

He was unimpressed by her strategy. 'I suppose you could ask him to fill in a survey.'

'Don't be ridiculous. You've got to be more subtle than that or it looks...artificial. Fake. Manufactured even.'

'You don't say.'

She was oblivious to his sarcasm. 'Seriously, it's vital. I decided the best thing I could do was spend time with Peter for information gathering purposes and that meant biding my time until the right opportunity came along. Before that happened though I had more good news, which I took to be in response to my helping Rhoda out. It wasn't exactly something I'd written on the original list, but it was a significant step forward for my friend.'

'Which friend are we talking about?'

'Lulu.' Violet jumped the video forward. 'It so happened that Culture Sunday fell on the day after Rhoda's move and it was Lulu's turn to choose. She bypassed the intellectual element, which is not unusual in her case. She's not big on art or literature or museums. Not that any of us minded the break. Sometimes you just want to let your hair down. But it meant she was able to drop her bombshell as soon as we were all gathered. Here, see for yourself.'

Mid-September

The five young women raced along the seafront, holding jacket hoods over their faces or umbrellas out to one side to stop the gusts of wind blown drizzle soaking them through. As one, they dived into the covered bench of a seaside shelter, perching on the seat and arms to accommodate them all, facing away from the elements. Issy opened a carrier bag and handed out parcels of fish and chips to each.

'Why didn't we do this in July when it was sunny?' Violet shivered.

Ayesha spoke through a mouthful of chips. 'We were too busy looking at piles of junk pretending to be art.'

'Philistine.' Violet chuckled.

Issy was still unwrapping her lunch. 'Why don't they wrap them in newspaper anymore? It's not the same eating out of polystyrene boxes with wooden forks.'

Kate was always the voice of reason. 'Food hygiene. Newspaper ink is probably poisonous or something.'

'Well I used to like it. I'm sure they tasted better that way.'

'I bet you wish they'd bring back TB and pounds and ounces too.' Ayesha ducked, as Issy launched a chip at her from the opposite end of the shelter.

'Girls, girls, girls. Behave.' Lulu intervened. 'It's human nature to be nostalgic about the good old days, but things change and we have to deal with it.'

'Hang on. Has anyone seen Lu? She seems to have been replaced by a fully grown adult,' Ayesha quipped. 'Like we wouldn't notice the difference.'

'Well, it comes to us all in the end.' Lulu dropped her package down on her lap, suddenly serious. 'And, actually, on that note, there's something I need to tell you all. I might not be able to make it to quite so many culture Sundays in future.'

There were a flurry of questions and horrified gasps, but Lulu waved them all away. 'I know, I know, but as Ayesha said, we all have to grow up, and I decided it's time I did.'

Eating halted as they listened.

'Obviously you know how much time I've spent in the hospital for the last year, two years even, but it's given me time to think, to take a good look at myself, and I've not always been the person I wanted to be.'

'But Lu, you're amazing the way you are.' Kate always saw the good in everyone.

'Yeah, yeah, you would say that, but I could be better, and now I have the chance to turn things around. I've been talking to one of the consultants at the hospital. He knows all about my history, dropping out of Uni, etc., but even so he's prepared to back me and if I do a year working as an orderly, he will stand as a referee for me next year, so I can restart my nursing degree.'

'What? That's wonderful news.' Violet was over the moon.

'Don't worry. I know it's going to be hard work and the money will be rubbish and I won't be able to stay out drinking all night, but to be honest, I think my wild days have run their course, and I'm ready for it. I really am.'

Kate threw her arms around her. 'I'm so proud of you. You'll be a fantastic nurse.'

'I'll try to be. You know, I watched the staff who were there for Rachael and they were amazing. When you're going through the total crap she went through, it is only them that keep you going.'

'You were there for her the whole way through too. Don't sell yourself short.'

'But I'm her sister and she means the world to me so I have good reason to be there. To them, she's just another patient, but at the same time, they didn't treat her like she was just another patient. They always went the extra mile, and that's what I want to do, the kind of nurse I want to be. So I'm afraid I'm going to be

working all sorts of hours, nights, weekends and culture Sundays included.'

There was a period of quiet as the group absorbed the information and what it would mean to their friendship group, until Issy perked up. 'I'm sure we can work something out, although it may take a bit more organising. But can I point out something even more momentous?' She paused for effect. 'Ayesha's blubbing.'

They turned to take in the unusual, but definite moistness of Ayesha's eyes, which she quickly whisked away with her hand. 'What?' She hollered, frowning deeply. 'It's the wind. Stop looking at me.' Then threw a chip at each one in turn.

CHAPTER 25

Violet was surprised to see a certain shine in the ombudsman's eyes also.

He coughed to clear his throat. 'She's come a long way, your friend, hasn't she?'

'Yes, she has. I'm very proud. And I believe she'll stick to it too, this time.' Her brow curled as a thought occurred to her. 'I suppose it was quite arrogant of me to think I had anything to do with it. Really, it's all down to her, and her experiences with Rachael. All of the credit goes to her.'

'Not a reward for your actions then?' His tone was light, with no hint of accusation.

'No, maybe not.' Her mind drifted off. This experience was challenging everything she had come to believe so heavily in for the last year, and there was nothing to replace it. If the deal was not as she had envisioned it, what was there? How could she make sense of her life?

It was too difficult a conundrum to solve so she closed the train of thought off. 'Anyway, it was only a couple of days after that I ran into Peter again, unblocking a drain or something of that nature, and we got to chatting. He said it was time he called in some of the favours I owed him, and asked me to help him on one of his street pastor shifts.'

The ombudsman's eyebrows rose sharply. 'Sort of full circle, you might say.'

'You might. I saw it as an opportunity to gather some data in advance of the blind date, so I jumped at the chance. Plus, I was intrigued by the whole flip flop delivery thing: why he wanted to do it; why he found it rewarding? I mean, to me, there's nothing positive about hanging around with a crowd of drunks, unless you're one of them, of course.'

'I shall refrain from commenting.'

'That makes a nice change.' She began to search the screen for the right day and time. 'I definitely learnt a lot, but it wasn't all about Peter. It was a real eye-opener, I can tell you.'

October

The pavement sparkled with a magic dusting of frost and Violet shivered despite the heavy coat she was wearing, and the hat and gloves.

'Why didn't we start earlier? It's freezing out here at this time of the night,' she grumbled.

Peter chuckled. 'Not many clubs kick out at eight o'clock these days. It's the wee small hours when people start to need our services. Here, have this.' He heaved a rucksack onto Violet's shoulder.

Her knees almost buckled under the weight and she shuffled it around to get comfortable. 'Blimey, what have you got in there? I thought we were taking flip flops, not gold bars.'

He hoisted another bag onto his own back. 'Flip flops and a few flasks of tea. On a night like this, chances are we'll happen upon a casualty or two in need of warmth as well as footwear. You never know, by midnight, you might fancy a cuppa yourself.'

She stamped her feet to aid circulation and encourage feeling back to her toes. 'Remind me why I'm doing this?'

'You're a good person, that's why. Come on.' He set off toward the centre of town. 'And because, if you remember, you owe me.'

Violet followed, dragging her feet and muttering under her breath.

'Come on, woman. It'll be good for the soul.'

They followed a path across the bridge, where months earlier Peter had come to her aid, and when they reached the point he had found her, he glanced around and laughed heartily. She shook her head and rolled her eyes, wondering if she would ever lay the night to rest, but then the events of later that night and the subsequent benefits to her friends came to mind and she figured it had all been worthwhile in the end. There wasn't a great deal left on her list to be sorted now, a few loose ends here and there, and of course, her love life still to catch fire, and if she put all her efforts into making this evening a success, who knew what tomorrow might bring. Niall de Havilland drifted into her mind, bringing a smile to her lips and a different kind of shiver to her bones, and she sped up to overtake Peter.

'Come on.' She nudged him with an elbow, as she passed. 'There could be vulnerable people in need of our footwear. Stop dallying.'

He half muttered, half chuckled. 'Dallying, is it?' Then sped up to keep stride with Violet's pace.

The night was a hectic one, with a surge at eleven when many of the pubs closed, sending hordes of inebriated people on to the streets, to head for home or on to another venue. The mood was generally good, with exchanges between groups taking the form of banter rather than ill will, and Peter and Violet assisted many a reveller who had broken heels or simply given up wearing their glamorous footwear for the sake of their bunions. Violet couldn't help but notice the amount of attention Peter got from the females they ran into, who blatantly bypassed her to get to him, but he dealt with it with aplomb with a simple 'Would you know it, I'm all out of mediums. You'd better have a word with my friend here,' and sending the more persistent ones back in her direction, buying himself some space. She wondered how he managed when he didn't have her there as back up.

By the early hours there was a different atmosphere altogether and Violet huddled closer to Peter for reassurance as they trudged the streets, her own ankles feeling the wear and tear.

By three their rucksacks were virtually empty and together they headed back to base and then home. As they rounded a corner with only a few hundred yards to go, a man staggered out of an alleyway and landed at their feet in a heap, his head meeting the ground with a disturbing thud. Violet stopped in her tracks, shock and panic interrupting her ability to think and act. Peter dropped his bag and immediately stepped forward to kneel by the scruffy pile of body and clothing.

'Whoa there, chap. Are you all right? Can you hear me?'

There were no words in reply, but a gruff, elongated moan seeped into the air around them, bringing goose pimples to Violet's flesh.

Peter looked up at her. 'He's in a bad way, not just in drink. From the look of his face, I'd say he's taken a battering. This calls for more than flip flops and tea. Call an ambulance, will you?'

Without waiting for a reply, his attention returned to the casualty. 'All right, buddy. There'll be someone here soon. I'm not going to move you in case your neck's had a bash, but I'll do all I can to make you comfortable, all right?' He straightened up to shrug off his coat. 'The poor guy's chilled to the bone. I wonder how long he's been out here.'

Watching Peter's busy response spurred Violet on and she scrabbled in her pocket for her phone. After hours in the cold her hands felt fat and numb and it took all her concentration to press the numbers. An operator answered quickly and she relayed as much information as she knew. When the woman asked for their address however, she was at a loss.

'I don't know. Near the top of town.' She stepped back to look for signage, but couldn't see any. 'Peter, where are we? What's this road?'

He stood up and held his hand out for the phone. 'Here. Talk to him. Make sure he knows he's not on his own. I'll run down to the junction and get a road name.' He started to move, but shouted over his shoulder. 'And don't let him push off the cover. He needs to warm up, but he's agitated and trying to get it off.'

Tentatively she approached the prone figure, uncomfortable in the presence of a drunk and quite possibly unpredictable character. She rested one hand on his shoulder and straightened Peter's jacket with the other, trying to block the gaps against the cold air. He continued to wriggle, although there was little strength to him, but as his head twisted against the concrete his bloodied face became visible and with a gasp she realised it was Ayesha's father.

'Oh, Geoff. What have you done?' She whispered under her breath, then glanced around to see where Peter had got to.

He ran up to her, stepped around the casualty and knelt the other side, handing her the phone. 'They'll be here in a few minutes. How's he looking?'

'It's my friend's dad.'

'You're joking.' He studied her face. 'Are you alright with this? If you need to step away...' He left the question open.

'No, no, I'm fine.' She shook her head. 'But I wish they would get here already. Ayesha's going to go out of her mind when she finds out about this. He's supposed to be sober.'

'Ah.' Peter nodded in understanding. 'Would he know you?'

'I think so. I don't know, it's been a while.'

'Will you talk to the fella? Keep him calm until they get here.' He reached around his back to unhook his scarf, clearly intending to offer this up to their charge as well.

Violet stopped him. 'No, here, have mine, or you'll be getting hypothermia too.'

He clearly saw the sense in what she was saying, as he settled back onto his knees. She carefully folded the scarf into a pillow and, as Ayesha's father thrashed his head to and fro, she slid it under his cheek and around his neck to prevent further damage. 'Here you are, Geoff. It's me, Violet, do you remember me?' She left a gap for him to reply and then shook her head at her own foolishness and forged on. 'Ayesha's friend from school. We used to drive you bonkers at sleepovers, talking all night. You used to say they should be called talk-overs instead because we didn't do any sleeping.'

There was no response.

'Keep going. You're doing a grand job.'

She continued to rattle on about anything and everything until sirens approached and blue lights swept the walls around her. Peter stood up to attract the attention of the ambulance crew and they took over the care of the casualty.

Violet and Peter stood back to one side, observing the professionals at work.

'I should phone Ayesha. She can meet us at the hospital.'

Peter slipped his arm around her quivering shoulders, sharing what little heat he had to share. 'Why don't you hang on a few minutes, and ring her with a proper idea of how he's doing once they've finished their assessment? You don't want to worry her unnecessarily.'

'I guess you're right.' She stamped her feet against the cold.

A paramedic handed Peter his coat. 'You might want to get that cleaned before you use it. Here.' He reached for a blanket from the back of the van. 'Put this around you. We don't want any more patients tonight.'

Peter swung it over his own shoulders and around Violet, so they were both wrapped in its warmth, as they watched.

Violet felt cheated. She had given up her whole evening to help the people on the street, and now this? Where was her reward? 'This is not how I imagined this evening ending. Poor Geoff.'

'I think he'll be alright. They don't seem overly concerned with his condition. They'll have him on the ambulance in a minute or two and be away. It's a good thing we ran into him when we did though. Goodness knows how long he would have laid there otherwise.'

Violet shuddered. 'It doesn't bear thinking about.'

Perhaps the fact she had been there at the right moment for him was reward in itself. She frowned. Of course, she was glad to have been of help, but rescuing Ayesha's dad had not been on her wish list. Perhaps it should have been.

Peter nudged her. 'Ok. It looks like they're about to be off.' He stepped forward, leaving her in the comfort of the blanket, contemplating the situation. After only a couple of minutes he returned to her side. 'Right, they're taking him straight to the local hospital. His condition is stable right now, but he is cold and pretty drunk, so he needs to go in to be sure there's nothing more serious. His phone and wallet were in his pockets, so if he was mugged they didn't get away with much. I've told them we'll follow on behind, and you'll phone his next of kin, to meet us there.'

'Yes, yes, of course, I can do that.' She reached for her phone and dialled. It rang several times, but if Violet knew Ayesha, she would have been tucked up in bed hours ago. It went to voicemail, so she dialled again. This time it was answered almost immediately.

'Violet, what's up?' Ayesha's voice sounded weary, but agitated. They were not in the habit of conversing in the middle of the night.

Violet explained, but was met with silence. 'Ayesha? Ayesha, did you hear me?'

Her voice was cold. 'Yes, I heard you. Tell them, I'll pick him up tomorrow.'

Violet was confused. 'But we're going to the hospital now. He'll be there in a few minutes. We can meet you there.'

'No, Violet. I'm not doing this again. Sitting by his bed all night, waiting to see if he wakes up. I'll pick him up when he's allowed home.' The line went dead.

Violet stared at the handset. 'She said no. She's not coming.'

Peter met her shocked gaze with narrowed eyes. 'I'm guessing this isn't a first.' He wrapped an arm around her shoulders and guided her back to the car. 'If you've had to deal with the same thing again and again, there comes a time when it all gets too much.'

'But he's her dad?' The truth of the situation sank in. 'I had no idea it was so bad.'

'Well, now you know. We'll go sit with him if she can't, then at least you can reassure her in the morning, and he won't be on his own if anything happens. She'd never forgive herself if it did.'

Violet allowed herself to be led. This was all so unreal. Her own parents, lacking though they were, had never given her a day's worry in her life. They simply hadn't supported her as fully as she had expected. What a contrast her and Ayesha's life had been.

***

Violet paused the footage and turned to the ombudsman. 'If I hadn't volunteered to go out with Peter on his rounds, who knows what would have happened. Geoff could have died of hypothermia if we hadn't come across him.'

'Don't dwell on the "what ifs", be grateful for the "what is".' He nodded sagely, then noticed Violet glaring down her nose at him. 'What? It's a quote. Somebody said it. I don't know who, but it's a great piece of advice. Spending time focusing on what *may* have happened is a drain on your energy.'

'You're so wise.' Her tone was dry. 'Anyway, we stayed with him all night. When he came round in the morning he recognised me and begged me not to tell Ayesha what had happened, but of course it was too late. She already knew. It cut me to the quick to see him so upset. This big, strong man I remembered from my childhood, sobbing about letting his little girl down, again. It was pathetic.'

'Perhaps it was the wakeup call he needed. I can see he's sober now.' He was reading from his tablet again.

'According to Ayesha there had been many similar wakeup calls before. This was nothing new. What was new was Peter's involvement, and that made a big difference.'

'How so?'

'Well, Geoff had punctured a lung. He hadn't been mugged by the way, he'd fallen down some steps, and his coat turned up in a bar off the High Street a couple of days later. Because of his injuries he had to stay in the hospital for several days, but Ayesha refused to visit. She gave me things to take in for him. Toothbrush, pyjamas and so forth, but she refused point blank to see him. I've never seen her so angry. And, because of that, Peter went in to visit him. Can you believe it? A complete stranger, but he went to visit him every day for a week. They just seemed to click.'

'So what happened next?'

'Geoff was due to be released and I was concerned because Ayesha... Hang on, let me show you.'

Violet fiddled with the controls, skipping scene after scene until she reached a point a few days later. Then, checking the ombudsman was paying attention, she pressed play.

October

Violet and Ayesha were sitting in the front room of the modest terraced house Ayesha shared with her father. Violet perched on the edge of her seat, checking her watch every couple of minutes, then peering out of the front window to the path leading to the front door, while Ayesha leaned back in her seat, her face utterly blank.

'I'm sure they'll be here any minute.' Violet checked her watch again. 'Do you want me to put the kettle on?'

'No. I've got work to do. I haven't got time for this.'

'I know, but he's doing well and I think it would do you both good to have a little chat before he settles back in. He's devastated he let you down and put you through this.'

Ayesha drummed her fingers on the chair and looked at the wall. '*Again*.'

'Yes, well, he's determined to do better this time.'

There was no response from Ayesha and Violet felt the tension rising as their wait extended. 'I'm sure they'll be here soon.'

'He's probably made your guy drop him at the pub on the way home. It wouldn't be the first time. Nothing better for broken ribs than hair of the dog.'

Ayesha's tone was as tired as it was angry and Violet felt ashamed she'd been so oblivious to what her friend had been dealing with all her life. 'Oh, Ayesha. I'm sorry.'

'What are you sorry for? You're not the one who thinks it's alright to drink yourself into oblivion every night with the money that's supposed to pay the mortgage, and you haven't thrown up on the carpet and left it for the cleaning fairies to clear up when they come home from school.'

A car pulled up in a space in front of the house and Violet heaved a sigh of relief when she recognised it as Peter's. She stood up. *'Here they are.'* But, then she realised Peter alone was striding up the path.

Ayesha stood next to her, took in the scene and sat back down. *'Told you. He'll be at the Golden Lion, or the Liberal Club.'*

Violet ran to the front door to give Peter access and hissed. *'Where is he?'*

Peter patted her shoulder and stepped into the hall. *'It's alright. Is she this way?'*

They passed through into the lounge and Violet attempted an introduction of sorts. *'Ayesha, this is Peter. Peter, Ayesha.'*

Ayesha continued to stare at a spot on the wall, but Peter, determined to communicate, sat on the arm of the chair closest to her line of sight and, furious as she was, in-built good manners forced her to give him her attention.

'Your father's not coming home right now.'

Ayesha looked at Violet and shrugged, acknowledging the inevitable. *'Is that so?'*

'I understand he's been leading you a merry dance these several years past and he's sorry.'

'So sorry he's propping up a bar somewhere, drowning his sorrows?' She shook her head and stared out of the window.

'Not this time.' Peter picked up her hand from the arm of the chair where it was resting. *'I told him about a place I know. A friend of mine works at this...'* he looked around for the right word. *'Facility. A community, where people with habits they need to kick can get help and support.'*

Ayesha's head pricked up. *'Rehab?'*

Violet sat down close to her. *'But that's great.'*

Peter addressed Ayesha's question. *'Yes and no. It's not as formal as your standard rehab clinic. It's like a farm. The people who go there have to work to pay their keep, take their meds, attend therapy sessions, stick to a pretty strict set of rules, but they can leave any time they want to. The aim is for them to reset their lives.'*

Ayesha frowned and shook hope out of her head. 'That's all very well, but he's tried it all before. A couple weeks of good intentions aren't enough. He'll come home and go straight back to square one.'

'As I said, this is different. It won't be a couple of weeks. It's more likely to be months and he won't come away until both they and he are confident he's ready, and then they'll make sure there's a support package in place. A job to give him routine, a buddy to go to AA meetings with, quite often a community he can join in with, like a church or something similar.'

'Months?'

'More than likely. He asked me to talk to you. He wanted me to tell you how sorry he is.' Peter's tone was gentle.

'Yeah, right.'

'Yes. But he also knows he's let you down too many times in the past, so he's not going to be in touch for a while. To begin with they're not allowed a lot of contact with the outside world anyway, but he told me to tell you he won't be in touch until he's able to hold his head up again. He's feeling pretty ashamed.'

'He's got a lot to be ashamed of.' Her words were harsh, but her tone had softened a little.

'He knows it. He also knows you have a firm set of friends around you for company, so you won't be alone and I think he figured you could use some time away from babysitting your old man.'

Violet wedged herself into the armchair next to Ayesha and slipped an arm around her shoulders. 'It's got to be a good thing. You can relax knowing he's in a safe place, being properly looked after.'

'But how will I know? When will I see him?' She was back in the role of carer, a role she had played since childhood and it felt strange to have the responsibility taken away.

'They send postcards. You know, like updates on how he's doing, and you can always check with me. I'll ring my friend and

get him to give you the latest. But for now, get some rest, and try and remember the good times you've had together in the past. This could be a new start for the both of you.' Peter stood to leave and turned to Violet. *'Do you need a lift, or are you staying put for the time being?'*

'No, I'll make my own way later, thanks.' She accompanied him to the door, lowering her voice. *'Thank you for this. A place on a program like that can't come along every day.'*

He shrugged. 'It was good timing, and I cashed in a few credits to make it happen, but it'll be worth it. Geoff wants to change, but he can't do it on his own.'

She looked sideways at him. 'You're pretty much a saint, aren't you? Go on, admit it.'

He waved her comments away and strolled to his car as she watched. Closing the door, Violet leaned back against it. Peter was one of a kind, good looking, funny. If she hadn't been convinced before, she was now. He was ideal boyfriend material. She might even have been tempted herself, if it wasn't for Niall. Her lips pursed in thought. What better way to repay his kindness than get on with setting him up on that date, and she knew Isobel was the perfect girl.

CHAPTER 26

'So that was that. Geoff went off to rehab and is still there as far as I know, although there's talk of him coming home for Christmas day. Ayesha got sent postcard updates every week or ten days, so she knew he was doing ok, and then a couple of weeks ago she was invited to go and visit for an open day. I wasn't sure she'd go, but I think by that time, having not seen him for almost two months, she was desperate to see how he was really getting on, and she came back fairly optimistic, so it must have gone well.'

'Good, good.' The ombudsman frowned as he made notes. 'So, are you saying this was a reward for your actions? For your night of flip flop delivery? Geoff beating his alcoholism certainly wasn't on your list, was it?'

Violet groaned. 'I don't even know any more. No, it wasn't on my list, but it most definitely was something my friend needed to be sorted. I suppose I took it as God fulfilling a need I hadn't been insightful enough to even recognise, let alone write down. Yes, I thought this was evidence for my case, but now, after everything we've seen and talked about, I don't know.' She took a few long, deep breaths in contemplation, a dull, uncomfortable acceptance settling in her gut. 'I'm beginning to doubt myself. I'm beginning to think there never was a deal. I mean, obviously I was working to my plan, and the list was there in black and white, but God... What

I'm trying to say is, the deal was pretty one sided.' It hurt her to say the words and each one left her mouth slowly and with several heart beats between each one. 'Like, maybe the deal didn't actually exist.'

He clamped his lips between his teeth, as if biting back a hasty response. 'I see.'

Part of her desperately wanted the Ombudsman to argue the fact, to say no, he was now on her side and she had been right from the beginning, but in her heart of hearts, she knew that wasn't going to happen. Her query was tentative. 'What do you think?'

His head leaned to one side as he considered his response, like an owl studying his prey. 'Well, I think… Obviously, as I said from the very beginning…' He stopped and smiled a soft, kind smile. 'I think you're probably right, but we've not seen all the evidence yet, and it would be quite remiss to make judgement at this point in time. Our review is almost up to date, so we may as well work through to the end.' He checked his watch. 'We have time and, just to be absolutely sure.'

She smiled a wry smile back. 'Well done on not saying "I told you so". It's very sportsmanlike of you.'

He raised his eyebrows. 'I don't know what you mean. I was always completely unbiased, as I'm sure you'll remember. Anyway, we need to see the rest of the story. I need closure.' He flexed stiff shoulders and crossed his legs in the other direction. 'Let's review your list. Firstly, Lulu, namely Rachael's recovery.'

'Tick. Rachael is doing better than I could ever have hoped. I know the cancer could come back, but for now…' She held up crossed fingers.

He tutted. 'If trying to barter with God wasn't enough, please don't insult my intelligence by suggesting entwining digits has any effect on anything. You'll be touching wood next.' His attention reverted to his notes. 'I would say results have gone far beyond expectations. Not only is Rachael in recovery, but Lulu has retaken control of her life and is working at the hospital.'

'Yes, she is. It's been a fantastic year for her.'

'Indeed. Secondly, Ayesha and a positive conclusion to her court case.'

Violet nodded. 'Again, tick. The case was dropped and Ayesha restarted the business. It was a steady build, helped by my introducing her to a couple of minor celebs I knew needed fresh representation, via their appearances on Prime, and also, of course, by her taking on Issy. I reckon, in a couple of years, she'll be back at the top of her game.'

'Hmm.' He angled the tablet so she couldn't see the screen. 'No spoilers, but you could be right. I suppose you could say Geoff's recovery is also a bonus. Right, thirdly, Kate's longing for a baby.'

'Big tick. I know the baby's not arrived yet, but for her to become pregnant, without the need for IVF, was absolutely amazing, and the fact she didn't find out until several months gone, meant she bypassed all the weeks of worry she would otherwise have had. It was the best possible result and it will only be a couple of weeks more before it arrives in person.'

'Yes. I believe he's due on the tenth...'

Violet interrupted, excited. 'He? Did you say he?'

The ombudsman waved a nonchalant hand. 'It was a generic "he". Doesn't mean anything.' He focused on his notes, but briefly peeked out the corner of his eye, to check she had taken his denial on board. 'Next, there's Isobel and the quest for self-respect. A little less tangible.'

'Also a tick. There's still work to do, I think, but taking on the bakery business, filling the slots on Prime and giving Martin the heave-ho goes a long way towards it. Actually, I thought matching her up with Peter would be the next step. You know, it would be a real confidence boost for her to date a kind man, who would treat her right, particularly one as attractive as him.'

The ombudsman sucked in his cheeks, trying not to grin. 'So Peter is attractive, kind, knows how to treat a woman. And you prefer Niall because?'

'Well, because we're meant for each other, obviously.'
'Because?'
'Because his joining my office was as a result of my good deeds. He was part of the deal.'

The ombudsman frowned. 'The deal you have now admitted more than likely never existed?'

Violet's mouth dropped open as the penny dropped. 'But, but…' She focused on the mid distance, as she tried to make sense of what she was saying. 'Wait a minute. Niall came into my life because I stuck up for Maggie in the office, when she was stressed out.'

'And what was she stressed out about?'

'Maggie was stressed about meeting Niall.' She turned to him, eyes wide. 'That's not possible, is it? That would mean Niall was both the problem and the reward, which is madness. I know God supposedly moves in mysterious ways, but that would be bonkers, even by those standards.'

His eyes narrowed. 'Indeed. Ok, now then, I'm assuming the next good deed you wish to put forward as evidence was your matchmaking between Peter and Isobel? Let's see how it played out, shall we?'

Violet bit her bottom lip as she remembered the event. 'Mmm, I guess. It wasn't my greatest moment though. It didn't go quite as I anticipated. Never mind, here goes.'

CHAPTER 27

'Actually.' Violet kept flicking forward and backward over a three-day period, unable to find what she was looking for. 'I can't show you.'

'What seems to be the problem?'

She turned to face him. 'Well, I was there for the set up, I arranged the whole blind date scenario. And, I was there for the fall out. For some reason, neither of them was terribly impressed. But obviously I wasn't actually there for the date, because that would have been a bit weird, although I did …,' her voice faded away, as she realised what she was admitting to.

The ombudsman was intrigued. 'What? What did you do?''

She clamped her lips closed, embarrassed to fill him in on the details.

'I'll only look it up, if you don't tell me.'

Her eyes rolled in frustration. 'Ok. I did go to the restaurant and watch for a while outside, through the window. I wasn't being creepy or anything. I just wanted to be sure things went to plan.'

He said nothing, but his expression spoke volumes.

'Seriously. Don't judge.'

'That is precisely my job description,' he replied, deadpan, then waved her concern away. 'Anyway, I wasn't judging your attendance there. It simply occurred to me that you summed your main problem up in a nutshell. You want to be sure things go to plan.'

Violet was taken aback by the accusation. 'Is there anything wrong with that?'

'To a certain extent, no, but you take it to a whole new level. If you ask me, that's what the whole deal concept was about in the first place, an attempt to control every aspect of your life. In fact, not only your life, but the lives of your friends too.'

'Are you calling me a control freak?'

His eyes narrowed. 'Yes. Absolutely.'

'Well... I don't... That's not...,' she made to deny his accusation, but the words caught in her throat. 'It's a very scary thing.'

'What is?'

'Life.' She shrugged. 'Literally anything can happen on a daily basis and you have no clue. I mean, how are you supposed to deal with that?'

He smiled a weak, understanding smile. 'It is scary, especially if you've been through a particularly rough patch, but people do. I think it's simply a case of taking one day at a time and doing the best you can with it. And maybe letting those around you take some of the strain, rather than trying to bear it all yourself.'

'I don't know about that. You know that saying about if you want something doing? There aren't a lot of people I trust enough and, when I do trust them, they either let me down or they're dealing with too much themselves already. It's a very unfair system.'

'I can see why you might feel that way. The last couple of years have been hard on you, haven't they? What with Ryan leaving like that, and your family being otherwise engaged, so far away.'

Her face hardened. 'Don't make excuses for them. They could have been here if they wanted to be.'

'It's not my job to make excuses for anyone. I'm only saying what I see, and I can see you've had it tough in the past, but this year… You've gone above and beyond for those around you. You've been a pillar of strength and you should be proud of that.'

His praise had taken the wind out of her sails and the weight of anger shifted in her chest. Having witnessed her own efforts on the big screen, and at times it had been far from an easy watch, remembering how uncomfortable she had been in certain circumstances, how out of her comfort zone, she was proud. Images of the past crept into her mind uninvited: the Mongolian throat singers shuffling into the hall, unable to speak a word of English; standing in front of her apartment in her apron with the neighbours watching as smoke billowed out of the windows; marching Martin along the pavement to Peter's van. A small smile found its way onto her lips.

'My friends weren't always grateful.'

'Good deeds can sometimes be misinterpreted.' He watched her face lighten. 'What is it? What are you thinking about?'

'Issy and Peter's date. I thought they'd have the time of their lives together.' A low chuckle escaped. 'Boy, was I wrong!'

November

Violet had been watching the hallway, through the spy hole in her front door, for almost an hour waiting for Peter to arrive. When at last he did, she strolled out, as if she just happened to be about to call on Naomi.

'Oh, hello. Fancy seeing you here.'

He harrumphed. 'It's like my home away from home.'

'Oh dear. Trouble with the lift again?'

He opened up a set of step ladders and leaned one elbow against them. 'Not this time. It's number two on my list of repeat offenders – bulb on landing of level three. Naomi sent me a message. Did you not notice it had blown again? It's right outside your door.'

'No. No, I hadn't noticed. Must have happened since I came in.' The moment had arrived to nudge the conversation in the direction she wanted it to turn. Now or never. 'I was talking to friends yesterday. They were telling me about this new restaurant in town, off the High Street. Have you heard of it?'

'I don't know.' He rifled through a toolbox, pulling out a couple of light bulb boxes, checking the specifications on the side, as he talked. 'What's it called?'

Good. He wasn't giving her all his attention. Perhaps he wouldn't notice her nerves. 'The Wardrobe, I think? It's supposed to be fantastic.'

'The Wardrobe? Small place, is it?' He chuckled at his own joke, but continued what he was doing.

'I think it's ironic, or something, but it's supposed to be fun.' Plunge right in before you chicken out. 'Do you fancy giving it a try?'

There was a perceivable pause in his actions as the invitation sunk in, but he didn't look up. 'Me?'

Butterflies took flight in her stomach. Was he going to go for it? This could be embarrassing. Act confident. 'Yes. Thursday evening, seven thirty. What do you say?'

He straightened up and looked at her through narrowed eyes. 'This Thursday?'

'Yes, this Thursday.' Her hands were clasped tight. 'Day after tomorrow.'

'Seven thirty, you say?'

He was making her work hard for this. 'Yes, seven thirty.'

He bent back to his toolbox. 'I don't see why not.'

Yes. Mission accomplished. 'Great, I'll text you the details.'

'Do you want me to pick you up on the way?'

'That's ok. Just be there at seven thirty.' She turned back to her own flat, ecstatic to have achieved her goal.

Peter pointed at Naomi's door. 'Were you not going...?'

'No, no.' *She had been caught out in her own deception and faked a glance at the watch on her arm. 'She's probably putting Arthur to bed now. I'll pop across later. See you.' As soon as the door closed behind her, she wiggled a silent dance of celebration, then peered through the spy hole.*

Peter was stood by his ladders, gazing at her door, a strange, wide smile on his face.

He had obviously been completely fooled. Turning to the sideboard, she spotted the good bulb, exchanged for a dud in the hall earlier, lying among the apples in the fruit bowl. She picked it up and tossed it into the air and caught it again, before slipping it into the drawer. Best hide the evidence.

Violet waited on the edge of the Daytime set for recording to end.

Issy's initial nerves had faded to a certain extent, now her appearances were a weekly event, but that didn't mean things always went to plan. She sidestepped past the rush of staff, stampeding in the opposite direction, to clear the kitchen area and give attention to Saffron and Robert, and halted in front of Violet.

Laughing, Violet pulled a tissue from her pocket and wiped a smear of cake batter from Issy's forehead. 'Had a falling out with the whisk again?'

'Mmm. At least I didn't point my arse at the camera this time.' She dodged around Violet's attentions and headed for the dressing room. 'I don't understand it. I never get in this mess in my own kitchen. I swear the equipment here is jinxed.' She peered into the mirror and reached for a wipe. 'Look at the state of me. I thought TV work was supposed to be glamorous.'

'Go on. You love it and, what's more, the public love you, so keep doing what you're doing.'

Issy grunted as she continued to clean her face, and peeled off what had once been chef's whites.

'Anyway, I've only popped in to cheer you up. Cinderella shall go to the ball. Assuming you don't have other plans tonight.'

Issy perked up and turned her attention to Violet's reflection in the mirror. 'Tonight? No, no plans. What did you have in mind? Although, I've an early start tomorrow, so I can't go wild.'

Violet backed slowly out of the room. 'No, nothing wild. I've booked a table at the new place off the High Street. My treat. The food's supposed to be top notch. Can you be there for seven thirty?'

'I should think so. Which place do you mean?'

'Listen, I've got to go, but I'll text you the details, ok?' *She hung onto the door, half in, half out. 'Seven thirty, yes?'*

'Yes, got it, seven thirty. See you there.'

Without replying, Violet allowed the door to close, and skipped back to her office. Yes. Step two, accomplished. She was doing such a good thing and could imagine the responses from both Issy and Peter after the event. They were going to be absolutely chuffed to bits with her.

***

'So far, so good.' Violet waved at the screen. 'You can see they were both up for it, so I don't see what their problem was. I thought most people liked surprises. I guess I chose the two on the planet who don't.'

'Perhaps the problem was they had no idea what was coming. They both thought they were having a nice quiet meal with you, and you alone. A blind date is a whole different ball game and you need to be mentally prepared for that kind of thing,' the ombudsman explained carefully.

'Well, personally I would have been very grateful if a friend paid for me to have an evening out with a gorgeous man. I think Issy's attitude was completely over the top.'

He raised an eyebrow. 'Issy wasn't happy, then? And what about Peter?'

Her brow furrowed. 'Peter was... odd. I asked him if he had a good time, and all he said was, yes, thank you and marched off. If I didn't know better, I would say he's been avoiding me. I've not run into him on the stairs or in the grounds once since, and yet before, he seemed to be everywhere I turned. I don't know what his problem is.'

'Don't you?'

The question took her by surprise. She had assumed the ombudsman would be sympathetic to her predicament, or have a wise response, not that he would question her lack of vision. 'No, not in the slightest.'

'How do you think you would feel, if someone you had had your eye on for some time invited you for a meal, then didn't turn up, but sent someone else instead?'

She thought about the question, but was unable to compute. 'But that would mean... Are you trying to say...? But Peter never gave me any sign... No. You've got it all wrong.'

'Have I?'

The idea was completely foreign to her, and her head ached with the concentration, so she gave up, shrugging the tension out of her shoulder muscles. 'Shall I show you the date? Or, just the aftermath?'

He allowed her to change the subject. 'Whatever you feel is appropriate.'

'Ok. In that case, you may as well see the whole thing. I may as well be hung for a sheep as a lamb.' She fiddled with the remote control, frowning. 'Whatever that saying actually means.'

CHAPTER 28

November

The venue for the date had been selected with care. Violet didn't like to leave anything to chance. Obviously she couldn't plan for every eventuality, but she liked to think she had considered the majority of situations.

Consideration one – neither Peter or Issy knew they were going on a date, which could mean some initial hesitation, and she didn't want either of them exiting prematurely, particularly as she was positive they were perfect for each other if they gave it some time. They had got on well at Issy's grand opening, although there had been so much to do that day they had barely given each other a second glance. With this in mind, the escape room dining experience cleverly fitted the bill, as they would have to work together, searching for clues, in order to leave a locked room, by which time she fully expected them to have bonded sufficiently to enjoy a cosy meal together.

Consideration two – Violet wanted to be able to observe their arrival and initial interaction, to be sure nothing unforeseen had happened to waylay her plans, but she didn't want Issy and Peter to be aware of her presence, so the venue needed to be in the right location too. Again, the escape room was ideal. She would conceal herself in the launderette opposite and, bonus, would get up to date with her washing at the same time. There was no doubt about it, something about the way the plans had slotted together definitely felt providential.

She arrived in good time, not wanting to risk running into either participant if they were to arrive early, heaving a large bag of dirty laundry with her, but leaning heavily against the launderette door, it refused to budge. Frowning, she stood back and spotted a sign stuck to the glass, handwritten in pink felt tip, stating that due to unforeseen circumstances the facility would be closed until Friday. Now what was she to do?

Standing back, she surveyed the other buildings along that side of the street for alternative viewpoints, but they appeared mainly to be offices, apart from a small supermarket at the end of the road and, A, if she hovered in the doorway there it was bound to rouse suspicion, and, B, the angle would be too deep and she wouldn't be able to see much, if anything, of the restaurant entrance. She sighed deeply, thinking, and her eyes slid up to the first floor. Light streamed from large picture windows, through which she could see people pounding away on running machines. Of course. If she carried on and took a left, there was an entrance to a gym she had joined in January as part of her New Year, new me resolution and only visited once, twice if you counted the fact she had to go back in to retrieve the large lemon cake she had bought on the way and left on top of the lockers. If she could position herself in one of those windows, overlooking the street, it would be the perfect spot.

Looking down at her tight jeans and jumper she realised she wasn't exactly dressed for a workout, but there was bound to be something in her laundry bag which would do the job, and it was about time she made the most of her monthly subscription. Humping the bag onto her shoulder, she marched around the corner.

The woman behind the reception desk used the last few moments of a phone call to look Violet up and down in a most scathing manner, and Violet felt her confidence shrinking. If she wasn't on a mission she would have made a run for it, but needs must.

'Can I help you?'

Violet couldn't decide if it was an offer of assistance or a rhetorical question, relating to Violet's ability to be brought back from the brink of slovenliness. 'Um, yes. I'm a member here, but I've forgotten my card. Can I still come in for a workout?' She added a shot of jolly to her tone to give the impression of keenness.

The woman's eyes narrowed. 'You're a member? I don't recall seeing you here before.'

Violet adopted a surprised expression. 'Really? I'm sure you'll find me on your system there, somewhere.' She tapped the side of the computer screen to encourage the woman to study it, rather than her.

The woman forced a smile. 'Name?'

Violet provided the details and after a long pause was rewarded with a, 'Yes. There you are. Who did you do your induction with? It's not been updated, and you can't use all the equipment unless you've done your induction.'

Violet hadn't done the induction. She'd done a tour on her first visit and been shown what she could and couldn't use until said induction had been completed, and had even got so far as booking it in twice, and cancelling it twice. But she needed access to the gym now and couldn't risk a box ticking exercise getting in the way, and besides, how hard could it be? Surely a running machine was a running machine and, over the years, she had tried most of the gyms in the area at least once. 'Oh, I can't remember his name, it was a while ago.' Wing it. 'A tall guy, with not much hair, but huge muscles.' She made fists and pumped up her own biceps, to emphasise the point.

The woman looked sceptical. 'Steve, was it?'

'Steve. Um, it could have been. Yes, now you come to mention it, I think it might have been Steve.'

Girl Plans, God Laughs

The woman harrumphed, and muttered something about being the only one who kept records up to date, and how she would have to be having words with someone, presumably Steve. She finished at the keyboard and shuffled out from behind the counter. 'I'll have to swipe you in.'

Thankfully the woman held the door open for her, as Violet had no recollection of which was the right way to go, and she hurried through with her washing. It took only a couple of minutes to locate the female changing room As soon as she was safely inside, she rummaged through the dirty items to find something suitable to put on and was relieved to pull out a pair of trousers, laughingly described as jogging bottoms, but which were generally used for lounging on the sofa, watching black and white films on a Sunday morning. She was not so lucky for her top half. There were plenty of blouses and a couple of jumpers, but no t-shirts of any description, unless she counted a pyjama top, which at a push could fall within a t-shirt sort of category.

A clock on the wall caught her eye, and the urgency of the situation struck her. Sighing she looked again in the bag, then at the pyjama top and begrudgingly pulled it over her head and checked in the mirror. The logo on the front read "I love snuggles", printed boldly above a picture of a penguin, and she felt herself blush at the thought of stepping into the gym dressed in such a way. She met her own eye in the reflection and scowled. 'Everybody will be too busy doing their own thing to be looking at you,' she told herself aloud, adding an afterthought. 'And, let's face it, the likelihood of you ever stepping foot in this place again is minimal.'

At the last moment, she grabbed a towel from the washing and, folding it over an arm, carried it against her chest out into the exercise room. She very quickly located the area with windows overlooking the restaurant, and was pleased to identify a spare treadmill, between two other runners. Almost as quickly, she stepped on and off again, having realised, not only were the controls far more complicated than merely stop and go, but the absence of a sports bra was going to seriously interfere with the level of enthusiasm she could throw into the exercise. Now what?

She glanced around the room, careful to avoid eye contact, still clutching the towel. The only other space was at the end of the row, at the last window, and the weights section. Ideal. No bouncing, merely lifting a few dumbbells up and down and, if she positioned herself correctly, a bird's eye view of the escape room reception.

The first weight she lifted down almost wrenched her arm out of its socket and she used both hands to replace it, before selecting an alternative nearer the apex of the pyramid stand, almost half the size. Better. Straightening out an arm, she curled it into her body, then relaxed it out again. She could do this. Then, as she got into a rhythm, she craned her neck to view the street. Too far away. She shuffled a couple of steps toward the window, continuing her bicep curls.

The view was perfect. In fact, she could see Peter with his hand on the door handle, about to enter. She crouched down slightly to follow his walk to the welcome desk, where he was greeted and obviously told to take a seat, as he moved back toward the window and sat down, picking up a newspaper from a table to one side. Clearly, Issy wasn't there yet then. Violet stretched, to be able to look up and down the pavement for her friend, until she spotted her climbing out of a taxi a few doors away. Issy studied the front of the building, and checked along the pavement, before entering, seemingly unsure she was in the correct place, then followed the same actions as Peter had. However, as she turned from the welcome desk, she must have seen Peter sitting there alone and spoken to him, as he folded his paper up and replaced it on the table. Violet could have hugged herself with pleasure. This was going to be brilliant.

'You need to stay on the mats with the weights.'

'Sorry?' Violet's attention was drawn back to the room.

A man, in a matching tracksuit to the woman in reception, was pointing back to the weights stand. 'You need to stay on the mats with the weights.'

Violet looked down to see her feet had moved off onto the carpet. 'Oh, sorry. Not concentrating.' She edged back a few inches and feigned giving all her attention to the job in hand, waiting for the man to move away.

He seemed to take an interminable amount of time, but as soon as he moved to the other end of the room, she turned her attention back to the window. Both Peter and Issy had disappeared. Violet's shoulders sagged with disappointment. She had wanted to see the moment when the pair had realised their situation, had wanted to witness their reactions, but now she had missed the chance, thanks to some busybody gym instructor. How frustrating.

'Excuse me, but you need to stay on the mats with the weights.' The man had returned and Violet was now in no frame of mind to take orders from him.

She frowned at his officious stance and looked at the dumbbell in her hand, then pushed it into his arms. 'Here, you take it. You clearly know what you're doing...' Leaning in, she read his name badge. 'Steve. I've had enough for one day.' She didn't clarify whether it was enough of exercise or of his interference, but her tone gave heavy clues. Then she marched back to the changing rooms, pulled a coat on over her pyjama top and left, determined to cancel the gym membership the moment she arrived home.

CHAPTER 29

'You can see I had very good intentions.'

'As you no doubt did in January, when you joined the gym.' The ombudsman had a humorous glint in his eye.

'Yes, well, what can I say? I have a busy life.' She nudged him with her elbow, well aware he was mocking her. 'As for your theory about my being a control freak, it clearly didn't do me any good on this occasion. My attempt at keeping an eye on the meeting was completely scuppered, so I had no idea of the sort of reaction I was going to get from Issy later that night. It came as quite a shock, I can tell you.'

'She didn't appreciate your match making attempt.' It was more statement than question.

'You could say that.' Violet pointed at the screen.

November

After a stressful day, Violet had treated herself to a long soak in a tub of warm, scented bubbles and finished it off by wrapping up in an enormous fluffy dressing gown and covering her face with a replenishing face mask. After all, she felt she deserved it, having repaid Peter's kindnesses and sorted out her friend's love life in one foul swoop. When the doorbell rang, she was dozing, floating on a cushion of pan pipe meditation music, a fragrant candle burning on the table, and was lurched out of it too urgently to be comfortable.

She glanced at the clock. It was gone ten, far too late for most of her acquaintances, and her best guess was that it was Naomi, who seemed to run on a different time scale to the rest of the world. A quick check through the peephole proved her wrong. It was Issy, no doubt unable to wait to pass on her thanks for a lovely evening first-hand.

Violet threw the door wide and Issy barged past. There was a noticeable lack of joy about her demeanour.

'Issy. Great. How did it go?'

Issy's face closed in on Violet's, so Violet had to lean away to create a comfortable distance between them. 'You, lady, have got some nerve.' She stuck a pointed finger into Violet's chest.

Violet couldn't think what to say, she hadn't anticipated a response like this. Her mouth opened, but nothing came out.

'I don't know which is worse, being set up with one of your ... your cast offs or being conned into going to a ... a ... a bloody escape room.' Issy's mind was struggling to keep up with her mouth. 'You know I don't like enclosed spaces. What were you thinking?'

Violet couldn't understand Issy's attitude. 'A fine dining escape room experience,' she qualified. 'But... but I thought you'd like it.'

'What, being shut in a small room, with almost a complete stranger, for an hour and a half?'

Violet's enthusiasm was waning very quickly. 'A rather handsome stranger. And anyway, you do know him, from your opening day and Rhoda's move. You've met him lots of times.'

Issy thrust her hands on her hips and huffed. 'And, at what point, did I give you any impression I would want to be shut in a room with him?'

Violet's face dropped. 'Well, if you put it like that.'

Issy flounced across the room into an armchair, getting her breath. Violet perched on the edge of the sofa adjacent to her, aware her facemask was threatening to crack under the pressure of her deep frown.

'Why, Vi? Why?'

'I honestly thought you'd like it.' She shrugged. 'A nice meal, with a gorgeous man, all paid for by me.'

'But you know my situation. You know I've only recently split with Martin. You know I've just started my own business. What on earth gave you the idea I had room in my life for something like this now? And why the hell would Peter want to go out with me, anyway?'

'I don't know. In my head it seemed like a good idea.'

'Good idea?' Issy slapped the arms of the chair with her palms. 'You're supposed to be one of my best friends, but now I'm beginning to wonder if you know me at all.' She jumped to her feet, ready to storm out.

Violet rushed to stop her. 'Don't go. Issy, I'm sorry. I thought I was doing something nice for you, but I promise I'll never do anything like that again.' Clearly the entire plan had been badly misjudged, but she was still confused by the level of Issy's annoyance.

Issy paused and Violet thrust herself between her and the door. 'I promise, never. I'm sorry.'

Issy let her gaze travel around the room, but then settled back on Violet and her mud pack. She sighed and shook her head. 'You do know you look ridiculous, don't you?'

'I wasn't expecting anyone to see me, and besides, it's not the most ridiculous I've looked tonight. I went to the gym in a pyjama top that said "I like snuggles" on it.'

'What?'

'It's a long story. Look, please, sit down. Let's talk about this.' She nudged Issy towards the sofa. 'I didn't mean to upset you.'

The wind had dropped out of Issy's sails. 'I know.' She flopped back on to the chair. 'But tonight has been one of the most embarrassing nights of my life. Ever.'

Violet bit her mud crusted lips together. 'What, more than going to the gym in your pyjamas?'

A twitch appeared at the side of Issy's mouth. 'Did you really?' At Violet's nod she continued. 'Yes, more embarrassing than that. All I'm saying is, if they're going to lock you in a room for an hour and a half, they should warn you, so you can go for a pee first.'

Violet's hand sprung to cover her mouth. 'Oh, no.'

'I was so desperate, I thought I was going to have to use one of the props as a potty. Apparently the room you signed us up for was the "advanced" room, for, how did the guy put it, "the most competent sleuths". In the end Peter had to pound on the door for someone to let us out. I honestly think we would have been in there all night if he hadn't made an enormous scene.'

'Oh, Issy, I'm sorry.'

'So you should be.' She picked at the pattern on a cushion next to her. 'I'm very cross with you.'

'I can tell. Can I get you a coffee or something to say sorry? I've got chocolate. And I must take this face pack off, or it's going to go solid.'

'It better be good chocolate.'

Sensing a thaw, Violet leapt to her feet and got busy in the kitchen, nipping through to the bathroom and cleaning her face, while the kettle boiled. Carrying the steaming cups back into the lounge, the air was still tense. She dropped a Tupperware box of chocolate treats onto Issy's lap.

'There, help yourself.'

They both sipped at their drinks, but conversation seemed to have dried up.

Violet tried again. 'Was there nothing good about the evening? Not even the food?'

'I was so mortified I couldn't eat. Peter certainly packed it away though, so it must have been all right.' Her tone remained slightly miffed, but the sugar hit had removed most of the venom.

'And there's no chance you and Peter might...?' The look on Issy's face prevented Violet from completing the sentence.

'No, never.'

They both sipped their drinks.

'He's a good looking guy.' Issy shuddered. 'But, he's too nice for me. I know it's crazy, but you know I like a bad guy.'

'Good looking? He's gorgeous. If it wasn't for Niall, I definitely would.'

'Yes, well, he's not interested in me either.' Her tone was adamant.

Violet assumed she was being modest. 'Of course he would. You're beautiful, funny, kind...'

'Yeah, whatever.' She rose from her seat, replacing an empty mug on a coaster. 'Look, I've got to go. I've an early start. My life is all mince pies and frosted cakes at this time of year.'

At the door, she turned to her friend. 'Violet, you know Peter's not interested in me, don't you?' She studied Violet through narrowed lids. 'I mean, you do know?'

Violet didn't want to appear stupid, but hadn't a clue what Issy meant. She frowned in concentration. Was Issy suggesting Peter was gay? No, surely not. Unable to make sense of the comment, she shrugged, non-committal, and pulled her friend in for a hug. 'Hey. I am sorry, and I'll never do anything like that again. Are we alright?'

'Of course we are. You're not off the hook yet, mind you, but I guess you're forgiven. Sort of.'

Violet sighed with relief. 'Good. Speak to you tomorrow.'

As she closed the door, she leaned back against it for support. She still wasn't totally sure how it worked, but she hoped points were awarded for effort, because all her energy had gone into today's debacle. In truth, she'd been counting on this one good deed being a success so as to give a final push towards the one outstanding objective on her list. For the last few weeks it had seemed she was on the brink of getting there. Niall had certainly shown an interest. There had been the odd suggestive remark, a cheeky wink, a couple of lingering looks which may or may not have meant something, an unexpected brush of his hand, on her back as they leaned over to study documents, down her arm as they chatted by the coffee machine, but there had been nothing concrete, nothing she could firmly pin her hopes to, and time was rushing by. Patience had never been one of her strong points.

Today had sapped every ounce of her strength, but she wasn't giving up. The haunting spectre of love was there, on the distant horizon, beckoning, egging her on, but always beyond her reach. Tomorrow had to be better, surely?

***

The frustration she had felt after the encounter with Issy re-emerged having witnessed it for a second time and Violet turned to the ombudsman with clenched hands. 'It was like right there. I knew we were meant for each other, obviously, but it just didn't quite happen. He never said anything outright, you know? So I couldn't be sure the situation or the timing was right and I didn't want to blow it, or I'd have made a move myself.'

'If it was meant to be, you couldn't have blown it, could you?'

She shrugged. 'I don't know, but maybe I could have delayed things even further, or made things more complicated than they needed to be, and I certainly didn't want that.'

'You? Make things complicated?' He sniggered, shaking his head. 'No, you definitely wouldn't want to do that.'

Violet pursed her lips, looking down her nose at him. 'You have no idea what it's like to be a modern woman, do you?'

'You've got me there.'

She frowned as she recalled the events of only a few weeks ago, not needing the visual reminder. 'I was very determined. I threw everything at it. I bought sandwiches for every homeless person I bumped into, gave up my seat on the bus for anyone who looked even slightly needy, put my change in the collection pots at the tills, made sure all my food was ethically produced, bought my Christmas gifts from local retailers, rather than online or chain stores.' She met his gaze to emphasize the point. 'And they were all fair trade.'

'Admirable, I'm sure.'

'You can mock, but it's incredibly difficult to be a good person in this day and age. Really hard work, but it paid off.'

The ombudsman's head bobbed to attention. 'It did? Are you putting this forward as additional evidence for your case?'

Violet slumped in her seat. 'No. I think that ship's well and truly sailed, but I did think it was real at the time. I believed my actions would have an effect on my life and they did seem to.' She began to skip the footage forward in chunks. 'There was no one event, but a few little things happened, Niall-related things that is, which, by the time of the office Christmas party, made me think it was a done deal.'

She paused on an image of herself approaching the party venue, her face alight with anticipation and perfectly made up, her hair and attire a picture of elegance. It was the same outfit she was wearing now, but it no longer had the same level of chic, and her hair had given up on any semblance of intentional style, long ago.

'That's not me anymore, is it?'

The ombudsman recognised an air of wistfulness to her tone, but couldn't place it. 'Of course it's still you. What do you mean?'

'I had it all in front of me then, or I thought I did. My life was about to start.'

'I hate to break it to you, but you're thirty years old. Life had been carrying on without you for an awfully long time.'

'You know what I mean.' She threw a pointed finger at the screen. 'Niall. Love. All that stuff. At that point, I had no idea it was all going to fall apart.'

'I assume Niall let you down?' His question was tentative, soft.

'Yes. Yes, he did. I didn't quite see it like that then, I allocated blame elsewhere entirely, but yes, it was Niall who let me down, entirely Niall.' She paused. 'With a little bit of my own arrogance in the mix, maybe. I'm almost ashamed to show you.'

He allowed her to wallow for a few moments, before nudging her elbow with his own. 'It can't be worse than the burnt cakes, or the bigging up Maggie thing.' He relaxed back in his seat, then immediately perked back up. 'Or the pyjamas at the gym. Or…'

'Yes, all right. You've made your point. I'm a walking disaster area. Well, here you go.' She pressed play. 'A little bit more fuel for the fire.'

CHAPTER 30

Christmas Party – Mid-December

If it wasn't for the fact the party was destined to change her entire life, Violet would have stayed at home. Her anticipation had been dented by Issy's constant badgering. If it wasn't one thing, it was another. "Are you sure you wouldn't rather go to the pictures?" "Why don't we go together later, after the meal? You don't want to sit at the stuffy old Managers' table really, do you?" "Do you think it's worth all this expense for one night out?" Like shoes were ever not worth the expense. Sometimes Issy's ideas were way beyond Violet's comprehension.

    Violet had tried to explain, slowly and carefully. No, she wouldn't rather be anywhere else on this one night of the year. Yes, the confidence boost the heels gave her were worth their weight in gold and of course she wanted to sit at the Managers' table, because that was where Niall would be, and it was Niall who had told her he would be looking forward to her company all evening. At least, he had dropped extremely heavy hints, about mistletoe in doorways and playing footsie under the table and something about Christmas bonuses and low hanging fruit which she hadn't quite understood, but sounded very much like flirtation.

Thankfully, for the last few days Issy had backed off, and her last text had consisted of a simple "See you there".

Tonight was the night. Finally. All previous attempts at her and Niall getting together had been scuppered by ridiculous and unforeseen circumstances, but she was determined nothing was going to come between them this time. It was going to be perfect. There would be champagne, though not too much, just enough to skim the top off her nerves, but not to deaden the senses, because there would also be snogging, and she wanted to enjoy every spine-tingling moment of it. She'd been imagining it long enough, it was about time the dream became reality.

So focused was she on everything going to plan, she had managed to break her normal habit of tardiness and arrived at the venue with minutes to spare. Floating on the promise of what the evening would bring, she drifted into the lobby, eyes sparkling with excitement and the cold. She beamed smiles at all and sundry, hugging surprised colleagues, unused to such a touchy feely approach from her, as she passed, then took the opportunity to touch up already perfect hair and make-up in the ladies.

The facilities were as luxurious as the rest of the hotel, with huge Victorian gilt mirrors and sparkling chandeliers. Whoever had got the short straw of arranging the festive gathering this year had pulled out all the stops. Next week, when she was back at her desk, she would be sure to find out who it was and send a thank you email. The idea of such thoughtfulness on her own part filled her with a sense of well-being and she sighed a deep, self-satisfied breath. A bevy of well-dressed females preened in front of the mirrors, applying lipstick and whispering to each other. Violet sat in a cubicle, listening to the excited chatter, ready to join them as soon as she was able, but, as she was about to unlock the door, the room cleared of all but a couple of voices she didn't recognise and the confidential tone of their conversation pulled her up short.

'I'm sure you've got it wrong, Sally. That's not the way he sold it to me.' There was a lot of shuffling and clicking and Violet could

imagine the pair rifling through bags for this, that or the other. 'I'm here as his guest. I only had to make my own way because he was coming straight from the office. We are together.'

'Yes, but I was talking to Carol, from costume, and she said he's definitely been seeing one of the make-up artists, I can't remember her name, but the one with the eyebrows, you know.' Sally's air was slightly desperate. She clearly wanted her friend to take the comments on board.

'That cow? Yes, I know the one, but she's old news. He was seeing her, but it ended weeks ago. He told me. I daresay she's been hanging around and wishing she could rekindle it, but he's simply not interested in anybody but me.'

There was a pause. 'And what about the other thing, with Andrea from HR?'

'We all have a past, Sally, and, let's face it, Andrea has more past than most. You can't blame him for giving in to temptation if she lays it on a plate.'

Violet listened, trying to picture the staff in HR. If her memory served her right, Andrea was a pretty, tall, young blonde who didn't look as if she would say boo to a goose. Violet would certainly view her with fresh eyes in future. As for the two on the other side of the door, she had no idea who they were. She would have liked to have put faces to the voices. Checking her watch, time was getting on and she should be making her way through to the dining room, but somehow, it would feel awkward to step out from the cubicle now. The pair clearly thought they were alone and to reveal her presence at this point would look strange to say the least.

'And what about the other thing?' Whoever Sally was, she was like a dog with a bone.

'What other thing?'

'With the exec. Frosty knickers. Khalid said...'

A burst of music filled the room as another group of women entered and the conversation stopped abruptly. Violet kicked herself. Just as the content was becoming most interesting. She had no idea who frosty knickers was, but she certainly knew Khalid and his reputation for knowing pretty much everything going on in the building, and how indiscreet he could be with the right provocation. She would be on the case first thing Monday morning. If there was gossip to be had, she didn't want to be left behind.

In the hustle and bustle of the once again busy room, Violet slipped out to wash her hands at the sink. She eyed the women around the room and wondered if any of them were Sally, or her mysterious companion with the complicated love life. Poor girl. Violet was glad her own love life was so straight forward, or at least, it would be by the end of the evening. Checking her own reflection, she smiled, allowing herself to feel a little smug.

Numbers in the lobby had dwindled and she swiftly mounted the stairs to the main event. If she wasn't careful, Niall would think she wasn't coming and she would hate to disappoint him. Quite a crowd had gathered by the double doors into the dining room, as people filtered through to huge round tables, each marked with Department names rather than allocated seats. Sensible idea, Violet thought. It was so easy to make the mistake of sitting someone who clashed with someone else together, unless you were all over office politics, and it was such a shifting landscape it was an almost impossible task. A white board inside the door showed the table plan and she could see the Managers and Execs were allocated three tables, all front and centre of the room, immediately below a low stage, already set up with a podium and microphones, ready for the customary pre-meal speeches.

She pushed through the crowds in the general direction, neck craned for Niall and the seat he had promised to save for her, but as she approached she could see him leaning over one of the other managers, his booming laugh providing bass to the general chatter of the room. What should she do? Go straight to him? Or, make her way directly to one of two empty seats on the other side of the curve, which she assumed were for him and her. She slowed down, hoping he would look up and spot her, stating his claim to both her and the spaces, but he finished his conversation, moved around to the gap and sat down. She edged her way around and was immediately behind him before, glancing over his shoulder, he noticed her arrival.

He stood and air brushed her cheek, taking the opportunity to whisper. 'Hey, Violet, looking good.'

Her knees turned to water and she breathed through the pleasure, waiting for the goose bumps to subside. 'Hi.' She made to pass behind and slip into the empty chair next to him, but another manager got there first, blocking her progress, allowing access to his own wife and leaving Violet with nowhere to go.

Niall seemed not to have noticed and she wasn't sure what to do. There were few people still standing and she felt awkward, particularly as the CEO chose that moment to take to the stage. There was a sudden rush for people to settle down for him to speak. Niall had surely said he was saving a place for her, but the table was now full.

'Violet.'

A hushed, but excited voice, grabbed her attention, and she turned to see Maggie, waving violently and gesticulating to a vacant chair alongside her own, one table along from Niall's. It wasn't what she had expected from the evening, but at that point in time, anything was preferable to being the centre of attention of the entire room. She crouched and made her way to join Maggie, as the CEO began his speech. A number of her closer colleagues were there with Maggie: Howard and a prim mousey woman, Violet assumed to be his wife; Khalid and his boyfriend, both resplendent in well-cut suits and matching paisley patterned shirts. Khalid raised his glass in toast to her, and Howard gave a wink, and she felt welcome in a way which had been missing at the celebrations of previous years. She realised a closer connection had built within the team, over the last few months. She wondered if this was a new thing, or if it was simply new to her. Certainly she had become more involved with her colleagues this year, perhaps opened up to them more than before. It was a pleasant feeling.

There was a rustle around the table, and she realised everyone was retrieving draw tickets from pockets and handbags, for the usual charity event of the evening. She had bought a couple of strips, but wasn't terribly interested in the results. Howard, on the other hand, had a book of various coloured numbers lined up on his placemat. Only half listening as numbers were announced and prizes were collected, she watched Niall out of the corner of her eye, chatting to his neighbours and laughing at comedy moments on the stage. He didn't seem to be missing her, but then, as part of the management team, he had to be seen to be social and cheerful and definitely couldn't appear withdrawn. That wouldn't do at all.

Her attention was abruptly brought back to proceedings, as Khalid whooped in joy as one of his numbers was called, and he made his way to the front, in his usual flamboyant style.

He returned to the table holding an envelope in front of his chest by the corners. 'My perfect prize.' Putting all his weight on one leg, his hip lurched to one side, as he proclaimed. 'A spa day.'

The rest of the table gave him a rowdy round of applause and he pretended to curtsey. Violet watched, smiling at his excitement, then felt Maggie's elbow in her side.

'This'll be interesting.' Maggie nodded at the stage, where Niall was striding up the stairs, amid a chorus of cheers and good-natured heckling. The CEO had been handed an enormous bouquet of flowers, and he peered out from behind them, waiting for Niall to reach the midpoint.

Niall seemed non-plussed by the floral prize, but the CEO was enjoying his discomfort. 'Come on de Havilland, a beautiful bouquet for you, you lucky man.'

Niall reached out to take it, but the CEO didn't let go. 'So, which lucky lady will you be giving these to? Anyone we know?'

There were a few calls from the crowd, offering to take them or suggesting he take them home for his mother. One joker recommended he split the bouquet and give one flower to each of the ladies in the room, but the CEO denied that possibility. 'No, no, we can't have that. This fantastic display should stay as is. Well, Niall? What's it to be?'

Niall stood, one hand on the bunch of flowers, staring out over the room, deliberating over what to do, everyone watching in anticipation. Violet held her breath. Was this the moment he announced their relationship to the entire staff? She was happy to shout it from the rooftops, but would have appreciated prewarning.

He coughed, putting on a show, but feigning shyness. 'Well, there is only one person I could possibly give them to. The most beautiful, charming and gracious lady I know. A genuine professional, who goes out of her way to ensure the show goes on, no matter what.'

Everyone waited with bated breath, Violet included. Was this to be a great declaration?

He pulled a single stemmed flower from the bunch with a flourish and held it out, peering through the strong lights on stage, at the tables beyond. 'Someone who makes my life a little better every day, in her own special way. Come on, stand up. You know who you are.'

In the moment he paused for breath, before announcing the lady in question's name, five women, at various tables around the room, including Violet, got to their feet.

Niall was oblivious to the confusion he had caused, unable to see past the stage lights. 'Saffron. Star and pillar of Daytime. Come on, darling. What would I do without you?'

While Saffron made a show of humility and surprise and received applause from the top table, as she made for the stage, there was much gasping and some sniggering from the guests farther out, who had witnessed the rising and confused gaping of the other women, as they first recognised their rejection, and then secondly became aware of each other.

Violet felt eyes briefly on her, until a cry went up from a busty auburn-haired girl, standing to the far right, who had suddenly realised that among the competition for Niall's affection was someone she knew. 'Andrea, you bitch.'

The voice belonged to the girl in the lavatories earlier, and very quickly Violet put two and two together, the depth of her stupidity slapping her to sense. Clearly, the complicated love life Violet had mocked the woman for, and her own love interest, were one and the same, and the unidentified friend, Sally's, warnings had been valid. The girl flew across the room toward the stunned Andrea, and a third girl, seated in the area allocated to costume and make up, joined the melee.

Violet watched in horror for a few moments, then felt the eyes of those at her own table fixed on her. In them she read questions, confusion and, worst of all, pity. Her face filled with heat, but she was determined to save herself. Her phone was in her hand and she lifted it as she met Maggie's gaze. She smiled as if unaware what was going on around her and grabbed her handbag and coat. 'Sorry, I've got to take this.'

The whole group watched her leave and she knew not all of them had been fooled. Khalid had shared a knowing look with his partner, and the shame of his awareness cut her to the bone. Maggie had simply looked confused, at first, but as her brain completed the computations required, the look had altered to pity, and it was more than Violet could take. She had maintained a steady pace until she reached the doorway to the hall, but, as the doors swung shut behind her, she ran as fast as her legs would allow.

Her heart thudded, her stomach churned and her head pounded with the pressure of contained tears. And whose fault was this whole debacle? Not Niall's - he was a handsome man, who was bound to attract attention, and who could blame him for giving in to temptation, outside of a steady relationship? And not hers - everything which had taken place during the months since the deal had led her to believe Niall was the man for her. God had allowed her to believe it, heart and soul, and God had allowed her to now become the butt of everyone's amusement. If anyone had charges to answer, it was God. That's who.

CHAPTER 31

Violet leaned forward, gripping the back of the seat in front with her fingers. She stared at the stationary image on the screen. 'I don't know how I didn't see it.'

The ombudsman sucked his lips between his teeth, but said nothing.

She turned to him and glared, as if it was his fault. 'That man's a complete arse.'

He shrugged. 'I couldn't possibly comment.'

'He's a selfish, self-centred, arrogant…' She searched the air for derogatory terms to add to the list, but failed. 'Arse.'

He shrugged again.

Violet stood up, sat down and stood up as various thoughts ran through her mind. 'What have I done? How could I ever have thought he was the man of my dreams? I've wasted a year of my life. And to think I was blaming God. I've been so blind.' She rested a hand on his shoulder. 'I need to get back to my body, right now. Where do I go? What do I do? Where…'

Taking her hand in both of his own, the ombudsman gently pulled her back down into her seat and checked his watch. 'Violet, wait a minute. We've got time and I think you should see this through to the end.'

'What more is there to see? Five minutes later I'm lying in the gutter with my skirt around my neck. I don't need to see that, believe me.'

He leaned toward her, patting her hand and maintaining steady eye contact in an attempt to keep her calm. 'Yes, but remember, life has carried on without you, or, at least, without your being an active part of it. Events have taken place around you and to those important to you, since you landed here and the fact you've not consciously witnessed them, make them no less vital to your future and your decision making processes.' He reclaimed ownership of the remote control with a firm hand. 'Will you let me show you? I would prefer it if you did.'

She considered his comments. He had patiently listened to her side of the story, watched scene after scene of her past life, the least she could do was hear him out. 'Are you sure there's time?'

'Absolutely positive. Trust me.'

A small smile curved her lips. 'Ok. Show me what I need to see.'

Christmas Party – Mid-December

Violet was lying on the pavement, a small trickle of blood dripping from her ear into the gutter. Tara had made no attempt to help, all her energies expended in screaming from the pit of her stomach. Tara's guest was equally useless, giving all his attentions to his prostate girlfriend rather than the injured body needing help at his feet. The only response which served any purpose came from the taxi driver who jumped from his seat and ran to where Violet lay, phone at the ready to call for an ambulance, and from a tuxedoed man who speeded down the steps to kneel at her body. The man was Peter.

***

'Hang on.' Violet had grabbed the handset to intervene. 'What's Peter doing outside my office Christmas party?'

'It's a long story, and anyway, it doesn't matter…' The ombudsman held out his hand for the controls.

'I beg to differ. I think it matters a great deal.' She held it at arm's length so he couldn't reach it. 'I don't believe for a minute it was a coincidence, so something was going on, and I want to know what.'

'I assure you there was nothing untoward going on and it will all become clear eventually, if you'll bear with me.'

She viewed him through slits, considering his comment, then discarding it. 'No. I want to know now.'

There was an undignified scuffle as he made a dive for the remote, but she managed to swap it hand to hand, keeping it out of his reach. He sat back with a huff. 'It's not on your timeline, it's on his. I'm not supposed to show that to you – you know, data protection and all that.'

'But, it is about me, isn't it? Don't I have a right to see it?'

His cheeks had pinked in the struggle. 'Ooh, you're a tricky customer. I've never had one like you before.'

'And you never will again. Come on, show me.' Violet threw the gadget onto his lap.

He looked over his shoulders in both directions. 'All right, but this stays strictly between you and me, ok? No letting the cat out of the bag, either here or back there.' He wiggled his fingers at the screen.

'Wouldn't dream of it. Go on. Quick before someone comes in.'

Early December

Issy was hovering on the corner by the entrance to Violet's flat, looking out for something or somebody, trying to conceal her shocking pink trench coat behind a clearly deficient tree trunk. Peter appeared from the opposite direction, a tool bag slung over one shoulder and a plunger in his hand. Issy leaned to one side and hissed before diving back to her original position. Peter stopped and looked around, but unable to identify where the sound had originated, soon carried on.

Undeterred, Issy leaned again, this time bolder with her approach. 'Oi, Peter. Over here.'

This time he spotted her, but confused by her actions, glanced around again to reassure himself she meant him, before heading in her direction. Issy grabbed him by the arm and pulled him behind the tree, which had failed miserably at concealing one body, let alone two.

'I need to talk to you.' Her voice was a hoarse whisper.

'Fire away.' He ignored her obvious desire for discretion and spoke in his normal tone.

Issy hushed him viciously. 'No, not here. Somewhere more hidden. Quick, round the corner. She won't see us there.'

'Who won't?' He found himself dragged by the shoulder. 'Hang on. I can't be messing around here, I'm on an emergency call out. One of my tenants has a blocked drain and I need ...'

'If you mean Naomi, she hasn't. It was all a ploy. I asked her to get you here under false pretences.' Issy looked excessively pleased with her powers of deception.

Peter bit his tongue and huffed. 'This better be good.'

'Oh, it is. Look.' She checked around for witnesses. 'Am I right in thinking you've got the hots for Vi?'

'What?' He pulled his bag onto his shoulder and turned to walk away in disgust.

'No, no, no.' She scurried around to prevent him leaving. 'Stay where you are. I'm serious. Answer me.'

'I'm a little old for playground games of "do you fancy my friend".'

She peered at him from beneath one raised eyebrow.

'Alright. Violet is ... Violet has ... I think Violet ... Ok, yes, I've got the hots for Vi. But, what of it? She's clearly got the hots for Mr Giant Ego Pants. No offence. I'm sure he's a nice guy. And I don't need the hassle or the heartache which goes with chasing somebody already spoken for. Been there, seen it, done it, bought the t-shirt. She obviously doesn't even like me.' What started as a statement of fact, ended as a tentative question. 'Does she?'

'Ego, shmeego!' She waved his comments away. 'Of course she likes you. Think about it. For a start, she tried to set us up on a date, and she wouldn't have done that unless she had you down as a good guy.'

'In my experience good guys nearly always finish last.'

She ignored him. 'For a second, this was her description of you, and I quote, "He's kind, he's thoughtful, he's really, really handsome, in fact, he's got the sexiest eyes I have ever seen and under those overalls he's got muscles on muscles. I'd have snapped him up by now if I didn't know for certain I was destined for Niall".'

His chin had risen a notch with every compliment, but came crashing down with the finale. 'And there you have it. Destined for Mr Giant Ego Pants.'

'But she doesn't know what she's talking about.' Issy flounced with exasperation. 'I don't know what happened when she started working with the man, but something did, and convinced her they'd been thrown together for some supernatural reason. But I know, in her heart of hearts, she doesn't even like him very much. Ok, he's easy on the eye, but personality wise he's a complete knob.'

'Don't hold back there now, Issy.'

'What else can I say? He is what he is and she knows it too. You should hear her mimic him when she's had a couple.' Issy took on a comedy voice. '"We've got to hit the ground running and run this idea up the flagpole and see if it puts all our ducks in a row, so we're all singing from the same hymn sheet." The man can't even string a proper sentence together. He's totally ridiculous and she knows it, at least subliminally.'

'Well, there's nothing I can do about it. It's not for me to tell her what he's like, you know, shooting the messenger and all that. Can't you tell her?'

She held a finger up as if making an important point. 'I won't have to.'

'Huh?'

'He's going to do it himself. Spectacularly, unless I'm very much mistaken.'

Peter waited for her to expand.

'I happen to know he's been putting it about at work.'

A confused frown formed on his brow. 'Putting it about?'

She nodded slowly. 'Yep. Rumour has it he's secretly been romancing Davina, who does the fashion articles on Daytime.'

'Not secretly enough apparently.'

She pressed on. 'And, at the same time, he's been seriously flirting with one of the HR girls, all legs and power suits, you know the type. And only this week I walked in on him playing tonsil tennis with someone from make-up. He's incorrigible.'

'You have such a way with words.'

'I know, it's the creative genes in me. You should see what I can do with modelling chocolate and a piping set.'

He tried to conjure up an image and then frowned. 'I'm not sure I want to.'

'Listen. The thing is, all these women are going to be at the same Christmas party and, one way or another, there's going to be massive fallout. It's an accident waiting to happen.'

Girl Plans, God Laughs

He paced a circle around Issy. 'So you're saying, Vi will get to hear about the other women and kick him into touch, and then I should make my move in the New Year when it's all died down?'

'No!' She rolled her eyes. 'No, you need to be there, on the night, ready to sweep her off her feet. When it all goes off she's going to feel stupid, humiliated, rejected and she needs a hero right there and then to build her back up, not six weeks later when the wound has had time to fester and she's anti men for the foreseeable.'

'But how's that going to work. I'm assuming it's a closed party, and I don't have an invite.'

Issy smirked in victory. 'You do now.'

His head jerked to one side so he could study her face.

'Only permanent staff are invited to the whole shebang, but lesser employees like me get to go in after the sit down do for drinks and the disco, and we all know if something's going to kick off its always during the drinks and disco.'

They were both quiet for a few moments as the idea percolated.

'Are you up for it?'

He rubbed his chin. 'I don't know. Do you think it'll work?'

'What could possible go wrong?'

'Plenty. Do you really think she'd be interested in me?'

'As I said, she would have snapped you up already if it wasn't for this silly idea she has about Niall de Havilland.'

'Snapped me up, ha.' Peter laughed lightly and studied his knuckles for a second. 'Alright, tell me where and when.'

'Yes!' Issy punched the air then reached into her pocket for an envelope. 'The details are all in there.' She started to walk away, but turned a few paces on. 'And don't forget, it's black tie.'

'What? A tux? You're joking me.'

She laughed and carried on walking. 'Too late. You've said you'll do it now.'

Violet's mouth was wide open. 'Is–o–bel!' She turned to the ombudsman. 'I didn't know she had it in her.'

'Hmm, a devious nature is not something I generally admire, but I have to say on this occasion... At least it was well intentioned.'

'Well intentioned, but not so well executed. She obviously hadn't been to one of our parties before. Something usually kicks off round about dessert. It's the high ratio of artistic temperaments in TV work.'

'If you say so.'

'So, Peter was on his way to the party to rescue me. Interesting.'

'Without being biased, I think I can safely say he's a pretty decent guy.'

She studied his image on the screen, muttering under her breath. 'He is a good guy. And a good looking one. Those biceps and that smile and those eyes. Oh, yes, those eyes.'

The ombudsman coughed. 'Moving on. So now you know what he was doing there. Can I go back to your timeline? Can I show you what happened after the fall?'

She was still thinking about Peter's eyes. 'You can show me whatever you like.'

CHAPTER 32

Late December

The hospital room was quiet apart from the rhythmic beeping and clicking of the monitoring equipment doing its job. Peter sat, head bowed, lulled into slumber by the repetitive sound and dim lighting.

Kate pushed through the swing door, carrying two cups of tea and a packet of sandwiches, jerking him awake. 'As you're determined to stay, I thought I'd bring you some supplies. Issy's gone home to get some sleep, bless her. She's in pieces.'

'I know. She won't hear it's not her fault, but I told her, it's de Havilland who behaved like an eejit, not her. She couldn't have known what'd happen.'

She pulled a chair up next to his so as to carry on the conversation at a low level. 'She thinks she should have told Vi before, about him and the other women. So it didn't come as such a shock. Perhaps Vi wouldn't have run off like that.'

He shook his head. 'Ah. Who knows what she'd have done? We're all capable of being rash.' He wiggled the sandwiches. 'Thanks for these.'

They sat quietly for a few moments, before Kate continued. 'I've told Ben I'm staying the night, and Lulu will be here early for her shift, so she'll be in and out whenever she can, and Ayesha's getting here for nine. I think there'll be someone here around the clock until her parents and Simone fly in. They were planning to come in by train on Wednesday anyway, but obviously now they don't want to wait.'

He nodded, sipping the scalding tea and wincing. 'You managed to get hold of them then?'

'Yes. I've been talking to Jan for a couple of weeks, sorting out their surprise visit for Christmas, so it wasn't hard. She's a lovely lady. It's a shame Vi took their relocation so badly. It was poor timing. Any other time and it wouldn't have mattered a jot, but as it was, Vi felt abandoned.'

'I'm sorry, I don't know the story. All I know is Violet doesn't have much to do with her family. What happened?'

'Jan married Vi's stepdad when Vi was five, six maybe. He already had a daughter the same age, Simone. Simone lived with her own mother, but she and Vi were great friends from the word go and everything was rosy. Then, when Simone's mum remarried, when the girls were about thirteen, Simone moved in with them. But Simone was much needier than Vi, always having some crisis or other, and Vi got a bit sick of it.'

'Was there a falling out?' He frowned, concentrating on the story.

'Not as such. Simone met a guy at Art College and moved to Spain, then France, running some sort of arty retreat, but their relationship was pretty volatile, so Jan and Roger were often getting calls and stuff. Anyway, when the parents took early retirement, they bought a camper and went off travelling. They stopped to visit Simone in the Pyrenees and fell in love with the place, so gradually they spent more and more time down there.'

'I'm guessing Violet didn't like that? Had her nose put out of joint?' He opened the pack of sandwiches and offered one to Kate.

'Ooo, no. I can't stomach mayo at the moment. Or chocolate worst luck. I hope it goes away after this one arrives.' A pat of the

full curve of her belly transformed into a protective caress as she returned to the story. 'No, to begin with Vi wasn't bothered in the slightest. She was living the high life, working in TV, meeting all kinds of people and living with Ryan. She didn't have time for family anyway. So, when they told her they were thinking of moving down there permanently, she was fine about it.'

'Obviously something changed.'

'Yeah, out of the blue Ryan decided he was too young to settle down and ran off with a sports instructor and left Vi in the lurch. She was in a right mess, not only the emotional stuff, but he left debts and all sorts. Course at that point she needed her mum, but at the same time Simone's partner walked out leaving her to run the business, with a mortgage on a property which was half falling down, and two months pregnant. Jan and Roger didn't know what to do, but Vi had always been so independent, they made the decision to stay put, apart from a quick weekend back in England. Vi expected them to race back, like they'd always raced to Simone when she called. She's never forgiven them.'

'Talk about being stuck between a rock and a hard place. They must have been torn. But poor Violet. I can see why she felt let down.'

'Vi's her own worst enemy. She played it down, like "I don't need you anyway" and they believed her. I think they were completely bemused when she started to blank them out of her life.' Kate shrugged. 'I tried to talk to her about it, but it's like talking to a brick wall. That's why between us, me and the girls decided enough was enough. I got in touch with Jan about a month ago to see if together we couldn't work something out. She decided they would all come back for Christmas as a surprise and try to build some bridges.'

Peter shook his head. 'And then this. I bet they're frantic.'

'Mmm,' she agreed. 'But at least we're here for her.'

'Yes, and I for one am going nowhere.'

They both turned their attention back to the figure in the bed and the gentle rise and fall as she breathed, a steady reminder there was still hope.

***

A small tear ran down Violet's cheek and she surreptitiously wiped it away while pretending to scratch her nose. The ombudsman pretended not to notice.

She cleared her throat. 'I'd like to say Kate made the story sound much simpler than it actually was. My family weren't there when I needed them.'

'I won't argue with that, but I would add they would have done a lot more if you'd opened up and shown how much you were struggling. They saw you surrounded by this friendship group, who were doing everything they could to support you in your time of need, and made a judgement call. People do the best they can with the information and resources they have available. No one's perfect.'

The silence stretched as she processed what she'd seen and heard.

'When you go back, do you think you'll be prepared to meet your parents halfway? Give them a chance?'

'Maybe. We'll see.' She studied her fingernails for a moment, then looked at him through narrowed eyes. 'I've definitely learnt one thing today.'

His face lit up. 'You have? That's good. What is it?'

'I have the most devious friends on the planet. First Issy setting me up with Peter at the party, and now Kate calling my mum. Honestly, I had no idea they were capable of such subterfuge. Those two have some serious questions to answer.'

He bit his lips together and frowned. 'Aah. I probably shouldn't say anything, but it wasn't all down to Kate. She was the instigator, but…'

'But?' Her head tipped to one side as she waited.

'But the entire group played their part.' He checked the auditorium was empty apart from themselves. 'In for a penny, in for a pound.' He pointed at the screen. 'Watch. This is how it all came about.'

CHAPTER 33

Late November

Lulu and Ayesha were chattering on Kate's doorstep and when Kate opened the door they stumbled across the threshold waving wine bottles.

'Come in, come in. Issy's already in the lounge. Let me get some glasses.'

Ben passed them in the hallway, heading in the opposite direction.

'Oh, Ben, are you not joining our girl's night?' Lulu chuckled at his quick exit. It was a constant source of amusement within their group that this man, who dealt with everything from drunken thugs to hardened criminals, turned to jelly when confronted with flirtatious girls.

He lifted his jacket from a hook and slipped it on. 'Not likely. I know what you lot are like after a couple. I'm keeping well clear.' He winked at Kate. 'See you later, hon. Have fun.'

Ayesha blew him a couple of noisy mock kisses. 'Mwah, mwah. Bye Ben, see you later.' Then, laughing, followed Lulu into the lounge. 'Ooh, Issy. Loving the hair.'

Greetings were exchanged and seats taken, while Kate followed with a tray of glasses and snacks and sorted everyone out with a drink. She fiddled with the controls on the stereo, and a raspy voice launched into song.

'Oh, I love this one.' Issy tapped her fingers on her knee in time with the rhythm.

'Me too.' Kate agreed, planting herself next to Ayesha on the sofa. 'Anyway, I've called you all here today to discuss something serious.'

'Should we wait for Vi?'

'Definitely not, it's about Vi. She's always late anyway, but I told her we were meeting fifteen minutes later than I told you, so I figure we've got half an hour to come up with a plan before she gets here.' Kate pulled out a notepad and tapped the rubber end of a pencil on it, as she gathered her thoughts. 'I don't know how you guys feel, but Vi has been an absolute rock for me this year. I know she's gone above and beyond for all of us in one way or another, and I feel like we owe her.'

'She's certainly helped me out, and my dad.' Ayesha ran her fingers through her hair. 'What are you thinking?'

'I was hoping one of you would have some suggestions. I've racked my brains, but I can't come up with anything suitable or affordable. Basically it needs to be cheap and cheerful from my point of view.'

'She was really there for me when Rachael was so poorly. I don't know what I'd have done without her, but what to get her?' Lulu rubbed her chin, in thought.

Ayesha nodded. 'If it wasn't for her I don't know where dad would be. He's come so far with the rehab. We were so close to our little family falling apart.'

Issy agreed. 'My whole career has taken off thanks to Vi. Calling me in to stand in on the show that day kick-started everything and, of course, she encouraged me to buy the business in the first place.'

'As your manager, I can second that. Her Prime contacts have been a boon.' Ayesha and Issy tapped glasses

'Well at the risk of TMI, if it wasn't for her giving me her award ceremony tickets, I might not be in the position I am today.' Kate pointed at her bump, blushing.

'Enough said.' Lulu waved her hand to stop any further revelations. 'So she helped Issy's business, my sister, Ayesha's dad and Kate's family plans. It's a shame we can't do something for her family. Can we?'

'I don't think so. I mean, what could we do? She doesn't even speak to them more than she has to. They invited her over for Christmas, but she's refused to go. Reckons she's got too many work commitments. It's such a shame.' Kate mulled it over.

'It's a pity they can't come back here. It might build a few bridges, but I guess they've got nowhere to stay since their house was sold, and Vi hasn't got room to put the four of them up.' Ayesha was ever practical.

'A hotel at Christmas would cost an arm and a leg and it's not ideal with such a small baby either,' Issy mused.

'Eureka!' Kate sat up straight. 'We're going to stay with my parents in Wales for Christmas. They could stay here while we're away and it wouldn't cost us a bean. Her parents could have our room and we've already started getting the nursery ready, so as long as Simone didn't mind a camp bed alongside the cot ... I'd have to run it past Ben, of course, but...'

'That's all very well, but then we're not doing anything for her. It's all down to you. What can the rest of us do?'

'How about we club together to give them Christmas? Turkey, trimmings, the works. You could make the cake, Issy.' Kate's imagination was running at full throttle.

'That wouldn't be a problem. In fact I could put together a whole hamper of goodies from the range we're doing at the shop, but is it enough?'

Ayesha was the voice of reason. 'Are we sure she'd thank us for this though? I mean, what if it all kicks off? We don't want to make things worse.'

'There is an element of risk. It's not like we can keep the receipt and get our money back if she doesn't like it, but Rachael is pretty much the most important thing in my life and if Vi and Simone could get a bit of that back...' Lulu shook her head. *'It has to be worth it, doesn't it?'*

'Let's have a vote. Hands up those in favour.' Four hands appeared in the air and Kate nodded, satisfied. *'It's agreed then. Ok, I tell you what. Leave it to me and I'll try and track down a number for Simone or Vi's mum and sound them out. If they can't make it, then we'll have a rethink. Ayesha can you set up a group on WhatsApp, and obviously don't include Vi. Lulu and Issy have a think about the finer details and let me know any thoughts. Remember guys, mum's the word.'*

***

'Mum's the word? They've being saying that non-stop for weeks. I assumed it was to do with Kate being pregnant, when in fact they've been planning this all along. What a bunch of ...' Violet broke off, flabbergasted by her friends' deceit.

The ombudsman's voice was gentle. 'It's surprising how far our loved ones will go to make us happy. You can see it was well intentioned.

Absent-mindedly, she picked at fluff on her dress, considering what she had learned. 'I'm very lucky, aren't I?'

His smile was poignant. 'And so are they. Look at what you've done for them over the last few months.'

'Only because I thought I was going to get something out of it.'

'And you did, possibly not what you thought you were going to get, but even so. There's a whole debate about whether true altruism can ever exist. Doing things for other people makes us feel good so it's impossible to be truly selfless. There is always a reward of some description, either tangible or otherwise, and I suspect this year has been a steep learning curve for you. I apologise for using de Havilland speak, but on the rare occasion it does fit the bill.'

'It has a bit.' She chewed on a fingernail, a small frown weighing down her brow. 'I didn't mean to be selfish. I don't know where it all started. Perhaps I was always like it, but I intend to do better when I get back.'

A rattle from the other end of the room as the door swung open made the ombudsman start and he quickly flicked the footage back to Violet's own timeline. Peter was still sitting close to the bed, his head supported by one hand, eyes closed in the dim light.

'He's still there then?'

Violet gazed at the image, taking in every detail.

'That's late on Sunday afternoon and he shows no signs of movement. It's now Monday morning there.'

A small cough at the end of the aisle drew their attention. Grace waved a clipboard. 'I'm sorry to interrupt, but we've had an alert downstairs. If we don't send Violet back now I'm afraid she'll have missed the boat, which will severely undermine operational protocol. I could do without the headache, believe me.'

The ombudsman's tone was professional. 'Thank you, Grace. I think we're done here anyway.' He turned to Violet. 'Aren't we Violet? Do you need any more proof with regard to the deal? Do you accept you were mistaken? Do you need to see any more?'

'No, I believe you. There are things I still don't understand, but that's down to me, not God. I guess I'm not supposed to have the answers to everything. Sometimes you have to let life be what it is and not try to control every last detail.'

'Then I'll mark your case as closed.'

Grace tapped her watch. 'Time is ticking. Come along, Violet.'

Violet shuffled to her feet and stretched, stiff after being sat in one place for so long. Peter's image caught her eye. He looked so sweet, nodding in his seat, a tuft of dark hair sticking up at right angles. He had been a part of her life for almost a year and yet she hardly knew him, often part of the backdrop, but rarely in focus. She paused and turned to the ombudsman.

'Is there any chance..?' She eyed Grace, nervous to issue a request in front of her. 'Could I possibly see one more thing before I go? It wouldn't take long.'

He glanced at Grace for a reaction.

Grace pursed her lips and sighed. 'I'll go and do the prep. You have five minutes and not one second more.'

He waited for the door to swing closed behind the retreating form. 'Well? What is it?'

'Have my parents arrived?'

He scrolled down the screen of his tablet. 'Yes. Yes, they arrived in the early hours of the morning and came straight from the airport to the hospital.'

'I know I'm going to see them soon anyway, but it's been a while since I looked at them through anything but angry eyes. I feel like I need to look again. Take some time to adjust my thinking, to get used to the idea they really do care about me. Is that possible?'

'It's on your timeline so I don't see why not.' He jumped the footage forward. 'It'll have to be brief though.'

'That's fine. Whatever you have time to show me.'

'Ok then. Here you go.'

Late December

A nurse led Violet's parents into the hospital room, waking Peter, who stood to attention at their entry, rubbing bleary eyes. Her mother was so overcome with emotion, she overlooked his presence, and immediately ran to the bed taking Violet's hand in one of her own, the other stroking Violet's cheek.

'Oh, you poor darling.'

The nurse was eager to reassure, but what she had to offer was limited. 'We're keeping her comfortable and the signs of distress she was showing in the early stages seem to have settled down. She's calm now. The doctor will be in first thing to review her status and decide what happens next.'

Violet's stepfather strode around the bed and held out his hand to shake Peter's. 'Hello. Roger. I'm sorry, I don't know your name. I take it you're Violet's young man.'

Peter accepted the hand, but shook his head. 'No, I'm Peter, but I'm just a friend.' He drew Violet's mother into the conversation as the nurse left the room. 'She's doing well. The change is subtle, but I'm certain she's headed in the right direction.'

'Do you think so? The reports we've had from the doctor haven't been at all encouraging. I was afraid I wouldn't get here in...' Her voice broke and Roger sped around the bed to support her with an embrace.

'Come on, love. Bear up. Where there's life there's hope, and Vi's a strong little madam, if ever there was one.'

Peter stepped forward, as if to intervene, but paused unsure of his place. 'I'm sure there'll be some progress soon. Hearing your voice will give her a boost.' He scratched his chin, torn. 'I suppose now you're here, I should be going.'

Roger studied Peter's pinched face. 'Now, don't you be rushing off. If you need a break, of course, get yourself home, but don't be going on our account. She can't have too much support, bless her. You're welcome to stay.'

Peter's face relaxed. 'Well, if you're sure. It's just, I'm convinced she'll be back with us soon and I wanted to be here, to let her know how everyone's rallied around.'

'Course you do, and so you should be. Go on, settle yourself back down, and keep an eye on Jan here, while I find another chair.' He drew a seat up alongside and pushed her into it. 'There you are, love. You stay there with young Peter.'

Another face appeared around the door. 'Is it all right to come in?'

Roger turned and smiled. 'Ah, Simone. Yes, come along in with Mum and Peter. I'm on my way to find chairs.'

She came through, a sleeping baby clutched in her arms. Peter jumped to his feet. 'Here, have mine. I've been sat down all day. I could do with stretching my legs.' He brushed the baby's head as he passed. 'What a little angel.'

Simone rolled her eyes. 'She is now I've fed and changed her, but she's been a proper handful on the journey. Travel and babies don't mix.' She leaned forward, straining to take in Violet's condition. 'I've been so looking forward to introducing her to her aunty and now... How is she doing? Any change?'

Jan merely shook her head, but Peter spoke up. 'No news is good news. But it's hopeful.' He ran out of steam and had to think before he continued. 'I'm hopeful, especially now you're all here. It's probably just what she needs to hear your voices and to know you're here waiting.'

'You think she can hear us then?' Simone studied Violet's face, searching for signs of recognition, anything.

'I'm sure she can, and she'll be fighting to come back to us, if I know Violet.'

Simone shuffled to her feet and gently laid the sleeping baby alongside her aunt, their faces only inches apart. Her voice was quiet, but steady. 'Violet, we've missed you. It's been such a long time. Too long. But this is your niece, Amelie Violette. And Amelie, this is your Aunty Vi. And one of these days, when she's feeling better, you're going to be really, really good friends.'

***

As the image stilled Violet's hand flew to her chest, where a painful knot had formed. She had been missing out on so much by refusing to go and see her family in France, by being so stubborn, and if she had any say in the matter, she would never make the same mistake again.

She jumped to her feet. 'I need to go. I need to put things right, right now.'

The ombudsman stood up too and sidled out of the row into the aisle to allow her to pass. 'I'm glad you've found the answers you were looking for.' He pointed to the door in the far right hand corner of the room. 'Head down that way. Grace will be back at any moment to take you through your paces.'

Violet ran halfway towards the walkway at the front, parallel with the screen, before she stopped in her tracks, turned and ran back up to pull the ombudsman into an embrace. 'Thank you.' She pulled away to look into his eyes. 'Thank you for everything. I'll try to do better in future.'

As she retraced her steps back to the front, he called out. 'Maybe I'll check up on you from time to time. See how you're doing.'

'Ok. You do that.' She yelled over her shoulder, pausing at the doorway. 'Not when I'm in the bathroom though, eh?'

'I'll do my best to avoid the bathroom breaks.' He laughed. 'Good luck Violet.'

'Thank you.' She placed one hand on the door to swing it open, took a deep breath and lunged through. 'And goodbye.'

The hall was light and bright and Violet had to squint to allow her eyes to acclimatise after the dimness of the auditorium. When she opened them wide, she spotted Grace huffing and puffing towards her from the far end.

When Grace spotted her she halted and waved frantically. 'Violet. Violet. Quick as you can and don't hold the horses.'

The urgency in Grace's voice spurred Violet on and she sprinted in the right direction. 'What's up? Has something happened?'

'We've lost some time.' Grace panted between sentences. 'I've told them before, we need to adjust the algorithms when we're dealing with the NHS. They always move faster than we ever think possible. I turned my back for a moment and the doctor declared your statistics as incompatible with life. He's in the process of telling your family it's time to let you go. We haven't a moment to spare.'

Violet easily kept stride with her older guide. 'But I've got to get back. I need to put things right and make a fresh start.'

'Then stop wittering on and get moving. Quick, through here.' Grace led her through another set of doors into the noisy lounge where they had first met, what seemed like an age ago. 'Come along. Come along.' She ushered her to a side room and pushed her inside what looked like a doctor's surgery, with a small desk and computer, and an examination table surrounded on three sides by pure white curtains.

'Quick, quick. Up on the bed and I'll get you strapped in.'

Violet did exactly as she was told, despite reservations, lying still as ties were attached to her ankles and wrists and a wide belt fastened around her waist. Grace went to the desk and tapped frantically at the keyboard before turning back and checking the ties.

As Grace's hand rested close to her own, Violet grabbed it, her heart thundering in her chest. 'Wait, Grace. I'm frightened. What will it be like?'

Grace's face softened and for a few brief moments she paused. 'There's nothing to be afraid of Violet, I can assure you.'

Violet's face remained tense, her eyes wide.

'Do you remember what it felt like getting here?'

'The falling? Yes, I remember.'

'Well, there you are. It's the same, but in reverse.' She smiled and patted Violet's upper arm, then turned back to the computer and pressed a button with deliberate force, before looking back at her charge. 'Only a little faster.'

The next instant Violet felt the world dissolve around her. Grace disappeared with everything else and Violet gasped in shock. She could see, hear and do nothing as she travelled at such speed, the skin on her face billowing with the g-force, the breath forced out of her body. She held on to consciousness for as long as she possibly could, after all, there was nothing else to hold on to, but eventually even that slipped out of her grasp and her world become dark.

CHAPTER 34

The hospital room was deathly quiet except for the medical paraphernalia. Peter had intended to slip away after the doctor informed them all hope was gone - he felt he had no right to feel the loss of Violet with such an intensity and no right to intrude on what should be a family only occasion, but her parents had fallen apart, clinging to each other for comfort; Ayesha had gathered up Simone, keeping her from slipping to the floor in her shock and distress, and somebody had to take the baby. He held the warm, oblivious bundle in his arms and strode from one end of the room to the other in an attempt to maintain the calm.

The doctor, with the aid of a middle-aged nurse, was removing equipment from Violet's body piece by piece, occasionally punctuating the silence by carefully explaining the process as he went. Finally, the doctor nodded at the nurse and she flicked off a bank of switches one by one, firstly halting the breathing apparatus and its rhythmic sighing of air into Violet's lungs, then stopping the onslaught of beeping as the monitor measuring her oxygen levels recognised the sudden drop as her breathing slowed to nothing. Without intending to, they all held their breath as they watched, waiting, hope dripping away with the seconds.

In the silence, the doctor leaned over Violet's face to detect any movement of air, then untangled a stethoscope from around his neck and listened to her chest, his gaze fixed on the far corner of the room above the heads of those observing. He made notes on the clipboard resting on the small bedside table, before lifting first one and then another of Violet's eyelids, and again noting his findings. The family gathered closer together as they waited for him to say the words they were dreading, and Peter paused in his journey, holding baby Amelie closer to his chest.

'Breathing has ceased, as has the heartbeat. There is no response to light by either pupils of Violet's eyes. All that remains is a check for response to pain, so I'm going to pinch the skin on her upper arm. In a few minutes, the checks will be repeated and then I'll complete the necessary documentation to declare Violet as deceased. I am sorry for your loss.' He adjusted the sleeve of Violet's gown and smartly pinched her arm between his forefinger and thumb.

'Ow!' Violet's left hand flew across to rub the site of the pinch. 'What are you doing?'

Roger grabbed Jan as she staggered to her feet and almost fell to her knees. Ayesha and Simone clung together even tighter in their astonishment and Peter very nearly released his grip on the baby. The doctor took a hasty step back and glanced in shock at the witnessing nurse.

Violet stared out from beneath her bandaged head, a shock of hair sticking out the top like a cockerel's comb. 'Good grief, it's hot in here. Can someone open a window before I pass out?'

In bewilderment they all looked at each other, then at the doctor, who seemed equally stunned. 'There are no windows. Nurse, can you adjust the thermostat please.' He quickly pulled out his stethoscope and reapplied it to Violet's chest, his eyes growing wider as he listened to the steady thump of her heartbeat. He thrust the equipment into a deep pocket in his white coat to study her closely. 'Violet, you've been very poorly. How do you feel?'

Violet flexed her shoulders, wiggled her toes and stretched like a cat, only wincing when she tried to lift her head from the pillow.

'I feel like I've been kicked in the head by a horse, but otherwise I'm good.' She shuffled so she could see her mother. 'Hi mum. Thanks for coming.'

Jan lurched forward to embrace her, but pulled back as Violet winced. 'Sorry, my darling, is it sore?'

'A bit, but what do I expect if I will throw myself on to the pavement head first. I'm sure it will be better soon. Dad? Dad, where are you?'

Roger moved into view, hovering behind his wife, rubbing his hands together. 'I'm here, bringing up the rear.'

She held her hand out to him. 'It's good to see you. I'm sorry you've had to drop everything and rush over here.'

He took her hand and bounced it on the bed in his own a couple of times. 'It's a sight worth travelling for. You had us all worried, you know.'

'Sorry about that. Protective headgear at all times in future.' She tried to laugh, but it turned into a yawn halfway through. 'Peter, stop showing off your babysitting skills and let Simone show me my niece.'

There was a rush of activity, as Simone retrieved her daughter and leaned over the bed to display the sleeping beauty.

Violet brushed the child's cheek with one finger. 'Hello, Amelie. Pleased to meet you.' Another yawn punctuated her words.

The doctor stepped in. 'Ok, well, I think Violet should be allowed to rest and I suspect it wouldn't do you all any harm to pop away for refreshment either. Let's say,' He glanced at his watch. 'No more visitors until three. Then I'll have time to run a couple of tests and make sure everything's as positive as it currently appears.' He moved to the door and held it open, waving them through one by one.

Ayesha dropped a kiss on Violet's cheek, whispering. 'I'll let the guys know you're back in the room. They'll be so happy.'

Then, when the doctor cleared his throat, she quick stepped out into the hall.

Peter made to follow.

'Peter?'

He stopped and turned at the sound of his own name from Violet's lips.

She held out a hand to him and he stepped forward one step and stopped.

'No, here, where I can reach you.' Her voice grew weaker with each word.

'I'm sure it will wait for later.' The doctor's tone was stern.

'Two minutes, doctor. I have a few things I need to say now before I forget.'

The doctor murmured under his breath, but exited the room, leaving the two of them alone.

Violet reached for Peter's hand. 'I owe you a big thank you.'

Peter's brow furrowed as his mind formed a denial, but Violet intervened.

'Don't start with the modesty. I know you've been here for hours and hours.'

He shrugged. 'I popped in and out, here and there.'

'Yea, right. You do a lot of popping up, on the bridge last New Year; when I tried to set fire to my kitchen; when the Mongolian throat singers disappeared.' She stroked the back of his hand with her fingertips. 'When my stupid arse boss humiliated me in public.'

'Go on. The only person he humiliated was himself. The whole world knows he's an arse now.'

Violet's eyebrows disappeared momentarily beneath her bandages. 'The whole world already knew, except for me. But, I've caught up at last.' A blush broke through the pallor of her cheeks. 'I think I can now tell a good guy when I see one.'

'In my experience, good guys always …'

She interrupted. 'Yeah, yeah. Good guys always come last.'

He clamped his lips together, disconcerted she seemed able to read his mind.

'On this occasion, this particular good guy, might just win the race.' She watched the changing expressions on his face and her nerve wavered. 'If he wants to be in the race, that is?'

He leaned down until his face was only inches away from her own, examining her features, a question in his eyes, a subtle smile playing on his lips. 'He's been standing on the starting line waiting for the frigging pistol to go off for ages.'

In spite of the pain in her head and the weariness of her body, she enjoyed the promise in his closeness. She moistened suddenly dry lips and smiled back, content she had made it back to her body in the nick of time. A whole future stretched in front of her and she had no clue what it held, and that was fine, though she intended to do all she could to ensure this man was a part of it.

Holding on to the last dregs of consciousness, her eyes fluttered closed and a single soft word escaped her lips. 'Bang.'

Sharon Francis

ABOUT THE AUTHOR

Sharon Francis

Born and bred in beautiful North Devon, Sharon is married with two grown up children. She studied Creative Writing with the Open University, completing her BA in 2017. Girl Plans, God Laughs is her debut novel, and first in the Limbo series. The second in the series is due to be released in 2021 and further works will be coming soon.

For more information about Sharon or her latest books go to: -

Facebook.com/Sharon-Francis-Author-110933057304441/

OR

www.foursirenspress.co.uk/authors/sharon-francis

Sharon Francis

KEEP UP TO DATE

If you have enjoyed this book, please remember to leave a review on Amazon, so other readers can have the benefit of your thoughts.

You could be the first to know when Sharon's next novel is available to purchase and receive free additional content by signing up for the newsletter at: -

www.foursirenspress.co.uk

Sharon Francis

ACKNOWLEDGEMENT

There are many people who deserve a mention for their practical help and moral support in the production of this novel. First and foremost, the Four Sirens Press crew, in particular Sue Hughes and Denise Smith, talented writers themselves, who have been a constant source of advice and motivation.

Big thanks also to Clare Beal and Christine Shorland, who were always on hand with a cup of coffee and encouragement whenever it was needed the most.

Even closer to home, I would never have got to the end without the support of my husband, David, and children Shaun and Beth, who have all contributed to the creative process in their own ways.

Printed in Great Britain
by Amazon